DREAM WEAVER

Sofia Simpson

DREAM WEAVER

The text of this book is set in 13-point Garamond

Cover art design by Erik Lopez

ISBN-10: 1495438996
ISBN-13: 978-1495438998

DEDICATION

To Matt, Matthew and Nicky, my three dreams
come true.

Also to Hannah- I promised and here it is.
Thank you for being my first fan.

Contents

Part One

Ari

Home of Disappearances

Before Arella Moira opened the door she knew something was wrong. The lights were out in the little cottage she shared with her grandmother. Not one twinkled through the window welcoming her home.

Arella trembled. She looked around the forest wondering what its unseen eyes may have witnessed. In all of her seventeen years, Gran always had a cheerful fire in the hearth and the oil lights lit at this early evening hour.

She had been home several hours earlier and had not seen her, so she had assumed Gran had taken a trip to the village. A sinking feeling had gripped her and Arella went to search for her in the village. A growing fear gnawed at her so she searched in all of Gran's favorite shops in the village, but had not found her.

Even now as she gripped the door handle, Arella tamped down her anxiety and tried to control her breathing. She had just ran home from the village, so she took a moment to take several calming breaths. Her thoughts were filled with visions of Gran taking care of her since her parents disappeared fifteen years earlier. Arella felt an overwhelming love for her grandmother just then. It gave her courage. Taking a deep breath, she opened the door cringing slightly from the creak of the hinges.

By now, it was early evening and the room was dark. She adjusted her eyes to the dim light and strained her ears for any sounds. Hoping to hear a quick response, she called out Gran's name.   Holding her breath, her heart sank as it remained silent.   Behind her in the meadow, the insects sung their early evening chorus, but she heard nothing else. Dread filled her heart. Holding her aching chest, she stepped over the threshold.

As she looked inside, her mind instinctively snapped a picture of the scene. The moon filtered through the open doorway and she could see the outlines of the small room.

Gran's favorite flowered teapot lay on its side slowly dripping drops of water. Flowers were left abandoned next to a vase half-filled with slightly wilted buds. Herbs hung in the window, recently strung. More herbs filled their small cracked kitchen sink abandoned and forgotten.   Gran's flowered hat and cane were at their usual places by the door.

She gasped quietly as she asked herself, 'Where is Gran?' The room may not have seemed out of character for some, but her grandmother had a penchant for neatness and order.   Arella couldn't let go of the door handle. She was frozen mid-step from the fear washing through her. Something must have gone wrong. When could this have happened, she asked herself?

When she had been home earlier, she had not seen the room this way. And, she had never seen Gran leave the house without her hat and cane. If those were here, Gran would have been too. Hoping to hear a response, she called out again in a cracked voice, "Gran?" Her name echoed around the cottage with no answer.

Her heart raced and Arella reminded herself that Gran was a Dream Catcher, nothing should have happened to her. With her abilities, Gran should have been able to easily defend herself. A powerful Dream Catcher, Gran had always kept her safe but never had

Arella felt so scared as she did now. Was Gran gone, like her parents had gone missing many years before? Beloved memories of Gran filtered through her mind among older scattered images of her parents' unfamiliar but loved faces. At two, in this very house, she had become homeless when her mother and father disappeared. Gran had moved in and it had been the two of them all of these years. Air forcefully left her lungs, as a cold fear for her beloved Gran again washed through her.

Squashing those feelings, she could not entertain those emotions right now. Gran was just somewhere else, she reasoned. She hadn't been able to find Gran anywhere in town she argued. Where else would she be, she questioned. Scanning the rooms, she tried keeping her composure. She needed a closer look, so she started running through their small home and searching every room to see if Gran's things were still there. Everything was in its place, except Gran. She was gone.

Remembering hours ago when unease had crawled through her in the village, she choked back tears and walked slowly back to the main room. Studying the room's details, she tried making sense of its history. Looking for anything she hadn't noticed before, she finally stood helpless as a bereft emptiness filled her.

She didn't know how she knew, she just did, that Gran was nowhere nearby. They shared an incredible bond, one she had never really appreciated until now when she felt its absence. Memories suddenly began surfacing tormenting her of when she was a toddler crying for her mother and father.

Shaking her head, her emotions finally boiled over. Falling down, she buried her face in her hands. Tears choked her as she screamed out Gran's name over and over. Her chest ached with pain as she realized Gran was gone. She was truly alone now. Sobbing, she cried for her beloved Gran who must have been kidnapped. She would never have left without any goodbye.

All strength left her as she wrapped her arms around herself crying hoarsely. Even when Delius, her best friend and neighbor reached her, she didn't have the strength to explain. Waving him off, she dimly watched as he tried to locate Gran.

Listening to his calls for her grandmother, she sat rocking herself on the floor, never wanting to step foot inside this home of disappearances again.

One Year Later

Early Decorations

"Stop kidding around Del, you're wrong, and you know it!" Arella argued from across the room to her best friend.

Hanging up decorations, she was struggling to reach a hammer just out of her reach when Del made an irritating prediction.

It was one year after her Grandmother vanished. She had missed several weeks of school in the subsequent searches for Gran, but she had caught up on her studies and Del and she were about to graduate. Del had stopped his studies also, claiming he couldn't concentrate with Arella in such grief. Arella couldn't have been more grateful. He was her one confidante, a support she could never have done without.

Today, Del's parents had surprised Arella and Del with decorations for the party. She was determined to decorate despite the party being three weeks away and she was forcing Del to help her.

"I am definitely *not* wrong Ari," he said dryly about his prediction, "and you will prove it in just one second," as he eyed her wobbling stance on the dining room chair.

"Well, why don't you use your fancy Dream Catching skills you just learned and bring the hammer to me, all magic-like," she teased.

"If we were dreaming, I would," he answered dryly. "I am a Dream Catcher, not a magician. Now, just stop being stubborn and get down and get it."

7

'Magician', Ari grumbled to herself, 'He could at least be a gentleman.' But she doubted she would get much more than a grudging cooperation in her quest to decorate.

As she eyed the hammer, she frowned when she looked over at him casually hanging the decorations. With his six-foot build, height would never been an issue for him, Ari thought, sulking over her minuscule proportions.

Seeing Del notice her frown, she turned away. She gave up reaching for the hammer and began to twist the streamer into a pretty braid, instead.

She returned her thoughts to her height, or lack of it, and decided she would trade her blue eyes for a few inches. Her eye color was rare among Dream Folk. Gran had alway said they were aquamarine, the color of the sea.

As part of a formerly elite family in Maone of Dream Catchers, Ari felt she was cursed to inherit unusual qualities.

Like Del, she would one day mature into her Dream Catching qualities, but if she had it her way, she would always remain a simple Dream Weaver, with the one task of weaving pleasant dreams for humans.

Being a respected Dream Catcher never did her family any good, she thought gloomily. Her Dream Catcher mother and father both disappeared when she was a toddler, and now Gran had been missing for a year.

Thinking of Gran was always painful, but today she refused to be in a bad mood.

It was as if Del could sense her moods because when she glanced over he was already watching her. He replaced his frown with an indecipherable one then gave her a wink. Warming, she turned away not acknowledging the gesture.

Was he flirting with her, she questioned? Turning red, she did not want to get into that kind of conversation now or ever. Controlling her awkward emotions was becoming difficult. Right now, it was debatable whether she wanted to hide under her chair, where she would probably fit, she thought disgustedly, or throw it at her infuriating friend. Either choice was a knee-jerk reaction that surprised her.

Unsure of his actions or her response to them, Ari glimpsed over at him again. She couldn't help but giggle when he wagged his eyes at her. She had to admit she was thankful for his attempt at humor.

She suddenly thought of Gran again and Gran's comical side. Closing her eyes, she smiled sadly. She had loved Gran's sense of humor. Gran was one of those types of people who called it like she saw it. Gran was the same size she was, a whole five-foot-two inches, but she had a sarcastic and brilliant comment for nearly every situation. One of her favorite expressions of Gran's was, 'I'd rather be shorter than someone than dumber than 'em.'

Ari brushed back her thick wavy hair and giggled at the memory. Ari knew Gran must have realized there was nothing she could have done about her pixie-like height. At this point, Arella realized she probably needed to adopt the same attitude.

At eighteen, she was pretty sure she'd stay little the rest of her life. She had to resign herself to the fact she would need to hand sew everything she wore or re-stitch pre-made pants and dresses to fit her small shape. Her recently developed curves had helped to make her look more like a woman lately, though.

"Thankfully," she breathed. She thought she would never round out like other girls her age.

"What did you say?" Del asked staring at her with an expectant look.

Beyond embarrassed, she cried, "Nothing!"

Putting up his hands in mock surrender he smiled a crooked grin and said, "Thinking about me again?"

Caught off guard by today's mode of teasing, Ari didn't know what to say. So, she said nothing. Del was her best friend, and friends just don't make those kinds of comments, she thought flustered.

What has gotten into him today, she wondered. Frustrated, she thought back and realized he has been acting strange all day.

The day started when Del's mom had brought her armloads of streamers and bags of balloons. "These are for yours and Del's graduation party," Gracius had said cheerfully.

Arella had taken one look at the decorations and immediately recruited Del to help. But, he didn't seem to be enjoying himself she grumbled to herself. In fact, he hadn't stopped complaining yet.

His bad mood was not like him, she thought for the thousandth time that morning. He was usually so patient and willing to help in any situation. She couldn't remember a time when he had refused to help.

Even now, when she had handed him decorations, he protested, "Are you kidding me?

More decorations?"

"Yes," she countered, "And stop complaining, because you owe me."

"For what?"

"For starters, the fact I've put up with you for eighteen very long years. Now decorate," she ordered.

"You're ridiculous," Del grumbled as he walked across the room. Leaning toward her, he growled, "I am a guy. Guys do not decorate."

"Well, you are going to," she said refusing to be intimidated, "Especially since this is your grad party as much as it is mine."

"You realize something," he said ducking his head to peer into her face, "This party is three weeks away. May I ask why you feel the need to decorate now?"

"Because," she answered defensively. "I want to be good and ready. And I like decorations. I always have," she finished softly.

"I know," he answered just as quietly.

"Then you'll help?" she asked, giving him her best pout.

Running his hands through his hair, he responded sounding exasperated, "Really, you and mom are crazy! You guys realize I am going to be hitting my head on paper streamers for a month. It's not fair," he finished with a resigned voice.

Feeling hopeful, she finished her argument with a little bit of guilt, "Hey, this is a big moment for both of us. Our next big moment is when we marry our bondmate. And since, that isn't happening any time soon, I say we enjoy this!"

"To do that you have to decorate right now?" he asked, his tone sounding guarded.

11

Ari knew Del well, but she didn't recognize this expression. Confused, she asked him, "Can't you be a little bit happy?"

He raised his eyebrow and she realized that was the nicest response she was going to get.

Ignoring his horrible mood and now piercing eyes, she made another lunge for the hammer but before she could stop it, the chair she was standing on began to tilt. She knew it was too late to catch herself but before she fell, her last thought was how she was going to kill Del.

Falling hard did not feel good and neither did the fact that Del's prediction came true. Fuming, she stayed on the ground for a minute trying to recover her breath and trying really hard to think of something smart to say about friends who let friends fall.

"Told 'ya you'd fall," he said walking to her.

Angry and not trusting herself to speak, she gingerly sat up. Rubbing her arms that had mercifully braced her from smashing her head onto the floor, she looked up at Del with a glare that made him back up.

"What?!" he asked as he held up his hands.

"Some gallant friend you've turned out to be," she said, not being able to think of anything more insulting.

"Gallant? You want a *gallant* friend now?" he asked crossing his arms.

He drilled into her, "Just a minute ago, you demanded to get on that chair. You wanted to hang those streamers *by yourself*. When I suggested you get the ladder, you suggested that I take a hike."

Holding his hand out, he finished with a soft look in his eyes, "I was just trying to help you not fall and now look at you."

Eyeing his hand, she questioned, "If you knew I was going to fall, then why didn't you come and help me hang the streamers?"

"Well, I was kind of hoping your clumsiness would not come into play today, but alas, I was wrong," he said obviously itching for a fight.

Ignoring his hand, she picked herself up off the floor still not trusting herself to speak.

He laughed, responding, "Well, that settles that argument."

"If I was arguing, Delius," she said sharply, "You would know it. This is me leaving," as she turned toward the door.

Surprising her, he grabbed her hand and said with a southern draw, "Well, I guess I should have just grabbed you off the chair and with great chivalry swept you off your feet preventing such a disastrous fall off a very old and rickety chair."

Before she could respond, he picked her up with ease cradling her to his chest smiling widely. With a softer voice, he continued, "Then I would announce to you, Arella, my friend, you are about to fall and I must save you." His eyes were twinkling and Ari was secretly thrilled to see him in his usual good mood.

"Yes. That would have been nice," she said trying not to laugh as she held a stern gaze to his.

She was suddenly breathless squeezed in his arms and she felt a giggle about to escape. Blaming her lack of air on his unusually strong arms, she refused to allow him this victory. When did he get so strong anyway, she asked herself. Still he should have helped her if he knew she was going to fall, she thought stubbornly.

After about a minute of a stare down, he sighed. He set her down and said, "Yea, well, you never would have listened to me, anyway."

Putting her hands on her hips, she argued, "Yes I would have!"

Turning his back to her, he seemed to resume his brooding and said, "Doubt it, kid. You are as stubborn as a mule." Looking back at her over his shoulder, he continued,

"When it comes to your pride, you would jump off a cliff before accepting help if you didn't think you needed it."

"I am *not* that prideful," she announced complaining, "I don't want to be thought of that way." Folding her arms across her chest, she asked, "I mean, haven't you noticed what all of these decorations are for anyway? To mark our entrance into the world and begin our Dream Weaving duties as adults?"

"What I'm *noticing*," Del said changing the argument, "is that I am already sick of looking at these ridiculous decorations."

Watching him give particular attention to a tangled streamer, she huffed and said, "You keep saying that. But, I'm surprised you would even notice them. You see nothing, unless it's right in front of you."

Quietly, almost to where she couldn't hear it, he said, "I see more than you think."

Running over to him, she began jumping up and down as she questioned excitedly, "Do you like my graduation gown you saw the other day then? Do you, do you?"

Cracking a smile, he answered, "As much as you've noticed my tux." Then eyeing her with a resigned look, said, "But, yeah, I like it. It should look...nice."

"Nice? It's more than nice, it's perfect!" she exclaimed tossing her hair back over her shoulder, noticing he was following the dark brown tresses with his eyes.

"What?" she asked. "Is there something wrong with my hair? What is with you anyway?" she demanded. "You've been acting so strange lately."

"Look," he snapped at her, "This is a big deal, and I'm just...preoccupied with everything right now, can you just get off my back?"

With that, he dropped his decorations and stormed out of his parent's little cottage.

Bewildered, she watched him walk with long strides out into the meadow that separated both of their homes. Trying to understand what could be putting a rift into their long-held friendship, she sighed and gave up for the moment.

Whatever it was, it will reveal itself soon, she hoped.

Noticed

A few days later, it surprised Ari to see Del waiting for her in the distance. She was coming home from her job at the bakery and he was waiting in the meadow. He had been avoiding her lately, which she could only assume was because of their strange argument the other day.

Frowning, she knew he was probably not happy she was walking home alone. He was a little protective, especially since she has been living alone this past year. But, she was relieved to see him. Today was Gran's birthday and Ari missed her. She never believed her grandmother was dead, she would have felt it if her Grandmother was gone forever.

Del had said she had a special bond with her Grandmother, which explained why she knew Gran was alive. She wondered if having Del as her best friend had created a type of bond as well. He knew her moods so well, it seemed that he could sense every time she needed a friend. But, their friendship had always been close and she couldn't help but feel relieved he made an appearance today. She needed a hug.

As she walked up the curved path leading to her cottage, she could see Del was leaning against a tree engrossed in a book. A warmth spread in her chest thinking about his faithful friendship.

The past year had been a trial and without Del's support, she would have been a mess.

He had been a good friend, lifting her low moods, never seeming to mind her tears. Anxiety inched through her as she remembered the day she came home to find Gran missing.

She had stood on the threshold of their cottage that day knowing she was completely alone. The memory of that moment still made her cry, especially today.

Wiping a tear away, she looked over at Del and saw he had put his book down and was watching her, smiling sympathetically.

Returning his smile, she liked that Del made her feel taken care of. It was nice. Her mood instantly lifted knowing he waited for her and she hoped he had gotten over whatever had upset him a few days ago. That was an odd day, one she did not want to repeat. She remembered another strange day she hadn't had time to figure out, the last time they went to the village.

Sighing, she recalled the day. It was an eye-opening experience and one she still didn't know what to think about. She had asked Del to go with her to the village, Maone, a thirty-minute walk away. If she hadn't asked, he would have resumed a long-held argument that she wasn't to travel the distance alone. There was always the threat of robbery during that walk and she hadn't been trained on how to defend herself, so Del, his parents or Gran would usually accompany her.

Wanting to ignore his request was not unusual, as she usually went against what he said to get a rise out of him, but she decided against it that day. She couldn't help but feel they were treating her like a child, but she knew they were right, she was vulnerable to attacks. Her powers hadn't formed so everyone had agreed with Del to stay on the safe side and continue accompanying her.

But of course Gran would have agreed to anything Del said. She used to sing his praises to the rafters. It had been annoying, since Del always took advantage of his charm factor when they were in a stalemate in an argument. Gran usually always took his side. Granted, Del was known to be cautious in any situation and Gran knew Ari's daring personality sometimes got them in trouble, so she would ask Del to keep an eye on her. It wasn't difficult to do since they have been inseparable since they could walk. She always laughed though when Gran would remark, "I asked him one time to keep an eye on you when you were both two years old and he did better than that, he kept two eyes peeled on you for good measure."

Laughing quietly, her thoughts returned to their village trip. It had been a quiet walk. Once in the village, they had walked among the quaint Swiss-type homes hardly speaking as she completed her errand. Del had been pensive and seemed to have something on his mind, so she stayed quiet and left him alone.

It had caught her attention as they had walked together that several girls stared at Del as they passed and giggling between each other. If she and Del had been engaged in conversation, she may not have noticed the silly girls and their ogling of her friend. His silence gave her no choice but to notice what was going on around them.

Funny, she had thought, over the past year, she had not considered dating or whether Del was interested in dating either. If she was going to be honest, she didn't even know some of the guys' names in her graduating class.

And she certainly hadn't noticed when Del had grown up. It wasn't until she had seen the girls' reactions to him that she had really looked at him. She saw him every day, but what she had seen surprised her. It had made her blush, which she promptly tried to hide by pretending to study a window display. She must have been become blind during her year of grieving for Gran.

His sun-bleached hair and tan was one reason he was attracting attention, she noticed.

He had filled out too, she thought with surprise. When he had time to do that, she had no idea, but it looked good on him. His warm brown eyes had looked over at the girls and he then glanced at her with a small smile.

Unsure if his smile was meant for the girls or for her, she hid her confused expression saying to herself, so what if he was good looking. His smile made his handsome features, well, more handsome. It softened his strong chin, which needed help in that department anyway and it made his teasing brown eyes look warmer. Well, surprise, surprise, she had thought sarcastically. No wonder he was the village idol lately.

Shaking herself out of her reminscing, she frowned despite herself. What was she doing thinking about her best friend's good looks anyway? He would always be her friend, she thought a little sadly. One day his attentions would go to a girl, but the question was, would they still be best friends when that happened, she wondered.

This was a topic she better not think about, she thought grimly. It was just far too unsettling to imagine Del *with* someone. It wasn't that he didn't deserve to have a girlfriend, she quickly thought. It's just that if he did decide to date someone she would be completely alone.

Picking up her pace, she hurried to reach him. She just wanted to have a great day with her best friend. Reaching him, he quietly told her he wanted to finish reading a chapter, so Ari settled herself comfortably by the tree. Looking up at him, Ari marveled again at Del's timing for a visit.

When her grandmother was alive and it was the two of them in their little cottage, it was her grandmother who had had the ability to sense her moods. Del had explained recently it was because of a family bond she had with her sweet and dear Grandmother.

Ari missed Gran's intuition desperately these days. But, Del's reaction to her moods has been a tremendous comfort.

It was a Dream Catcher quality, she thought wrinkling her nose. She was glad Del had those abilities, but she didn't want them. Not all Dream Weavers were Catchers. They had enhanced abilities Dream Weavers did not possess. Among their many talents, they could sense moods, by touch and in close distances.

Sighing, she reflected how she was a Catcher, also. Her signs have been emerging lately, but she was far from able to sense moods like Gran and Del. His powers were emerging quicker than hers.

If life had turned out her way, she would have been content as a simple Dream Weaver but with a mischievous personality. Life didn't turn out that way for her. She was a Dream Catcher and potentially, a powerful one. An irritation filled her at that thought, but she needed to accept the facts and embrace them.

Because of her kind, Dream Folk, a race made up of Dream Weavers and the more esteemed Dream Catchers, children all over Earth had the ability to dream peacefully.

And the Dream Maker kept everything running in peaceful order. All Dream Weavers relied on the Maker to assign them children to weave dreams with. If a Dream Weaver can teach a child to dream, they can then dream peacefully on their own, as adults.

Dream Weavers access humans' memories and weave them together creating a satisfying dream. Dream Catchers, among other talents they possess in Oneiro, also help humans dream, but mainly they thwart nightmares.

Sometimes, however, the bad dreams continue. These are usually inflicted by fallen Dream Weavers and Catchers, called Outcasts. They are former Dream Weavers, who have chosen to weave terrible nightmares.

Outcasts had been taught to weave vibrant, peaceful dreams, but having severed all communication with the Dream Maker they have chosen to defy Him by invoking nightmares on humans. Cutting themselves off from all that is good in Oneiro and the dreamworld, they have been banned from villages and lived in Outcast hideaways.

Dream Folk lived in a world suspended between reality and fantasy. It's an invisible, mythical-like place humans cannot access, called Oneiro, a place of dreams or rather, Dream Weaving.

It's a world that looked much like Earth did years ago, without technology. Where small communities thrived and Dream Folk ate and lived off of the land. Villages nestled themselves among grassy valleys, at the base of tree-studded mountains, by frothy seasides and clear lakes.

Ari's village, Maone, was situated in a cleared forest with a beautiful waterfall nearby. Her and Del's cottages were about a thirty-minute walk from the village.

Because of Gran's disappearance, however, Del had been asking her to spend more time with him and his parents. It was dangerous for her to live alone, he said. Outcasts were known to raid for food and clothing. Injuries happened when Dream Weavers attempted to protect themselves from theft.

The raids most often happened to secluded homes, on the outskirts of the village. Catchers, with their enhanced senses, however, could usually predict when Outcasts were in the area. But, their village did not have many local Catchers to protect them.

Thinking of Catchers, she looked up at one of the most recent ones. Del had his book down and was watching her.

"Hey," she greeted him, color steeling over her cheeks. Sheepishly, she asked, "When did you finish reading? I didn't notice you had stopped."

"I noticed," he said quietly.

Looking away, she examined her feelings. She sat quietly wondering what he was going to say next.

"You miss her, don't you?" he asked quietly.

Remembering her constant yearning to know what happened to her grandmother, she answered truthfully, "Yes, I only wish I knew how to find her." Blinking away tears, she paused so she could find her voice and said quietly, "To have her gone is as if half of my life is missing."

"Well," he replied, "She's raised you from the time you were a little girl. All of your memories are centered around her. And, every time you look in the mirror, I'm sure you're reminded of her."

People in Maone claimed she looked just like her dark-haired, light-skinned grandmother compared to her fair-haired mother and father.

Sighing, she said, "Maybe, I'll transform into a new shape to stop reminding myself she's gone."

Reacting quickly, he crouched next to her and said, "Just because Dream Weavers can transform into any shape they want, doesn't mean they should. The ancient Dream Weavers set the standard that we should act as human as we can, and that means keeping your human look."

"Look at you," he gestured, "You're adorable, just like she is." Suddenly shifting away, he looked embarrassed and added quickly, "If Gran is small in height, then what she misses in inches she makes up for in personality."

Wondering at the quick switch in subjects, she went along with it agreeing with him. "She's also the smartest Dream Weaver I know."

"And you wanted to stop reminding yourself that you're just like her," Del teased. "What a way to waste your intelligence."

Her temper flaring at his jab, she asked in a hard voice, "Would you also agree with the village-folk, Del, that I have a temper, like Gran's?"

Despite his answering smile, she said, "Then I'd watch your words, Delius, I'm not in the mood today for an argument."

"I know," he said softly as he studied her face. "Do you want to talk about it?"

Her temper deflated immediately and she turned her face to hide the rush of tears that sprang into her eyes again. His concern never ceased to amaze her.

"Come here, I've got two shoulders," he said reaching for her. "Pick the one you want."

She accepted and stepped into his arms. She released the rest of the tears she had been holding and cried about missing Gran and all the family she had lost.

"You'd think I'd get used to being alone by now, but it's just hard to accept that Gran is gone," she whispered into his shoulder.

Del held onto her tightly, as he softly patted her head and back.

After crying for a few more minutes, she tried leaning back from Del not wanting to bother him or his shirt anymore. But, Del wouldn't let go, instead tightening his arms around her, whispered, "Don't worry, Ari, I don't mind. Keep crying, I don't mind." Without knowing why, she lay her head back on his strong shoulder until her tears finally stopped.

Del shifted so they could both sit by the spot she had abandoned. Sitting down and tucking herself back into his arms, she thought back to her parents. Del played with the ends of her hair as her memories washed over her.

She wished she could have known them, but they were two people she could not remember. Like Gran, their disappearances sixteen years ago remained unsolved. She couldn't help but wonder if that was more than a coincidence.

Looking up from Del's shoulder, she asked, "How can three people in the same family, in a small peaceful village, go missing?"

"Not sure," he answered seeming to study her then looking away quickly . Pushing her softly away, he said solemnly, "But, I know somewhere you could investigate it, though. D.C. would be the perfect place to find answers."

Unable to hide her quick frustration, she argued, "No one there showed any interest in searching for Gran. And the few who did only searched for a few days and gave up looking. I am not going to repeat that disappointment by asking them to care about my education."

Getting up, she walked away from Del and fumed as she stormed into her cottage locking the door.

This was an argument she and Del have been having for a year now. He thought she needed to go to Dream Catcher School, known as D.C. Any teen who showed signs of Dream Catching were sent to this prestigious school, but she did not want to join their ranks. Among other things, they learned how to battle the Outcasts.

But, she wanted to track them, not fight them.

The Outcasts were who she suspected of taking both her grandmother and her parents. It was no secret her family tended to produce incredible Catchers. Without a doubt, she knew if she could find the Outcasts, she would find Gran.

Frustrated with her village's lack of response to Gran's disappearance, she refused to let the elders know her Dream Catcher qualities had begun to develop, Del was the only one who knew. If the Elders had known, they would have requested she attend the prestigious training program.

Besides, she didn't have the time. Her job at the Sugalle Bakery kept her very busy and she only needed to save a few hundred more denarii before she could leave Maone in search of Gran. And her bosses, Franz and Helga Sugalle, were mercifully giving her plenty of work lately.

The problem was, she needed to know more about her adversaries, the fallen Dream Weavers. Del was taking a preliminary course at D.C., and was learning more about Outcasts, but since she refused to attend, she was missing those lessons.

Thankfully, however, she had managed to convince Del to show her his daily work. He agreed as long as she didn't experiment with what she learned without his supervision.

Leaning against her door, she regretted her outburst outside. Frustrated at her temper, she wished she hadn't argued with him, since now she lost her chance to study from his Dream Catching books.

She thought about their friendship. Where would it go she wondered as they grew older? Past images of his calm, serious face that hid sarcasm as well as affection filled her mind. She watched him through the window leave her yard and cross the field that separated their homes.

When he closed the door to his neighboring house, she decided quickly to apologize.

She didn't want to argue anymore and she needed his help, so she jumped up and ran out of her house crossing the field as quickly as she could. Reaching his door, she rapped on the door.

He answered with a knowing smile. Ignoring his smirk and trying in vain to catch her breath, she asked, "Can we just forget about our argument?" Smiling sheepishly, she said, "I'd like to get started on today's lesson."

Without saying a word, he reached inside for his bag of books and led the way to her cottage.

She would start a search to find her grandmother, with or without her powers fully formed. Three weeks, that's all the time she had. She had to make the most of it.

Lessons

"Dream Weavers, as you know, are given a human child to weave dreams with," Del said as he found a comfortable seat at her kitchen table. "We are responsible for helping that child control their dreams," he explained his brown eyes serious on hers. "We can't allow worries and fears to leak into their unconscious state," he emphasized.

"That's what creates nightmares," Ari said as she tried to stifle a yawn. This is all information she has been given many times before.

"Yes, especially during childhood they can't seem to manage their dreams on their own, we have to help them. The older they become the better they get at it, so by the time they have matured we can move on."

"Matured?" she asked. Her face coloring, she had no idea why she was asking this, especially when she knew the answer.

She knew when human boys and girls became interested in dating, their dreams became unmanageable to weave through. They became obsessively focused on their love interest and Dream Weavers would frankly rather give them their space than try to help weave dreams through *that*.

But, why she would ask such an embarrassing question, was completely beyond her. It was like she wanted to see Del in a new light, but the idea of such a vision terrified her completely. So, what was she thinking? She realized when she lifted her head, however, it was too late to back down from her strange line of questioning.

He raised his eyebrow and waited for her to continue, which she wouldn't. She deserved whatever sarcastic comment was coming.

Deciding she needed to give a reason for her silliness, she blurted out the first excuse she could think of and said quickly, "Well, you know, it's just that we went over that so long ago..." Taking a deep breath she put her head back down to hide her heated blush.

She must be scarlet red by now, since she was completely mortified.

After it was quiet for a few minutes, she took a quick peek and then quickly turned away when she saw his expression.

He was studying her smiling that crooked grin of his.

Embarrassed and feeling silly for even bringing up such a question she knew the answer to was ridiculous. Why would she bring up an embarrassing topic, like maturing. What game was she playing anyway?

Finally, unable to stop herself, she picked her head up and questioned, "What?"

He was leaning back in his chair with his arms folded across his chest. "I was just wondering why you just now decided to try flirting," he said still smiling.

Flustered, she replied, "Flirting? Me? Flirting? I only brought up...!"

Leaning closer, he said, "If that's what this is, then I think you can do better than that."

Taken aback, she was speechless and her heart was beating a strange wild rhythm in her chest. Finally finding her voice, she found her temper and said angrily, "Better than what? What are you talking about?"

Leaning back again, he said, "You know, if you want to practice flirting, I don't mind if you try your techniques out on me."

Jumping out her chair, she tried to come up with something that didn't sound like a lame excuse. Furious with herself for not thinking this through, she said, "I am not trying to practice flirting! And, well, I just had a question about it, and *you* are making mountains out of...you know, molehills!" Putting her hands on her hips she waited for an apology.

She thought her excuse was pretty good, what could he say now?

His voice deepened as he asked, "Ok, then what's your question?" He looked at her with a far from innocent expression.

Feeling the blood drain out of her face, she stuttered again, "Wha, what do..do you mean?" She hadn't thought of an actual question. And looking at him, she knew he very well knew it.

Still grinning, he said, "Well, you should remember all of this from school. What do I need to explain that you don't remember?"

A question suddenly popped into her head, so triumphantly, she asked in a rush, "Well, um, I know that when they get interested in dating, we stop Dream Weaving with them and are given another assignment."

"Yes, so?" he said slowly as a look of disappointment crossed his face.

Just now remembering a genuine question she had had a while ago, asked him, "So do we ever Dream Weave with that person again, when they get older?"

Looking down at his notes, he answered in a neutral voice, "Yes, sometimes. It all depends on whether the Dream Maker needs us to help them weave peaceful dreams again. Anything else?"

Looking at her with an expectant expression, he waited.

Feeling victorious, she was suddenly let down, like she missed something. But, she only said innocently, "No, I just hadn't heard that answer before, is all."

Happy to have dodged an uncomfortable situation, she returned her attention to a book they were reading together.

Thinking of Del's reaction to her strange question, she wondered why she *had* never gotten interested in the whole boy thing. She guessed it had to do with her year of mourning Gran.

It seems like she has missed a lot. She was beginning to see that maybe Del was missing out on things too, by helping her through this hard time.

Looking over at him warmly, her brows furrowed when she saw him writing notes in his notebook furiously.

Was he avoiding dating because of her grief? She could easily see him doing that for her.

Deciding to ask a safer question, she asked, "Del?"

He still had his head down writing notes when he answered, "Mm'hmm?"

"What happens if you were to show up in someone's dream?"

The only indicator Del had heard her question was that his pen slowed. Finally answering, he said quietly, "Only Dream Catcher's can do that."

"I know that," she said trying to be patient with his non-informative answer. "But, what happens? Anything?"

Looking out of the window they were seated by, he didn't answer right away.

Clearing his voice he replied softly, "You begin to create a bond with them."

"A bond?" she repeated.

Hesitating again, he explained, "You begin to share their emotions, in small increments at first, but the more you frequent their dreams, the stronger the bond becomes."

Looking at her, his blue eyes seemed to be telling her something, but what she couldn't figure out. Finally he said, "You could possibly be melded to their emotions permanently."

Gathering up his books, he put his notes he had just written next to her saying softly, "Study these tonight and I'll see you tomorrow."

Before she could say goodbye or remark on the lesson, he was gone.

Wondering what just happened to make him leave so suddenly, she decided to leave it alone. Grabbing the notes he left for her, she carried them into her room and began studying them like he had asked.

Grumbling, she said to herself, "What is up with that boy, anyway?"

Throwing the notes to the side she glared at the papers. After a few minutes of fuming, she knew it was pointless to be upset, so she reached over, picked them back up and began to study.

"Hope you know what you are writing about, Del," she said under her breath. "I'm going to need all the help I can get."

Revealed Abilities

The next day, Ari was happy when Del agreed, albeit grudgingly to share with her his notes. His attitude was completely business-like, all trace of the previous day's teasing was gone. Trying to be a good student since he seemed to be in a testy mood, she listened carefully.

In this lesson, Del pronounced his words carefully, "You have to be careful with your thoughts, Ari, when you are Dream Weaving..."

Having heard her elementary professors exclaim that knowledge many times, she was unable to help herself,. She interrupted, "I know, I know!"

Ignoring her outburst, he continued, "If your motives are off, if there's *any* negative emotion in you, it will come out in that child's dream."

"And into their daily life," she added in a monotone voice.

"Yes," he agreed solemnly, "It's serious, Ari, you have to be careful. Dreams are fickle, "he continued. "Normally most Dream Weavers just help manage the dream, guiding the child's emotions and memories into a dream that is both peaceful and satisfying."

Not sure how to ask her next question, she fingered her grandmother's afghan on the couch they were sitting on as Del gave his lesson.

When Del's fingers covered her own nervous ones, she looked away afraid to meet his eyes.

"What happened today that you are not telling me?" he asked.

"Nothing," she mumbled feeling guilty.

"It doesn't sound like, 'Nothing'", Ari, now what is it, what happened?" Kneeling next to her, he kept his hand over hers.

Her hand was tingling strangely under his and she was having a hard time concentrating on anything. The thought that she could turn her hand over to hold his suddenly popped in her head.

Squashing the thought quickly, she pulled her hand away ignoring his hurt look. She'd held his hand before, what would have been the big deal, she asked herself, annoyed.

"Are you ok, Ari?" he asked in a subdued voice.

Did she trace a note of disappointment? Brushing the suspicion aside, she crossed her arms, and decided to be honest with him.

"I've been practicing my sensory abilities you had me study the other day."

Exploding off the floor, he loomed over her and yelled, "You did what?"

Shocked at his reaction, she hung limply as he pulled her up and grabbed her shoulders.

"You cannot do that, Ari!"

Letting her go, he ran his fingers through his hair, "By sensing other's emotions, you're marking their moods, recognizing them anywhere. Sometimes, it's permanent!"

He turned away saying heatedly, "I cannot believe you."

Turning back to face her, he questioned, "I thought we agreed you wouldn't try anything new without me. How could you have been so foolish?"

Before she could answer or even respond, he urgently asked, "Who? Who did you reach into today, whose emotions did you try to sense? Whose?"

Quietly, she answered, "Franz and Helga's."

"Well, they seem simple enough," he said, noticeably relieved.

"Those emotions and memories shouldn't last, they should wear off in a few days."

Grabbing her shoulders again, he asked, "Are you feeling what they're doing now?

As he watched her carefully, she concentrated as she reached into her own emotions to see if she could still sense Franz and Helga's current emotional climate.

"Yes," she answered slowly. Concentrating, she said, "They're arguing, that's funny," she said softly, "'cause they never argue."

Worried about her bosses, she wondered if she should go over to the bakery to help them. Maybe they were unable to finish their baking for tomorrow's clientele.

"Couples do that," Del assured her, "trust me, it's nothing to worry about."

"But, listen," he said capturing her attention again, "Stop. No more reaching into folk's subconscious. You don't know what you'll find and it could alter both of you completely."

Reaching for her hand, he begged, "Promise me, Ari. No more Dream Catching. You're not ready. I haven't learned enough to be able to tell you much yet. Just promise me you'll wait until I am with you to try anything new."

Schooling her face, she knew she needed to hide from him that she would be leaving when he went to D.C. She would be practicing Dream Catching all the time then.

She wouldn't be home when he returned on breaks, and she knew he wouldn't like that.

Her being off by herself tracking who knows what kind of creatures these fallen

Dream Weavers had turned into would be the last thing he would want her to do.

Finally, she lied, "I promise Big Brother," reverting back to a nickname she had given him years ago. "You have my word."

She just caught the frown that came over his face as he turned away, saying as he left, "See you tomorrow. And Ari, sweet dreams."

'Sweet dreams?' she thought.

He was being so cryptic lately. Well, she was going to have to drag it out of him, whatever his problem was.

Dreams

"Delius, I'm warning you, you come one step closer and I'll, I'll..."

"You'll what? Hit me? I'm not too afraid, not of a little girl, anyway, now stop running

away from me."

"Don't call me a little girl!"

"Well, you're acting like one."

"No, I'm not!"

"Well, then come here and show me how old you are, I just want to try something."

"No! You are not *coming any closer to me."*

Sighing, he stopped circling around the room after her. "I think you're just afraid."

"Afraid of what!?"

Successfully distracting her, he raced across the room before she could react again and

grabbed her in his arms.

Gruffly, he said, "Of this."

And with that, he kissed her.

She jumped up from her bed sweating out her latest dream, this one more disturbing

than the others. Del was her best friend and the feelings coursing through her right now were not, well, very friend-like.

She would die if he ever found out about these dreams lately. They were disturbing because she had never, never thought of Del in that way. And all of last week, when she dreamed, that's all she could imagine. It frightened her to see things changing like this. And he would never let her live them down. And he might...

A thought suddenly hit her. She put her hand on her head, willing the thought out of her brain. But, there it was creeping into her, chilling her muscles. Which was a very different feeling from how she had just woken up.

As her body got adjusted to the drop in temperature, she wondered, was Del impressing these dreams on her? She knew he could, he had already been demonstrating Dream Catcher abilities. He very well could make her dream of him, if he wanted her to.

Angry, she threw off the covers and questioned the thought again. Would he cross that line of their long-held friendship?

Dream Catchers could walk into and become part of any dream they chose. They could catch on to any dream and become a character in it.

It was heavily frowned on, however, and she would be shocked if her best friend had tried that power on her.

But, what if, she thought uneasily, she had dreamt all that on her own?

This was not something she could ever bring up to her best friend, because that's just it, he's her *friend*, and this would undeniably put a strain on their long-held *friendship*, she told herself.

Well, this was one dream she would keep as a dream *and* to herself, she firmly decided.

Then, she remembered something that had happened not too long ago.

She had snuck up on him in the meadow and sprang an attack, like when they were kids. She had had the surprise element, and soon had him pinned beneath her after she had tackled him.

But after his initial surprise, he surprised her by rolling her around until she was the one being pinned down instead of the other way around.

Laughing, she had said, "Well, this is a surprise, Del, usually I do that move on you!"

Sticking her tongue out, she struggled to get up.

Pinning her down easily, he said quietly, "We're not kids anymore, Ari. Haven't you noticed?"

The teasing had gone from just that to...something different.

She searched his eyes for an explanation. His golden-streaked hair fell around his eyes, but even then she could see a change in them.

They were dark brown, deeper brown than normal, and darkening by the moment. He seemed to be struggling for words, but he wasn't saying anything. He just stared at her.

Finally, she said in a small voice, "Del? You're hurting my arms."

He lightened the mood by laughing quietly. Jumping up off the ground he pulled her up, abruptly ruffling her hair.

"Hey!" she had cried out. "This took me forever to untangle this morning," she grumbled. Still unsure of what had just happened, she had stalked off without a second glance behind her.

Shaking off the memory, she could still feel his eyes on her back, like a warm presence enveloping her.

They were two weeks apart in age, with a lifetime of friendship ahead of them, she hoped.

But, as their 18th birthdays neared, she feared things were beginning to change.

It seemed like they might have already.

Fear crept into her chest. Could their friendship withstand these strains on the bond they've had since toddler-hood?

And would he force himself into her dreams? Except it didn't feel forced, it felt...right.

Remembering how it felt to be in his arms with his warm lips on hers in her dream, she recalled she had wound her arms around his neck and returned his kiss enjoying it, a bit too much.

"No. This is not happening. I am not falling for *anyone*," she announced to herself.

There is too much going on.

Graduation was coming up signifying her entrance into adulthood and her life as a Dream Weaver and eventually a Dream Catcher. Her secret search for her grandmother was the one adventure she needed to focus on right now. And least of all, their graduation party was coming up setting all of this into motion.

Considering her and Del's party for a moment, she wondered if it was a good idea now. She and Del had decided to celebrate their momentous occasion together. That decision had been made years ago, but now she wondered if they shouldn't have their own space.

Especially after that strange moment in the meadow and her dreams of late. Things had begun changing in her life and it was all happening before she was ready.

.

Aware

Plopping down on her Grandmother's stuffed chair, her thinking chair, Ari tried to think of something to do.

It was evening, dusk had just left the horizon. And thanks to Del's wonderful parents, there wasn't anything she needed to do. Del's mom brought her meals; she was only responsible for keeping her Gran's house tidy.

Thinking of the recent loss of Gran, who had taken care of and loved her throughout her life, grief constricted her heart once again.

Disbelief continued to threaten her peace as she struggled to retain fragile control of her emotions. Gran would never have liked to see her fall apart this way every time she had time to think.

Wiping away her tears, she hugged her arms across her chest as she got up from her painful reminder of a happy childhood.

Looking down at the floral overstuffed chair, she almost smiled as she remembered how many sweet memories it contained of times she had spent curled up on her grandmother's small lap.

She almost couldn't stand it. As she looked away, another tear fell down her face; reminders like these were why she spent so much time at Del's cottage with him and his parents.

The memories of her recent dreams had stopped her from arranging any lessons this past week. She was too confused to even face him. And other strange things were happening, things she could not even begin to figure out.

She wasn't sure what to do about the dreams however, or what to do without Del. As she internally wrestled with the desire to see him and talk to him about it, she threw away the notion as quickly as it came. She was too horrified to imagine that conversation.

She only needed to keep the dreams from him a little while longer, she decided.

Plans for her trip were underway, but the thought of not having her best friend beside her made her chest tighten with anxiety. They've been inseparable for as long as she could remember.

Looking out over the moonlit meadow that separated her grandmother's cottage from his, she thought back to the past year and wondered how she would have survived without him.

If he hadn't helped her cope with her grief, it would have destroyed her. His friendship changed a very dangerous situation into something she grew from...and she became stronger for it.

Feeling a familiar warmth come around her, she suddenly knew he was standing behind her.

So lost in her thoughts, she hadn't noticed him walk in.

Before she could say anything, his arms came around her. Resting his chin on her shoulder, he said softly, "I saw you crying, what's wrong?"

"Pfsh, saw," she sniffed wiping her tears away with the back of her hand trying to dismiss the sudden jolt of electricity that had sparked when he hugged her. "You sensed it, like you always do."

When she referred to his advanced abilities as a Dream Catcher, his arms tensed but still held her.

"You could too, if it were me," he responded.

"You never cry, you're too strong for that," she retorted.

"Yea, but if I did, I'm pretty sure you would know it before anyone else."

"Why is that, I wonder?" she asked for the first time voicing her suspicions.

Sighing, he said patiently, "If you were going to D.C., you would know. They explain it in the preliminary classes."

Talking about Dream Catcher school finally forced the rest of her tears to come full force.

Putting her hands to her face, she bowed her head and cried silently. If Gran were

here, she would be going with Del to school. Not going on some crazy quest to find her.

Gently turning her around, Del murmured, "Don't worry, you don't have to go. I think

that it's a bad idea you won't go and that you refuse to tell anyone about your powers.

But, I won't tell anyone. You know I won't."

Burying her face into his jacket, she cried for a few more minutes then lifted her face to see his.

Gazing up at him, she explained, "You know why I won't. Gran was a Dream Catcher and look at what happened to her. She's gone, missing. Her entire life was to help others and train other Dream Catchers and do you see anyone making any effort to find her?"

Angry, she looked away as he waited out her tirade then said, " You think I want to waste my time going to that school when I could be looking for her? Absolutely not. I won't." Pausing, she said quietly, "She devoted her life to writing training materials for that place, and just when she needed them most, they deserted her."

Looking away, she was surprised...again. She was starting to feel Del's emotions again, it's like they poured into her at different times. What he felt, she felt. After the last dream, she swore she could sense his emotions more often.

She was becoming better and and better at reading him, even at a distance. The higher the emotion, the easier it was to find him.

She thought, when it first happened, that she was going crazy. At the time, she had suddenly felt a tremendous amount of anguish coming from across the meadow when she was in her cottage.

Not thinking, just reacting, she had sprinted over to his house and found him hunched over as a hammer had just slammed his finger.

She couldn't believe then, and she couldn't believe now that she could sense that.

She couldn't tell him what was happening, she didn't want to be accused of losing her mind. So, she had explained that she had heard him yell from her cottage and had raced over.

But she could also tell when he was hiding an emotion. And she could feel that he was blocking something pretty powerful right now.

Searching his chocolate brown eyes that looked tormented at the moment, she reached up and touched his cheek.

Finally deciding to brave her irrational questions, she asked, "What is it, Del? What are you hiding from me?

And why can I feel this? I mean, I know I've known you my whole life, but why this connection between us? What's happened?"

Her cheeks still wet from her recent tears, he slid his finger over the trails the tears had left on her skin. His gaze wandered over her forehead, to her eyes, down to her lips where they stayed.

Her heart catching, she found she couldn't breathe.

There was that same intense look, his dark brown eyes becoming darker and were also coming closer.

Why would he bring his face closer to her's unless, he wanted to...

Putting her hands on his chest, she stopped him and asked, "Del, I don't know..."

Before she could say anything more, he dropped his emotional guard and in an instant an intense heat flooded over her as she felt his every emotion, *for her.*

Inhaling deeply, she struggled for words as her eyes searched for his again, and before she could react or say anything, his hand had found the back of her neck and he had closed the distance between them.

He was kissing her with an intensity that overwhelmed her, yet surprisingly thrilled her at the same time.

She couldn't help but feel joy when his joy was flooding into her that she was responding to him.

And she realized she *was* responding to him. She wanted this kiss as much as he did.

Like in her dream, she circled her arms around his neck. Twining her fingers into his hair she brought him closer.

Pulling back, he stopped their kiss and said, "I have been dreaming of this, of you, for so long now," only to claim her lips again.

Pulled into a maelstrom of emotions coursing through her, she could only grab onto his jacket and hold on as her knees began to buckle from under her.

"Oh no, you don't," he growled as he stepped back to pick her up and cradle her to his chest.

Walking over to her grandmother's chair, he sat down with her on his lap and looking at her tenderly, he kissed the tip of her nose and cupped her face with his hand.

"You are *not* going to faint on me, now," he whispered. "There's something you need to hear first."

Her eyes widening, she couldn't believe she was sitting on Del's lap like this and that she was *feeling* all of this.

Claiming her attention, he said, "Ari, *you* are who I've chosen. I've known it's been you for a long time now, but you were never ready for me to tell you...until now."

Hugging her tightly, he kissed the top of her head and continued, "But with Gran gone, there's been a lot going on, and...you've missed a lot of explanations."

Raising her head to look at him again, confusion settled over her features. She asked, unsure of where this conversation was going. "What do you mean?" she asked nervously.

"Gran wasn't here to tell you about choosing someone for your bondmate was she?" he asked quietly moving a strand of hair from her eyes.

"No, not really," she said, relieved this wasn't the conversation she thought it was going to be. "But, it can't be rocket science," she said waving her hand in the air, "I mean, you just *know* don't you?

Looking at her tenderly, he answered, "Yes, you do, but there's a little more to it than that."

Looking down, he sighed and said, "I knew my mom should have talked to you about this." Looking up again, he said smiling nervously, "But, it's a little too late for that now, isn't it?"

Frustrated with the information she wasn't getting, Ari began to feel anxious as she started to realize how much she didn't know.

"What are you not telling me, Del," she said pointedly, "What have you done?"

Raising his eyebrows, his handsome features looking surprised, he answered, "It's not anything I've done, it just happened!"

"What happened?" she implored feeling panicked.

Finding her hand that was still wrapped around his neck, he said quietly, "I've fallen in love with you Ari, and that will never change," he said his eyes blazing. "Not for as long as I live will that change. You are who I've chosen, I'll never love anyone else."

Her stomach felt like it had dropped out of her and climbing out his lap, said, "Delius, this kind of sounds serious. Am I supposed to fall in love with you too...permanently, like this?" she asked her voice shaking.

Terrified at having to make such a life-long commitment so quickly, she explained as she backed up slowly. "I mean, I love you. I do. And that kiss, well it was amazing, but, to tell you that, that, I'll spend the rest of my life with you right now..."

Stopping, she searched his expression for answers.

Leaning over with his elbows on his knees, he hung his head, and said quietly, "Ari, I shouldn't be the one to tell you all of this, I'm not objective enough."

Shaking her head, she strode back over to him, she dropped to her knees and took his head in her hands so they were eye-to-eye.

"Delius Forgrove, you will tell me what all of this means, and you will tell me now. No way am I going to run over, wake your mom up and..."

Before she had a chance to finish, she was silenced with a kiss. Keeping her wits was proving to be a difficult thing. As soon as he laid his warm lips on hers, she lost all train of thought. She wrapped both her arms around his neck like before and returned his kiss.

Pulling her back slightly, Del growled, "Ari, you cannot do that."

His eyes were anguished and wondering why, she asked, "*You* kissed me. What did *I* do?"

Standing up and moving her away to arm's length, he said patiently, "When a guy, like me, tells you he loves you and will love you for a very long time, like forever, he kind of needs to hear your response. And a good response is, generally, what he is looking for, hoping for. You kissing me back without that answer is a little...well, it's driving me crazy," he finished, subdued and waiting for her decision.

Saddened, she looked at him, and said softly, "I thought I did tell you." Her voice rising, she said fervently, "And I can't seem to help kissing you back; when you kiss me, I just..."

Unable to explain her feelings, she said instead, "I can't tell you right now how I feel, about all of this."

Remembering her approaching venture and his school commitment, she said, "And you are going off to school and I'm going to be..."

"Waiting, right?" he asked hopefully.

"In a sense," she answered, fighting the urge to fess up to her travel plans. Good sense overcame a spontaneous confession and she said instead, "I'll be thinking, a lot. About all of this, you and me. I *will* be thinking," she promised.

Knowing she was telling that much of the truth, she ignored the guilty feeling that it would devastate Del when he discovered her gone. She shuddered as she realized he would probably be very angry.

Keeping her quest to herself was not easy when it came to Del. She'd never had very many secrets from him and none that were this life changing and dangerous.

"Look," he said, as he kept the distance between them, "You know how I feel. This is not a simple thing. It's actually kind of complicated and it's definitely very permanent. I can't explain any more. The rest, you need to find out on your own," he said sighing, "I mean there's only so much I can do, I'm not capable of much else right now."

Looking down, he shook his head, "I've come into your dreams, Ari," he confessed, "which is..."

"Not right!" she finished for him. Heat surged through her as she realized he had used his powers on her.

"Did it *feel* wrong though?" he asked bringing his intense gaze back to her.

"Well, no..." she answered slowly, "But, you should have told me first how you felt and not..."

"I was. That's how I was telling you, it's all part of my choosing you," he said, resigned.

Looking away, he dropped his arms from her shoulders and said, "Like I said, you know how I feel. Find out about all of this and then come and talk to me."

Relieved he was giving her time, she said, "Del, when I know more, I'll find you. It's not like I have to look far. And besides," she said adding, "you can feel my emotions, can't you?"

Smiling, he answered, "Yeah, so I'll probably know before you tell me, since you haven't been trained on how to block your feelings yet," his eyes twinkling.

Pointing her finger to his chest, "Well, that's convenient! You are something else!" she said shaking her head surprised she was laughing, surprised about all of this. Crossing her arms over her chest, her mood sobered and she said, "You know, it's really not fair, you have the whole advantage here. And the dream thing..." She said, her voice trailing off.

"Is totally fair," he finished as he began walking to the door. He seemed reluctant to leave, but opening it, he turned around saying with a crooked smile, "All's fair in love and war, right?"

"War?" she asked.

"If I have to fight for you, I will," he promised. "I've loved you a long time, Ari, I won't give you up easily."

"You may not have to," she responded her heart in her throat.

"I'm planning on that."

With that he walked through the door and into the night that had begun a battle for her heart.

Revelations

It was a long night.

She had tried sleeping, but whenever she was almost under, a flash of memory would remind her of Del's abilities inside and outside of her dreams.

Flustered by her memories, she tried thinking of what questions she would ask Del's mom, Gracius.

She had always been able to talk to Gracius so easily before; she hoped this conversation would not be awkward.

Burying her head under her pillows, she moaned, "*How* is this *not* going to be awkward? Her son is in love with me and I'm not even sure what that means, or how I feel!"

Turning over, she gave up on sleep and got up to make a cup of tea.

A few moments later, she sipped the relaxing liquid, and sat at the same table where she and Del had studied for hours since first starting school.

Tracing scratch patterns on the table top, she looked out the window and caught sight of him leaving his cottage with a bag slung over his shoulder.

"It's barely dawn," she whispered to herself wondering where he was going so early.

After a moment, she decided he must be leaving for his preliminary classes. Suddenly, a thought occurred to her. He must *know* she wanted to talk to his mom. She exhaled her pent-up breath, in one big rush of air. Not realizing she had been holding her breath, her temper began to rise.

"Does he know what I'm *thinking* now too?" she hissed.

Grabbing the list of questions she had ended up jotting down, she threw open the door and stomped over to Gracius, Del's mom, and Del's father, Don's home.

Not bothering to knock, she slung open the front door. Searching the small area, her eyes landed on a woman, who looked young enough to be in her thirtie's, but who she knew was much older.

She sat at a small table with two cups of steaming tea in front of her.

"Ari?" Gracius asked hesitantly. "Would you care to have some tea with me?"

"Well, at least you are *asking* me and not trying to read my mind, like *some people*!" Ari exclaimed, frustrated.

"Now, that would be impossible even for a Dream Catcher, and I am only a Dream Weaver, so that couldn't have happened, now could it?" she asked softly.

Her temper settling with Gracius' soft voice, she nodded and crossed the room to stand behind the chair Gracius was offering her.

"Do you know why I am here?" Ari asked, needing to know if Del knew her intentions to come over.

"Yes," she answered quietly. "And, can't say I'm surprised, Del's father and I have been expecting it to happen for some time now."

"For what to happen?" she asked fearing she would hear an embellishment of what Del had tried explaining the night before.

"For him to bond with you," she said looking directly into Ari's eyes.

Her mind in a whirl, Ari, dropped into the offered seat, and put her head in her hands.

"And why did no one try explaining this whole thing to me before this happened?" Ari asked her voice cracking.

Before Gracius could answer, she picked her head up quickly and argued, "I mean, what am I supposed to do?! He keeps reading my thoughts and... and, I feel like I have no privacy, at all!" she cried.

"Now, he can't read your thoughts, Ari, just your moods," she corrected. "You're the only one he can do that with, now that he's bonded with you."

"Should it just happen to me like that too? I mean, I don't know... I mean, this is crazy! What if I don't..." noticing Gracius' stricken look, she stopped talking.

"You don't love him yet," Gracious stated, rather than asked.

"I *do love him*!" she disagreed jumping up out of her seat, "but, I just don't know if it's the same as his love is...yet," she added quickly when Gracious' eyes spilled over with tears.

"I was afraid of this happening," she said sniffing quietly. "Every mother is. There's always a risk of a bond not being reciprocated."

Calming down and sensitive of Gracius' tender feelings for Del, Ari requested, "Please tell me of this bond, what exactly does it mean?"

Wiping her tears away, Gracius sat up straight in the chair, and began, "Ari, when Dream Folks love, it's never partially. It is with your entire being and is unconditionally irrevocable."

"Are you telling me," she asked her, "that Del's decision to love me will never change?

Not even if I don't love him that way back?"

Panicking, her heart felt like it was racing as she watched with horrified eyes as Gracius nodded slowly.

"It's not that I don't!" she assured his mother. "It's just that I *just* realized that things could even be different for me and Del. I mean, doesn't it take time for this to develop into what Del feels?"

"Yes, it usually starts about a year before you *consciously* know you love them," she explained.

"You mean the dreams," Ari said remembering Del's comment about her dreams.

"Well," Gracius said folding her hands over the scarred table, "usually that starts about a year before the bond occurs."

Speaking slowly, from her own memories it seemed, she continued, "You start by dreaming of the person you are falling in love with in a natural dream state. Which means, Del did not begin by visiting your dreams, but by imagining you in his."

"I never knew," Ari said with wonder in her voice.

Shaking her head slowly, Ari thought back over the year they shared together. All the times he had held her when she cried, taking a year off from school to help her through her grieving. The memories were endless. The amount of concern he's shown her should have tipped her off to his true feelings.

Talking without realizing, she said softly, "The year off school, our lessons," she said faltering, "but, he's my *best friend.*"

"All the signs of someone in love," Gracius said softly with understanding in her eyes.

Noticing Del's mother again, she asked, suddenly curious, "Who began the bond first, you or your husband?"

Getting up from her seat, the older woman began clearing the still-full cups of tea from the table.

"Sometimes, the boy and the girl will start the natural dreams, the first dreams, at the same time," she began speaking softly. "And then they go through it together, discovering their love for each other eventually." With a far away look in her eye, she said quietly, "Don and I were one of those fortunate couples."

Smiling, she carried the dishes away to the sink crossing their main room over to the bright kitchen. Light came through cheerfully through the sunny yellow curtains that were pulled back. They sweetly framed the kitchen windows.

Maybe, she thought sadly, if things had happened differently, what had happened with Del's parents could have happened with her and Del.

Despite their conversation, Gracius seemed happy. Watching her work in the kitchen, she could see one reason why her mood was lifted. Their kitchen made up the entire left side of the house. And even though the cottage wasn't spacious, there was a certain charm to it.

Giggling quietly, she looked at all the decorations she had forced Del to help her hang falling from all areas of the house.

But, even without the cheerful stringers and signs, the kitchen brightened up the entire house.

Spices hung in one of its corners where she knew their aromas were easy to notice if you walked by them. A colorful display of serving spoons lined the wall under one window, complimenting the blue-green paint the kitchen boasted.

The same colorful exhibit could be seen repeated on canisters filled with, she knew cookies and fresh baked treats. They were lined up on a counter made up beautiful pebbles swirled into an elegant design.

She could understand Gracius' mood being in a kitchen like that, she thought morosely. Slumping in her seat, Ari sighed loudly. She wondered if she would ever have a home like this. She hadn't thought much further than finding Gran.

What she would do once she found her, she had no idea. She was kind of hoping Gran would have some ideas when it came to their escape.

So wrapped up in her thoughts, she hardly heard Gracius calling out from the sink. "Ari, have you started having dreams of Del?"

Horrified to have to answer such a personal question, Ari was sure her cheeks were purple they were so flushed. Not sure she wanted to answer, she said, "Ummm..."

"You don't need to be embarrassed, Ari," Gracius said turning around drying her hands with a towel. "Yes, I'm Del's mother and I'm not a trained Dream Catcher, but I do have experience as a guide, so I can enlighten you on this very complicated subject."

Seeming to study her face, Gracius paused and continued, "Isn't that what you came here for? We've always been friends, right? And you've never been shy with me before, but I certainly don't want to make you uncomfortable. So, you don't have to tell me what your dreams are, you can just answer, 'Yes' or 'No' to my questions, ok?"

Happy to have returned to more comfortable ground, Ari mutely nodded.

"Ok, so let's get started," she began, "Have you been dreaming of Del?"

"Yes," Ari answered.

"Now, I know that some of that may be Del, considering he's already formed a bond with you, but I wonder how much of that is you," she said her eyes questioning Ari's.

"I really don't know," Ari answered. "I mean, maybe you should ask Del that, because he did tell me he has been coming into my dreams, lately," she said her face coloring slightly.

"Yes, he may have started the dreams, but it takes a trained Dream Catcher quite a bit of practice to come into someone's dreams every night. How long have you been having your dreams?" she asked.

Her throat suddenly dry, Ari could only whisper, "For about a week, a solid week."

"Seven days," Gracius said her eyes sparkling. "There's no possible way Del could have caught your dreams for *seven* dreams in a row."

"So, I'm starting my bond with Del, now?" Ari could hardly whisper. Her mind trying to wrap itself around that idea, she tried to listen, but all she could hear was ringing in her ears.

Looking up, her forehead began to form little beads of moisture and her heart began palpitating very quickly. Trying to see Gracius, she could barely make her out as there were two, no, three of her now.

Before she could register the fact that she was going to pass out, everything went black.

Dreams Again?

"What happened? How long has she been out?" someone asked. Her forehead was being gently wiped with cool water.

Her body was overheated, where was the air? Turning her head searching for cool air, her movement caused a commotion around her.

"She's coming around," someone else said close to her.

"She needs space! Give her space!" Wait, she knew that voice, was she dreaming again? It was the voice of peace in her life. Trying to see if she was dreaming, she lifted her hand reaching for the source of the voice that has been haunting her dreams as of late.

Searching for his face, her fingers finally found a smooth cheek, with a familiar mouth.

Opening her eyes, the light blinding her momentarily, she said, "Del? Is that you?"

"Yes, sweetie," he answered, his expression completely relieved. "I'm here. Got here as fast as I could," his eyes especially warm. "I'm just sorry it took me so long," he said as he continued to blot her forehead with cold water.

"Where were you?" she asked confused.

"At D.C.," he said, hanging his head down. "I never would have gone on that completely unnecessary trip, if I thought, for one second, that this would happen."

Looking up at her, he asked, his forehead creasing, "What did happen anyway? I could only feel..."

Her expression must have stopped him, because she could see his cheek turn a slight red, as he turned his head away from her.

"You *can* feel my emotions," she said softly. Ari realized she was in Del's room, where she must have been carried and that they had it to themselves. His parents had just left.

Returning her gaze to his, she asked, "Del, how do you do that?"

He didn't answer at first, but her feelings began slowly changing as she waited.

Knowing he must be as nervous as she was, and seeing how sensitive he was being to her feelings, her emotions quickly began blossoming into something warmer, stronger.

His eyes widening, he looked over at her quickly. Her heart quickening, she said quickly, "Now, wait a minute. You've got to give me time, ok? I mean, you've had a year, *a year* to get used to this idea. You've got to let me have some time too, ok?" she asked nervously.

His head bowing onto the bed he was kneeling against, he found her hands and brought them to his lips. "You know I will, Ari. I'll wait," he promised her his eyes shining.

Not sure what she just promised, she returned his smile, timidly at first, then with a confidence that everything would work out.

They had to, she could never give up on Del, he was all she had ever known.

Forgiven

Walking slowly among the fallen leaves and mossy rocks that covered the embankment of a rushing river, she followed it's fast course toward its source, a spot she liked to go when she needed a peaceful moment.

Stopping just when she came around the final bend, she gazed up at the terrific display before her.

As the sun bathed her skin, she lifted her face enjoying the warmth. Ari closed her eyes. Her mind went over the details she just painted there of the magnificent waterfall she had witnessed.

The thousands of tendrils of water cascading down its descent into the rushing river below soothed her nerves, something she needed desperately right now.

The Dream Maker could help her too, she thought grudgingly. Guilt began to rise within her as she thought of the times she used to go to him as a child. They would talk over her day, her frustrations in school and with classmates, something she always seemed to have.

The Dream Maker ruled over them all, accessible only by thought. Legend had it that he would one day appear among them, but that day had yet to come.

Dream Folk could connect with their Maker at any time, if they so chose. It amazed her that their Maker could connect with so many of them at the same time.

Randomly she wondered if he would be able to do that when he physically came to be with them. That seems absolutely impossible, she resolutely thought.

But, it seemed impossible what he did now. She only had to call him in her thoughts and he was there.

Her deep loss this past year, however, had driven her to reject her Maker's comfort. Del had encouraged her to keep up her talks with him, but she had been too angry.

The Dream Maker had not only created the first Dream Weavers, it was by his design that the rest were even here. He orchestrated all the moves of the Dream Folk.

Not by puppet strings, but by their conversations with him, he guided them in their daily decisions. He also assigned them humans to Dream Weave with, mostly children.

The Dream Weavers who ultimately rejected the Dream Maker and chose to make theirown decisions were the Outcasts, those who wreaked havoc on the minds of those they were designed to protect.

Taking a deep breath, she exhaled all of her frustration, wondering how she was going to face the dangerous trek she was taking without her best friend, and her Dream Maker.

Shaking her head, she knew she was acting like a fallen Dream Weaver, an Outcast, in cutting off all talks with the Maker.

She had been too angry, however, to face his voice in her mind. He could have helped by warning her of what happened a year ago. She was convinced he deliberately kept it from her.

And for that she could not seem to forgive him.

Sighing, she thought back to Del and their recent development. Still numb from all of the information she had talked over with Del's mom, she searched her heart and found she didn't seem to mind Del's intrusion on her heart lately.

Laughing quietly, she remembered Del's expression when she had first felt her deeper feelings for him.

Even though she felt his feelings, whenever he chose to show them to her, she was as surprised as he was when she began to feel a love for him too.

In comparison to Del's complete love for her, hers was small but blossoming. But, it had yet to feel permanent to her.

She could still get angry with him and it almost lessened the ground he had gained on her heart.

Pondering what the next year will hold and still confused about this entire process, she took in the waterfall again, memorizing as much detail as she could. It's portrait was a calming presence she always carried in her mind when she needed a peaceful transfusion.

She wanted to carry this memory with her. For the next week and a half, she was going to need as much peace as she could find so as to not tip Del off before he went to D.C.

Skipping out on Del was going to prove difficult.

His bond with her gave him easy access to her whereabouts. He could always seem to find just where she was whenever he searched her out.

She had yet to sense him, however. Knowing that worried Del, they would practice daily, but she still was unable to find him. He remained patient, however, promising her it would happen, eventually.

Among the lessons, they'd also been getting ready for their coming party. Every time she decorated, however, it served as a reminder that the party was a deadline. It was where she would have to say goodbye to Del.

That was more than she could think about right now.

Firmly pushing that thought to the back of her mind, she was surprised with how easily she was conforming to this whole bonding process with her best friend.

She had noticed, lately, more peace in her heart than she had felt in the entire past year. She didn't know who to thank for that, Del or the Dream Maker.

She smiled as she thought of how personal and loving the Maker was to have thrown Del and her together at such a young age. He must have known she could never have survived such devastation on her own.

And maybe, Gran's kidnapping or death, whichever it was, she grimly thought, was not by His design at all.

He does not control any of their decisions, so if the Outcasts had taken her grandmother, that was not the Maker's fault. She had to stop laying blame at His feet, she thought guiltily.

Curling up next to a tree stump, she decided to resume her long overdue conversation with her Maker.

She wrapped her arms around her knees and waited as she opened herself up for his voice to come into her mind.

"Ari,"

His voice resounded in her mind, and her tears began falling one after another. Choked up, she could hardly reply,

"Yes?"

"Why have you forsaken me?"

"Oh, Maker, I am sorry. I have placed the wrong judgment on you."

"It was not I who took your grandmother, Ari."

"I know, now. I just realized how we all make decisions, even the Outcasts, that can go against your design. I did that too, by ignoring you, and I am sorry."

Hanging her head, she put her face in her hands and cried silently.

"I forgive you, my child."

Feeling his warmth, his forgiveness, spread through her, she looked up at the skies and rejoiced at his love for her.

"Maker, I am ready."

"Ready to receive your assignment?"

"Yes. Is this a task I can do while I search for my Grandmother?"

"Yes, and I will tell you at the right time who you will Dream Weave with. Are you sure you want to make this journey?"

"Yes."

"It will be long and trying. You will face many difficult situations, but remember, my child, I am with you."

Unable to speak she reached up to the skies and brought her hands to her chest, grateful feelings pouring out to him, who loved her so much.

"I love you, Maker, thank you."

"And I love you, my child. Never forget, I am always here, no matter if you can hear me or not."

With that, she stayed huddled in her seat on the ground, tears of joy pouring down her face as she rejoiced in her reunion with her Maker.

Hearing footsteps coming quickly from a distance, Ari knew Del was coming for her.

He wouldn't have to try to find her, she knew, since this was a spot she had ventured to often after Del had introduced her to it several years ago.

Wanting to share with him that she had just spoken to the Maker, she knew Del would be as overjoyed as she was.

Getting up, brushing off her pants, she ran in the direction of crunching leaves and waited to see him.

She was caught off guard, however, to see Del racing around the bend through a stand of trees with a terrified expression on his face.

Stopping suddenly, he stared at her, a storm of expressions coming over his features. At first, he looked incredibly relieved. Then he looked...angry.

Striding over to her, he grabbed her arms asking, "Arella, where were you? I felt you...having a hard time and, and I raced over to find you and then suddenly you were gone! Did you place a guard over yourself?!"

Encasing her in his arms, he exhaled and said roughly, "I have never been so scared. You just vanished from my head, and I thought I was going to..." burying his head into her hair, he held her tightly.

"I'm sorry, Del. I was just talking with the Maker," she said completely taken by surprise.

She realized Del must not be able to sense her when she was in conversation with the Maker.

He held her tightly for a few moments but when she squirmed trying to catch her breath, he relaxed his hold until he was holding her more gently.

Pulling away, she looked up at him and shared, "Del, did you hear me? I talked with our Maker!"

As his expression changed completely, Del brought her to him again in another crushing hug.

"I've been hoping you would do that," he said with relief in his voice. "I guess that's one reason why I wouldn't be able to feel your presence."

Stepping back to look at her, he said teasing, "You know, I thought I had fallen in love with a fallen Dream Catcher for a while there."

Relieved he was no longer angry, she answered him, "I was just being incredibly stubborn and was placing the blame on the wrong doorstep," she confessed. "But, Del, it's incredible, He *forgave* me," she said her voice breaking.

"Of course He would!" Del exclaimed, "He will never let you go. You can let go of Him, but He'll never abandon you."

Walking back into his arms, she held onto him as she thought back to the past year and how abandoned she had felt.

She had done it to herself, preventing the Maker from comforting her, just when she needed him most, and He had forgiven her for it *all*.

Still reeling from his grace, she held onto her anchor, the only person who cared for her as much as Gran had, maybe more.

Love swirling through her, she had to force herself not to think of their impending separation. She knew she had to make this journey alone. She couldn't risk involving Del. This was her fight, not his.

Wanting to know something, she pulled away so she could see him better, and asked, "How long have you, you know, loved me?

Laughing, he ran his hand through his hair, and she smiled. She recognized whenever he was nervous. His trademark signature was when he messed with his hair.

"Gran guessed it before she disappeared," he answered softly.

"Oh Del," she breathed, a rush of feelings rising into her chest. Not sure what to say, she could only say the truth. "I had no idea."

"I know, believe me," he said with a strained voice, hanging his head.

"I couldn't stand not knowing how you felt anymore," he said quietly, pacing back and forth as he began to gesture with his hands. "I thought I was going to go crazy, you have no idea how hard it was to keep all of this a secret from you. And then Gran disappeared." Pausing, he finished, "I thought I had given you enough time to mourn your grandmother. I didn't want to push things on you before you were ready...so, I stepped into your dream over a week ago."

Nodding slowly, she said wondering something, "When you caught my dream, what was it like?"

Stopping short, he looked over at her, a smile coming over his face settling his anxious features.

"It was great," he answered simply. "Your mind is quite interesting," he said laughing.

"Did you expect anything else?" she asked quickly, to cover her embarrassment.

"Look," he said seriously, "I have to leave soon. I hate the fact I am going, but I need to be sure of something before I do go."

He took a deep breath and asked, hesitating for a moment, "Is it true you've been dreaming of me?"

Blushing deeply, she couldn't believe she would have to talk about this subject *again* and with the subject of her dream fantasies. Looking down, anywhere but at him, she whispered, "Yes," as her throat constricted.

"Now, don't faint on me, like you did with my mom," he said gently teasing.

Walking over to her, he hooked his finger under her chin and lifted it until her eyes met his again and knowingly asked, "You know what I mean, right?"

She tried turning her head away but he held on fast saying, "Ari, please just answer me."

Giving up her embarrassment, she finally answered hardly able to meet his intense gaze, "Yes, but could you please tell me when you started them?"

"Ok," he answered smiling. "How about you tell me first; how many dreams have you had?"

"Oh, I don't know..." she answered, not sure she wanted to tell him, yet.

"Ari, it will help you to know this too, please just tell me," he asked.

"Ok, about nine times," she answered brusquely.

As he nodded slowly, she could see he was very happy with her news. She asked again, "How many of those times did you instigate them?"

His eyes suddenly shining, he answered, "Twice."

"Oh," she said. It was about all she could say. "Did you know my dreams were changing?" she finally asked.

"I knew the week you began avoiding me, that something was changing with you."

"You knew that I was dreaming of you on my own," she stated trying to grasp all of this.

"Yes. Come here," he said reaching for her, "This must all be so much for you to take in."

She walked into his arms, grateful for his comfort. After a couple of minutes, and unsure how to ask her next question, she was happy her face was hidden from his.

"So you really were chasing me around the room?" she squeaked, her voice closing up again.

A throaty chuckle was his only answer.

Pulling away, she said a little outraged. "Since when do you think you could ever catch me, anyway?"

With that, she had an sudden idea. Pulling away from him she ran off toward her home.

She was glad she had worn her broken in brown leather pants as she took cuts through trees and bushes, racing away from him.

Realizing he was gaining on her she made a split-second decision to dive into some bushes. Giggling into her hand, she waited for him to run past her hiding place.

Instead, she heard his footsteps approach and quickly acting, she dove out of the bushes racing away again.

This time, however, he closed in easily and grabbed her.

Both of them laughing, she held onto his arms to balance herself. She could hardly get a breath from their run.

Looking at her, he was grinning, hardly out of breath, when he said, "Yea, and just like in our dream, you couldn't outrun me then and you can't out-trick me now."

Letting her hands slide down his arms finding his hands, she said seriously, "Del, this is *all* confusing, crazy confusing," she amended as she turned around so she could concentrate.

"But, I am beginning to understand that time will tell if we're meant to be together."

Turning back around, she said as she held his gaze, "This doesn't sound like anything we can rush anyway."

Then she stepped over to him and giving him a little push smirked and asked, "Now, how did you do it anyway? How do you know where I am?"

"Let's just say," he answered, "you have a presence I can spot anywhere. And, look," he said switching gears, "I told you before, I can wait, we have plenty of time for this to happen."

Taking in the information, she asked, "How did I get such a patient guy?" her eyes twinkling.

"I'm not that patient, actually," he said in a low voice. "I *should* be really mad that you ran away from me just when I was very happy to be holding you."

"I'm just lucky you don't have a temper," she said jokingly.

"You don't know that, Ari," he disagreed his eyes intent on hers. "I've changed, lately. But I'll forgive you this one time," his tone lightening.

Holding his hand, she turned and pulled him along the path that led to their homes. As the warmth of his hand seeped into hers, she didn't allow herself to think that the next time she ran away he may not be as forgiving.

Graduation

Plans were underway for one of the biggest parties the village had seen. Several of their graduating classmates were celebrating the same night she and Del were.

Several groups were also organized to travel together as they walked from party to party. Always conscious of Outcast raiders, villagers never knew when they would strike and no one wanted to take any chances tonight.

Ari and Del were knee deep in decorations and flowers the night of their party as they finished putting the final touches they had began three weeks earlier.

Del, a little subdued as he worked, was stuffing the leftover stringers and balloons into a bag when Ari stopped him, "Aren't you going to get ready?" she asked quietly.

"Yes, I guess I should start that," he answered.

Feeling his melancholy and guessing at how deep it went, her heart constricted. "Del, I'll see you soon, I promise," she said half-heartedly.

"Will I?" he asked quietly, looking up at her.

Trying to calm her heart that had just jumped in her throat, she said looking down, "You know you will," she said, lying as well she could.

"I don't know," he sighed, "I just have a bad feeling."

Thinking of the bag full of traveling items she had hidden in her attic, she squashed the guilty feelings that had just crashed through her, and said lightly, "You worry too much, Del."

That was for his own good, she swore to herself. He does *not* need to be in any danger over her.

Knowing she was doing the right thing, she continued her charade, pushed him to his room, and said, "Now go and look as handsome as you can, I feel like having some eye candy to look at tonight."

Stopping her efforts just as he reached his room, he said with a small smile, "I've been waiting for a long while for you to feel that way."

Reaching for her, she dodged his hands and skipping away, flirting, said laughing, "Oh, no you don't! Not until I'm ready!"

"Ready?" he questioned.

"I want you to see my dress," she said laughing. "Like I told you, it's perfect and I want tonight to be perfect."

"So, do I," he said under his breath as he moved into his room and closed his door.

As the guests started piling into the small cottage, Ari peeked out from behind Gracius' bedroom door and guessed now was as good a time as any to emerge.

Feeling very elegant in her long gown, she opened the door only to be surprised to find Del leaning against the wall next to the bedroom.

Meeting his eyes, she was surprised to find him so astonished.

Holding the edges of her skirt, she asked nervously, "Well, how do I look?"

Bedecked in a strapless shimmery gold gown that hugged her curves down to her waist, she hoped, belatedly, it wasn't too revealing.

Having never worn a ball gown before, she folded her hands and watched as Del seemed to find his words.

"Ari, you look...stunning," he said faltering momentarily. Gaining his voice back, he reached for her gloved hand and promised, "You will not be leaving my side tonight."

"Oh, really," she said flashing her mother's jeweled earrings as she tossed her head to look over at the crowd of villagers who were talking quietly as she had made her entrance into the room.

"I can't see what the big deal is," she protested. "I don't look any differently than normal," she said looking down at herself, only to look away quickly, blushing furiously.

"Yes," he said dryly, "I can see you really believe that, too."

Glad to see some of the old Del come out, she smiled as her blush began to fade and said stubbornly, "I do."

Holding his arm out, he waited as she took it and walked out into the room of guests.

"Well, if it isn't our little Arella, turned into a princess," commented Cy, a long-time friend of theirs from school who approached them first.

Decked out in a blue suit, he wasn't as dashing as Del was in his black tuxedo, but with his dark looks, he still looked nice, she observed neutrally.

Feeling Del's arm stiffen under hers, she placed her other hand on his arm preventing any rude comments and said, "Thank you, Cy, you have always been a good friend. We appreciate you coming to our party."

His eyes twinkling and looking from Del to her said, smiling good-naturedly, "Yes, well, it really came as no surprise to see you two staying such good *friends* these past few years."

A smile coming over her face, she looked up at Del seeing his face relaxing into a smile also.

"Well," Del's warm voice adding, "You know what they say, you know what kind of person you are by the company you keep."

Laughing, Cy responded, "Well! So, that's the reason why I've not seen you this entire past year!"

She couldn't help chuckling at Del's choice words, and watched as the two grabbed each other's hands in a friendly shake.

Turning around to leave, Cy looked over his shoulder and said, "Ari, you look beautiful, breathtaking, if I might add," with a sly look at Del. But, he continued in a different vein, probably because of Del's glare.

"I am happy for you both. It seems like things have developed while you both stayed hidden from us villagers, lately. Truly, I wish you both well." Looking over at Del, he said, "I will see you at D.C. tomorrow, right?"

Del paused then gave a curt nod. Ari speculated if he was suspicious of her plans.

After Cy left the cottage, she and Del joined the other guests. Occasionally, throughout the night, Ari would find find herself separated from Del as she caught up with old classmates. Each time she would look up she found herself the object of his attention.

At one point, standing by the fireplace, she looked up from her plate of refreshments and jumped when she saw Del standing right in front of her looking at her with a soft look in his eyes.

"You look like a pixie standing there, the firelight glowing off your skin," he said softly.

Blushing, she looked down and just then someone called out, "Let's play a game!"

Everyone agreed calling out some suggestions, "The Frog Chase!"

"Hide and Seek!"

"The Mole Run!"

Finally, when someone called out, "Blind Match!" everyone agreed heartily. It was decided they would be play outside, so everyone started filing out the door into the cool night air.

When she saw Del was still watching her, she blushed. She toyed with her glove as she asked, "Do you want to play?"

"Do you?" he countered.

She knew how the game was played, but did not want to play unless he did. She stayed quiet as she looked out the door with a wistfully.

Del must have read her expression and gently took her by the elbow and led the way out into the front yard.

"Come on, my shy little Ari. Since when have you been shy with me?"

"Good question," she whispered under her breath but allowed him to guide her to a spot under a tree.

"Now," yelled Rudy, a rotund teen not yet graduated from Dream Weaver school, but taking advantage of his audience. "The person playing the Blind Bat will be blindfolded and put in the middle of a crowd, that being the rest of us," he explained.

"He will try to find the girl of his choice as he walks around the meadow, while we whisper hints as he walks by, trying to confuse him. We may not move as he walks by, we have to stand our ground, but we may say anything we choose!"

Raising his voice, he called out, "They may not both be bonded yet, to play this game!"

After some grumbling, several couples moved to the edges of the crowd that had circled around the boisterous speaker. As the rules of the game were explained, Ari was surprised by how many bondings had occurred over the past year.

"Those of us who are single, raise your hands!" he yelled.

She raised her hand. "Technically, I'm not bonded, yet," she whispered. Del frowned and raised his hand reluctantly.

Noticing Del's and Ari's hands raised, Rudy ambled over and pulling a white handkerchief out of his coat pocket, he handed it to Del immediately.

"Well, since you are the guest of honor, Del, you should be the Blind Bat," he announced.

"Now, you have to tell me who the lucky lady is so we can all try to confuse you," he ordered.

Once Del whispered into Rudy's ear, his raised eyebrows were the only indication he had heard the name. He marched away pulling Ari with him as he spoke quietly to the rest of the party guests and then barked orders for all of them to disperse throughout the flower-studded yard.

Once Del had tied his blindfold on, Rudy hid Ari behind a stand of trees at the edge of the surrounding forest.

After smiling at her, his eyes friendly, he said, "Congratulations Ari, he will make a great husband and is already turning into a great Dream Catcher. Hope your bond happens soon!"

Before he could see her embarrassed flush he strode away to take his place in the meadow.

Someone turned Del around several times, and let go him. He cocked his head to the side and looked straight in her direction, smiling.

Even though he bumped into several pretty girls, Ari was very pleased to see that he politely nodded to each of them, but then moved them out of his way as he walked slowly toward her.

Making his preference known, he walked purposefully in her direction. No matter the suggestions called out to him, he ignored the subversions and finding her hiding place, came around the trees, and found her hiding.

Reaching for her waist, he pulled her to him as she laughed and reached up to pull off his handkerchief.

Still laughing softly Ari looked up into his warm chocolate brown eyes. As she stared up at him she barely noticed the last rule of the game being called out.

"Once you've found your girl, you have to kiss her!" yelled a laughing Rudy.

Glancing appreciatively at the game announcer, Del returned his gaze back at her and said softly, "Are you ready for this, Ari?"

Her heart beginning to race, she jumped when she heard Rudy call out, "Aww, Del, she can't decide on this! You deserve a kiss!"

"Ari?" he asked again, as her attention returned to Del.

"Ready?" she asked breathless.

She realized this was the first time he had held her like this since that night so long ago, it seemed, when he had first told her he loved her and had kissed her.

Knowing she was being given a choice, she suddenly became nervous having an audience. "Can we go somewhere else?" she asked Del quietly so no one could overhear.

Looking around, he smiled and said, "Sure, just give me a second." She watched as he let go of her and jogged over to Rudy gesturing with his hands as he spoke to him.

Coming back, he held her hand and pulled her into the forest, leading the way to the waterfall she had grown to love.

Goodbyes

The stars caught the river's currents, sending their lights sparkling onto the water. Ari watched dreamily as she stood beside the embankment in her favorite spot in the forest.

Looking up at Del, she lost her smile as she took in his expression.

"What is it, Del?" she asked.

With troubled eyes, he said, "I need to tell you one more thing about the bonding process."

His eyes roving over her upswept hair and the soft curls falling delicately to her shoulders, he seemed unwilling to continue.

"There's something you need to know," he began slowly. "I still can't believe you don't know all of this already, but I guess, with your grandma disappearing, you weren't around when all of this began happening to some of our classmates."

"But," he continued, looking at her sadly, " There's a chance you may not complete the bond with me."

Alarm racing into her chest, she asked, "What do you mean? I sense you, I can feel your emotions, when they're not guarded, anyway."

"That's the chance, the risk of a bond being made early. If you don't complete the bond with me, I'll always love you and you'll always know it. Eventually, no matter what guard I try to use, you'll always sense my emotions. You may begin to resent it if you don't share my feelings."

"But, the bond is started, how can it be stopped?" she asked worry for him taking over her feelings.

"It's more like, it can be interrupted," he answered, turning away.

"Ari," he said, turning back around and closing his eyes for a moment, "I have to leave you after the graduation party," he reminded her.

Opening his eyes, his searched hers for a moment before continuing. "Someone else could get to you before our bond completes," he said, his suffering eyes roaming the area once.

"I was hoping," he said settling his eyes on hers, "to have seen some more of the signs of a bond between us taking place for you. I mean, mine has been settled for some time now."

Panic settled into her chest. She couldn't imagine being the cause of constant torment in Del's life-or of someone else starting a connection with her. Shuddering, she couldn't help but thinking that this was hard enough to have happen with *Del*.

"That can't happen," she said forcefully.

Nodding his head, he sighed and said, "It doesn't happen often, but it has happened before. We need to be careful; you need to stay pretty much to yourself this next..."

"Year, right? Isn't that what you told me?! I can't stay cooped up, Del. That's crazy!

I'm not a hermit!" she exclaimed.

Resting his forehead on hers, he entreated, "I don't want you to be. If you would just come with me to study, this wouldn't worry me as much."

"You don't need to worry, I will *not* be feeling this way with any other Dream Weaver," she insisted.

"If I could just be sure of how you feel," he whispered. Looking down at her, her gown sparkling in the starlight, he said softly, "I wonder...," as he reached for her face.

Bringing it up to meet his, his lips grazed hers, swiping from one side to the other gently.

Sweet new feelings for Del began pouring out of her. She stood as still as she could and she suddenly wanted, at that moment, to feel something more for him. But when she remembered her trip in the morning, her heart broke.

So many other blossoming emotions began overlapping her conflicting feelings, however, which made their tender kiss sweeter.

As she returned his kiss, he held her tightly before he finally broke their contact.

Taking a full step back, studying her, he asked quietly, "Now, think about it, how do you feel?"

Examining her feelings, she closed her eyes and said, "Different, a little more...wait, I think I can see you with my eyes shut now!"

"Del, start moving around, I'm going to try to find you...," she said excitedly.

Keeping her eyes closed, she followed the windy patterns his warmth left behind as he made subtle moves to the left and right.

Knowing she was following him correctly, she twisted as he suddenly circled her.

Grabbing him, she commanded, breathlessly, "Stop."

As she opened her eyes, he looked as astonished as she felt at what she had just done.

"Del, I wanted for this to happen, so you can see that everything is going to be all right," she whispered, her eyes glistening.

"That sounds like a goodbye already," he said forcefully.

"Well, with you leaving in the morning, I'd rather say our goodbye out here tonight than when you leave," she said working hard to keep herself from becoming upset.

Looking out at the waterfall, she breathed deeply, drinking in the vision of the soothing scene and said, "I'm going to miss not seeing you all of the time."

Taking her in his arms, he asked quietly, "And you think I will be any better?"

"No," she answered, "but I want you to know I will be careful of meeting anyone I don't know. That whole bonding-with-someone-else-thing, will not happen," she promised.

Looking at her strangely, he asked carefully, "Where are you planning on spending your time?" he asked.

"Oh, at the bakery mostly," remembering her job for the first time. She had asked for some time off for her sensory abilities to wear off. She didn't want to be able to sense Franz and Helga's emotions while working with them.

Thinking she should check on them in the morning before she left, she returned her attention back to Del.

"What were you just thinking of?" he asked reaching up to play with a strand of her curls.

"Just of Franz and Helga," she answered throwing her arms around his neck.

"But," she said softly, "I'd like to be thinking of something else," trying not to feel her heart breaking.

Feeling her intent, he lowered his head until his lips met hers. It was the hardest goodbye she'd ever had to endure; as she wiped the tear coming down her cheek she tried to hide her plummeting feelings.

Reaching up to cup her face, Del whispered in her ear, "I'll be back every chance I get.

Don't cry, my Ari," pulling back to look at her, said with conviction, "You are my everything, I *will* take care of you."

Resting her head on his shoulder she knew he would. By these memories, he would carry her through what lay ahead.

It Begins

Ari had never even gone as far as a few miles outside of the village before, at least not without Del to guide her back home.

Having gotten up before the break of dawn, she woke up knowing she needed to go.

Everything inside of her was screaming to get started soon. Her grandmother needed her, she could just feel it.

As she threw aside her covers, her mind snapped to attention. Everything was ready, and as Del was sleeping, she shouldn't have any problems leaving today.

Memories of the previous night rested softly on her mind. Her heart warmed at the thought of Del and the past week, and it's enlightening revelations of their bond something she wanted to reciprocate, but couldn't yet.

As resolve formed for her to leave and soon, she felt her nerves stretching with tension winding around her muscles. She forced herself to calm down.

She would not let herself down. This was the moment she had been anticipating for a year now.

To vindicate her Gran, she thought as she hurriedly dressed, she would have to find her. She had already prepared a route through the forest she would travel. But, as she tied on her shoes, she couldn't ignore a strong feeling, a second sense, that was telling her to visit the Sugalle Bakery.

Frustrated, she couldn't figure out why she should go there. It was in the opposite direction she needed to go. But, she decided to trust her gut.

To head into the village this early could be tricky, she thought. Hopefully, many of the villagers who had attended the party were sleeping the morning through. Many of the Dream Folk took advantage of morning hours to sleep, as they had Dream Weaved the entire night, sometimes needing further rest to recoup.

As she climbed down the ladder from the attic, where she had hidden her travel bag and dried foods for the past three weeks, the thought crept its way in before she could stop it.

The weight of leaving her future bond-mate laid heavily on her. Fighting her emotions before they revealed themselves to a sleeping Del, she thought of happier times wishing those memories were what she was experiencing right now, instead of these darker ones.

Righting herself again, she strode purposefully toward the back door, the only door not visible to the cottage across from hers, and burst into the dark predawn air. Breathing in its heady, woodsy scent, she purposefully avoided looking at the house that knew her heartbeat as well as she did.

To cover the sound of her running footsteps, she tread on the soft mosses lining the worn path the two families used to travel to the village.

She covered a lot of distance quickly, and soon felt it was safe to begin a brisk walk to the bakery. Not wanting to lose her advantage of an early start, she thought only to check in the bakery to be sure all was well.

Unsure of the reason for her uneasiness, she hurriedly walked the final leg into the village.

Keeping to the outskirts of the cottages edging the small village, she hoped no one would notice her presence as she made her way to the small bakery that was only three buildings down from the main lane.

Reaching the side of the bakery, she breathed a sigh of relief and peeked into one of the windows. Not seeing Franz or Helga, she turned around and keeping her back to the brown and white checkered building, Ari reached into her mind to see if she could track their presence with her newly discovered abilities.

Her eyes closed, she sensed a faint trail of the familiar tone of their feelings noticing with a sense of alarm they were experiencing a high amount of stress. Unable to tell which room they would be in, she decided to enter, through the back door.

Surprised she couldn't hear them, only feel them, she wondered where they could possibly be.

As she walked the familiar halls the unease she had felt since this morning heightened to a degree that kept her back to the walls and her guard up.

If her bosses were in trouble, she wanted to help, but not get caught in it, that was for sure. Her mission was too important for her to be stuck in Maone during an investigation. She would just help and leave.

Why she knew there was something definitely wrong, she couldn't say, but all of her senses were on alert as she tiptoed down the hall.

Looking through every doorway cautiously, she had passed several rooms when everything in her began to scream for her to get out of the cottage. She was in danger!

As she sprinted toward the front door, she heard running footsteps behind her. Before she could get the door open, a heavy bag dropped over her head and trapped her arms to her sides. Her captors cinched it shut tightly.

Sightless, terror took over her and she began screaming.

The bag quickly came off and as her vision returned, her screams stopped in her throat when she saw who had attacked her.

Franz and Helga with their faces twisted into ugly sneers were coming for her again, but with a white cloth.

Backing into the door, shock made her helpless for a second. That was all the time it took for them to turn the cloth into a gag and to wind several ropes around her body trapping her arms again.

Her wits returned and anger flared at their deception. As she breathed heavily into the gag, trying to get used to her limited air supply, she could taste and smell that the white cloth had been treated with something.

Screaming, she couldn't believe her cries were noiseless.

"Now, don't bother with those screams, honey, you'll just wear yourself out," Helga purred.

Helga continued with a sinister smile on her face, "No one will be able to hear you, dear, no, not even your sweet and handsome boyfriend."

Turning to her husband, she said quickly, "When do you want to leave? The morning is about to break."

Speaking quietly, he answered, "Let's get started now. Even though he can't sense her, he can still see her. We haven't perfected that one yet. We can't cloak her. Our cloaking abilities will not hide anyone other than ourselves."

As they turned back to her, Ari began to kick over furniture near the door, and anything else her feet could reach trying to make as much noise as possible,

Scrambling to stop her before she could make it to a nearby glass case, Franz reached her first and roughly turned her around, holding her in a vise-like grip as Helga came at her with more rope.

Tying her legs securely, Helga looked at Franz meaningfully. He turned her back around and then slung her across his shoulder.

She had wished no one would notice her presence before. Now she was screaming tearfully begging for someone to see them as they slipped out of the fake bakery and into the breaking dawn air.

Even if they had enveloped themselves with some kind of invisible cloak, it still would look strange for her to be floating in midair as Franz carried her over his shoulder, she thought desperately.

After a few moments of walking hurriedly through the village, Franz' shoulder dug into her stomach painfully, causing her to moan.

They made it out of the village and into the surrounding forest without any interruptions. She was surprised they kept to the worn path. They must not be afraid of getting caught, she thought morosely.

She could see they were heading south, just the direction she had wanted to travel. Wondering if these two impersonators were responsible for Gran's disappearance too, she thought it must be connected.

But, why the interest in her family, she questioned fiercely? Ari's captors stopped suddenly. She was granted a reprieve for a moment, from her uncomfortable perch only to be thrown into nearby bushes.

91

Not bothering to hide themselves, Franz and Helga tore off as many branches as they could get their hands on and threw them over her.

She was still bound tightly, but she knew she had to try to attract attention. Rolling furiously from side to side, she managed to make the bush shake with her.

Spotting the disturbance, Helga ran to where Ari was hidden, crashing through the brush to reach her. Franz joined her and they both held her from behind as whoever they had heard approached.

What they all didn't realize was that it was Del who began to stalk by.

Captured

Watching Del walk by searching for her with a grim and determined look on his face tore her heart into pieces she didn't think it capable of.

Wanting to scream out from where she was, she sobbed into her gag and wished her tears had voices of their own.

Surely, he could feel her anguish! Not understanding what the Sugalle's had put into the gag that hid her screams, she struggled against her restraints needing desperately to feel the security of Del's arms.

Her hair was yanked backward, the combined strength from Franz and Helga prevented her from making the smallest movement.

As Del neared her hiding place, Ari couldn't bear feeling his emotions. When he walked slowly past her, they had crashed into her like a wrecking ball; it was more than she could bear. Now, like he, they receded the further he got from her.

He couldn't feel her. Helga had been right about that. Not wanting to believe her, she had depended on his bond with her to save her, for him to find her so easily. All hope dropping from her chest, she realized she had nothing else to hold onto-no one else in the world who cared enough to try to find her.

Hopelessness settled into her being and she couldn't form a coherent thought. She allowed the pain to take over the place where hope had been.

Not knowing how to cope with this new and frightful feeling, she gave up on holding onto consciousness. As a merciful darkness took over her vision, her last thought was of Del. Her screams taking over her thoughts, her torment finally ended as her last thought repeated itself over and over again; "Del... Del... Del."

After a couple of miles of cooperating, her captors finally allowed her to walk on her own. Relieved she didn't have to be jostled around callously on Franz' shoulder, she kept up their brisk walk as best she could.

Physically, she was fine, but she couldn't stop the flow of tears that ran continually down her face.

Still unable to make a noise, she did the only thing she could think of. She decided to cry out to the Dream Maker.

"Maker, why have you abandoned me?"

"I will never leave you or forsake you, Ari."

"But, how could this all have happened?!"

"My child, I have created all that you see, are you questioning my way?"

"How can I not? My Grandma has been gone for a year. And how long will I be held captive? How do I know I will survive this?"

"You have to trust in me, I will never abandon you."

"How can I? This seems so hopeless."

She hung her head as she stumbled along, and despair rushed at her full force.

"Ari, I have a plan for you, a plan to prosper you and not to forsake you, a plan to give you hope and a future. Trust in me."

"Maker, I will try."

"Do not despair, my child. Trust in me."

As she felt his presence leave her mind, she held onto his promises. He would not abandon her.

When she had thought no one cared enough to find her, she had felt a terrible hopelessness. But, with her Maker's whispered proclamations, she now felt a new hope surge through her.

Wondering what could be his plan for her in the Outcast's camp, she trudged on.

Her tears ended, the only sign she gave for her bolstered attitude. She had a feeling it was better for Franz and Helga to think her hopelessness had weakened her. They would be less vigilant. She did not want to be considered a threat.

Plans to attack them were useless, she knew. She had no idea how to fight. But, if she could escape them, she would at least have a chance.

First, she needed to listen, and find out as much as possible before she attempted to break away.

She was rewarded only a few moments later, when Helga mentioned her voice.

"Franz, do you think our formula has worn off, yet?"

"Not sure, we should test it and see if she can make a sound," he answered brusquely as he threw a glance behind him.

"When?" she questioned curtly.

"In a few moments, follow my lead," he answered.

Ari kept her head down, as if she were lost in own little world as she waited for their next move. She decided, whatever it was, she would remain noiseless. If her voice had returned, she would know it, but would make sure not to show it. She would need her voice once she'd made her escape.

As they rounded a bend she thought she heard her name whispered from a nearby thicket.

Not wanting to attract attention, she subtly glanced in the direction of the noise. Poking out of the bushes were two unmistakable markings of an Outcast.

Two long, rounded ears that came to a point at the end were in view while the rest of the creature was hidden behind the thick brush.

As she looked, however, the figure slowly rose, revealing a furry face that reminded her of a teddy bear. It had a strangely pleading expression that looked like it was begging her to be quiet, to trust him or her.

Stunned at being hunted by yet another Outcast, she wasn't sure what to do. Alert the Sugalle's of this new Outcast?

Which camp would be worse to tolerate, she wondered?

The Sugalle's were forcing her to make a punishing trek through the forest. Would it be so bad to trust this strange face who was looking at her so innocently?

After thinking a minute, she looked back and the ears and face that went with it were gone.

Suddenly feeling alone, she tried not to look around to find this new creature that was following her. She kept her head down, straining her ears to catch any more speech from her tracker.

Hearing a whisper of leaves rustling, she quickly became alert. "Don't scream," the furry Outcast whispered so softly she hardly heard it.

Suddenly, in a blur of leaves and shouts, the Outcast's limber, lean body came flying out of the bushes toward Franz and Helga.

Recovering quickly from their surprise, the two Sugalle's quickly went into attack mode.

Ari huddled herself into a nearby bush, shoving herself in as best as she could with her arms trapped in the tight ropes.

Franz and Helga jumped with surprising lightness into the air and met their attacker head on.

She watched as the bear-thing roared with fury, knocking Helga through the trees with one swipe of his fur-coated hand.

His back was turned as Franz came at him with a huge tree limb, so Ari cried out hoarsely, "Watch out!"

Not knowing why she had just defended the new Outcast, she shrunk back into the bushes and watched as Franz's attack was thwarted.

The beast turned around just in time and ducked under the huge branch swung at him.

Roaring again, he jumped high and Franz, with the sun in his eyes, wasn't able to see the attacher.

This new Outcast knew Franz would lose his vision, she thought with wonder. A fierceness instantly gripped and surprised her as she wished she could fight like this.

Franz stood looking around with an angry and confused expression. Noticing her in the bushes, he pointed at her and promised angrily, "We will fix your voice as soon as this is over."

Just then, the Outcast seemed to come out of nowhere. He jumped off a high branch, right on to Franz' back, knocking his head into the ground.

She watched as the creature jumped off Franz's back and paced over to his head.

Studying the unconscious form, he watched it for a few moments before he sighed heavily, his features relaxing.

Looking around, he found her easily as she cowered in the bushes.

Walking carefully over to her, he said, "Now, don't be afraid of me, lil' Ari. My name is Wuz, and I was sent to find you," he said in a surprisingly gently voice.

Her wits left her then, and she burst out laughing. She couldn't seem to stop her outburst. Ashamed, she tried to control her reaction to his name.

Finally, she found the breath to answer his confused expression, "You mean to tell me, you are named after...a nursery rhyme? Sorry, but after what you just did, I find that hard to take in."

Of all things, a bashful look came over his features as he said, "Well, it's a name someone gave me, and it kind of stuck."

Still giggling, she said, "So it's kind of like, fuzzy wuzzy was a bear, fuzzy wuzzy had no..."

Frustrated, he interrupted, "Yes, yes. You have to admit, don't I kind of look like one?"

Looking at his features, his rounded ears, his black nose, and teddy-bear-mouth, she answered, trying to stifle a laugh, "What? A bear? Umm, kind of, I guess." Unable to help herself, she laughed again. "But, excuse me for saying this," she said in between a bout of giggles, "but you aren't exactly a fuzzy little bear."

Putting his hands on his hips, he waited as she finished her new outburst. Looking at her patiently, he said, "You know, I'm used to that reaction, but usually when someone does it, they dearly regret saying their true feelings. And, I did just save your life."

Sobering quickly, she said, "Yes, I know, and I'm very thankful. Remembering he had called her by name, she asked, "How do you know who I am?"

"Let's just say I know someone very special to you. And I have to say, you look just like her."

She struggled to sit up as hope flared in her chest.

"Who? Please tell me you are talking about my Gran!"

Watching her, he nodded.

Tears sprung to her eyes and she struggled to remain calm as she asked, "Did she send you here to me?"

"Yes," he said gently, "She knew you got yourself in a mess of trouble."

"Oh, Gran," she whispered, wishing she could use her hands to cover her now awkward display of emotion.

Wuz pulled out a pocketknife and began to cut away the ropes that bound her.

"Now, we've got a long journey ahead of us and we better get going," he said while she rubbed the marks on her arms.

As he helped her up carefully, Ari tried not to grimace when her skin brushed his cropped short furry hand. She had never met a Outcast. She was uncomfortable knowing he had willingly traded human looks for those of a monster.

She tried to shrug off the shiver traveling down her spine and be more accepting, but she was having a hard time being comfortable around him.

As she tried to match his long stride, he kept his gaze forward darting glances around to be sure of her safety.

She knew if Gran had been responsible for his conversion to good, it had to have been very thorough.

Studying him, she realized she had a weapon in her new friend Wuz. His agility and tracking skills were talents she wanted on her side.

If that required trusting him, then she needed to start now. Stopping in her tracks she remembered that Del was trying to find her. She turned around and began to scan the area. She needed a few moments to see if he was near.

Reaching into the innermost recesses of her mind, Ari drew up her feelings and applied them to her search in the region. Just as she was reveling in her emotions, hoping for the transfusion of Del's feelings to hers, she was roughly interrupted.

Ari!!" Wuz yelled, grabbing her arm and pulling her off the path. "You can't be doing that! They've spotted us now for sure!"

Disoriented, she was horrified at her use of Dream Catching without knowing the repercussions. She hid behind Wuz's back as they stood on the edge of the path while he searched around them for the best hiding place.

"It's no use. They'll find us," he muttered darkly.

Just then, great piercing noises filled the air.

Loyalties

Before she could look up and see what great creature could make such a noise, Wuz grabbed her and began speaking urgently to her.

"Time is running out here, Ari. And your Gran, she needs you, so stay out of trouble and follow my orders. I've got to act a little differently once they've reached us. But don't worry that I've lost my mind, ok? I'll protect you."

Looking up, he searched the skies for the creatures that were still making shrill calls to each other.

Alarmed, she asked quickly, "Wuz, are you saying Gran was taken by these things too?"

"Yes, it was a trap she allowed. I can't tell you anything, that's your Gran's right. I just didn't know I wouldn't be able to tell you *anything*. Didn't figure *you knew* how to Dream Catch, that's what did it for sure."

The birds or creatures were coming closer. Trying to remember her lessons on the fallen Dream Weavers she tried to concentrate on Wuz' words.

"Figuring as how you already know the basics, you need to know something very important. With Outcasts, judge them by your heart. You can sense true evil if you tried, and the same for goodness. And the judging is easier by touching them."

Holding her hand he projected such a sense of peace she was overwhelmed by how comforted she felt in such a terrifying moment.

"We all have it, and you just need a moment to test their intentions. It's advanced Catching but I think you can figure it out soon enough."

Feeling a rush of wind all around her, she barely had time to look up when two monstrous clawed feet grabbed her by the shoulders and effortlessly picked her up into the sky.

Closing her eyes as she was flung vertically in the bird's attempt to make flight, she fervently hoped it kept its strong grip on her shoulders.

Not sure she wanted to open her eyes, she did when she realized Wuz could be in danger for aiding her.

Her heart made a home in her throat when she saw how high they already were. Looking around she searched for the other bird.

Seeing nothing, she craned her neck to look behind her and with great relief saw Wuz hanging in just the same position she was in.

Grabbing at the talons that were surprisingly not digging into her skin, she looked desperately around at the ground trying to see where they were taking her and her rescuer.

The Outcast was covering a lot of ground quickly and soaring upwards above the clouds. She realized it must not want her to see the flight path it was taking her and Wuz.

She was having trouble breathing since the air was rushing past her so quickly. Gulping small breaths, she concentrated on getting enough air so she wouldn't faint. She needed consciousness.

After seemingly endless hours of flying over dense cloud cover, Ari noticed that they began to slowly descend. She panicked at the thought of what she would find below.

She started imagining the worst of all the tales she had been told of Outcast hideaways.

Desperate to talk to the Dream Maker, she wondered if she would find his voice louder this high up. She had always wondered if the Maker made his home in the skies.

Without further thought, she closed her eyes to the rush of air meeting her face, and in her mind, reached out to speak to him.

Maker?

Yes, my Ari.

What *do I do? I am in a fix here.*

Trust in me.

O..k…

Trust in me, Ari. My plan does not always make sense. I will be here to protect you and comfort you when you need me…

Umm, Maker? No disrespect intended, but is this your version of protecting me?

Look where I am.

At the moment, they were descending toward a tree-studded border. In the distance, a clearing revealed scores of tents surrounding a formidable looking stone castle.

Her eyes wide with disbelief that she was entering Outcast territory. She shut them quickly and listened as the Maker continued their conversation.

Ari, how can you question me? Didn't I create our world? Didn't I create you?

Trust in me.

Maker, I can see that you created me, I'm not evil. But, did you create all of that down there?

Even the thought of entering that realm made her stop and catch her breath. She had no idea what to expect and it thoroughly terrified her.

I did not create evil, little Ari. Just remember I am with you always. And sometimes I am carried in the hearts of the most unexpected Dream Weavers.

At that, the Outcast carrying her began making shrill calls to its partner and Ari grabbed tighter to her hold of its clawed feet.

Screaming, she held on as tightly as she could as the beast dove downward swinging her forward again. Dodging the tops of trees, the Outcast finally dropped her to the ground.

Despite the rough landing, she was relieved to have her feet on land again. With the Outcast hovering over her, she tried to regain her bearings. As she leaned over and braced herself on her knees, she peeked behind her at the Outcast. She could see more clearly he had the distinct look of an ugly vulture, but in monstrous proportions.

With its black hooked beak and yellow head it eyed her much the same as she did it. Not sure which gender to give it, she realized she didn't follow Wuz's last instructions.

Not once during her flight did she test the Outcast's intentions of good or evil. She leaned down to check her shoe, but unsure what this thing could sense, she hesitated to test it.

Deciding Wuz would not have steered her wrong, she went ahead and barely skimmed her fingertips across the rough skin on it's leg as she stretched her arms up from her crouched position.

What she didn't expect was such a rush of anger, loneliness and despair assaulting her.

At her touch the vulture screeched at her. It flapped its wings staring at her with its black eye as it moved away.

She couldn't tell whether it was angry with her for trying to sense its emotions or whether it was just reacting to the terrible emotions it hosted.

'What must it be like to live with that kind of hatred and ill will?' she thought to herself.

With a surprising tenderness toward to this fallen Dream Weaver, she wanted to talk to it and see if she could help it in some way.

Before she could try, however, Wuz yelled out as he landed roughly in the area next to her. Jumping up quickly, he glared at her for a moment. Just before he bent down however, to catch his breath, he slyly winked at her.

He must be warning me, she thought to herself. This is not the time for saving Outcasts. Nodding to herself, she began to look around and noticed the second bird had landed a short distance away.

It seemed to be keeping its distance from Wuzzy.

Trying to keep the confusion from showing on her face, she watched Wuz' performance. It wasn't difficult to figure out why the two vultures kept their distance.

Friendly and gentle Wuz had turned into a raving madman. He was stalking around the area, sniffing the area as if he were looking for his next meal.

Turning his eyes to her, she had to force herself from not crying out in fear. He was absolutely terrifying when he wanted to be.

Growling at her, he advanced on her, grabbing her arm roughly.

"If you know what's good for you, you better be moving along, now, you rotten little Dream Weaver," he sneered.

Speechless, she ran to keep up with his long strides, but her short legs no match with the furious pace he was setting.

Rushing through the few trees they had landed in, they walked into a field of downtrodden green grass toward the expanse of tents she had spotted from the air.

Despite the terrifying demeanor, his touch allowed her to feel he meant her no harm. A calm settled over her.

But, their frantic pace was soon too much for her lungs and she began begging for Wuz to slow down. "Please, please, I can't go like this much longer," she said gasping for air.

Stopping, she almost dropped to the ground when she found herself being hauled up onto Wuz' shoulder.

"Oh no," she groaned, "not this again."

"You don't leave me much choice Ari. Just hang on," he said quietly so only she could hear.

Wuz set a pace the vultures couldn't keep up with on ground. The birds were soon gliding over them, casting their shadows on Ari and Wuz.

Making sure they couldn't hear her, she asked, "What is your Outcast name, anyway?"

"Don't ask, it's better you didn't know. I can't show any favoritism at all," he answered brusquely.

Frustrated, she watched as they passed the tents quickly. She was just beginning to notice who were in the tents. They were milling about or peeking their heads out at her.

Her eyes widened and she wished she could get a better look. She couldn't believe what she was seeing.

The Outcasts were creatures she couldn't have imagined in her wildest dreams. She knew that someone had obviously imagined these monsters, however. These Outcasts all turned someone's nightmare into reality.

There were all manner of reptiles ranging from snakes with legs and crocodiles snapping their huge teeth, to lumbering, enormous dinosaurs. She could see other monsters too. Troll-like creatures, giant monsters with drooling mouths, others with sharp and razor-like teeth, and still more with no teeth all staring back at her.

She was almost glad she could hardly see all of them as they rushed past them. It was too much to take in, she decided.

She could see that they were making quite an entrance. Creatures great and small stopped what they were doing to glare at them as they passed.

She wondered if the smaller Outcasts were as vicious as the bigger ones. She was sure they were as she flew by one tiny Outcast who screwed up its ugly face and screamed at her, shaking its fist.

Shuddering, she couldn't look at them anymore. It was too frightening. She was horrified that they haunted children's dreams at night. One look at them was enough, but to be forced to dream of them for hours must be truly awful.

They soon began to pass through another area of the tent encampment. Noticing the tents were now changing in colors, she looked up to see what these Outcasts looked like.

Beautiful but terrifying women seemed to occupy this area. She guessed beauty had appealed to these once good female Dream Weavers. But theirs was a cruel beauty. She could see it in the set of their eyes looking at her with disgust.

They must attract their human prey in their dreams, only to frighten them in terrifying ways. Shaking her head sadly, she couldn't help but notice they were clothed in strange and varying outfits. Their clothing featured different styles, from ripped leather to torn jean cutoffs.

As they quickly ran past, she could see some had extra limbs, while one looked much like the famed Medusa, with her head covered in writhing snakes. She did all she could to look away from their strangeness.

The one consistency she couldn't help but notice in all the camps they ran through was the most frightening. She cowered under the lack of noise as soon as Wuz and she entered their domains. From the first tent, all talk ceased.

It terrified her too that hate-filled eyes turned her way as they advanced through the camp. Wuz instinctively tightened his hold on her when they first encountered these antagonistic stares. As uncomfortable as her position on his shoulder was, she appreciated his protection.

She had a feeling that if she were left alone in this camp, she wouldn't survive five minutes. Every creature seemed to intensely resent her.

She even appreciated the two great vultures flying above her now. They seemed to invoke fear among the Outcasts as they flew over.

Each time the Outcasts began to crowd the path she and Wuz were racing down, the two vultures swooped down and snapped their great beaks, barely missing the Outcast's heads as they ducked out of the way. The great birds soared upwards, cackling at the havoc they invoked.

Trying to see beyond the creatures these former Dream Weavers had transformed themselves into, she craned her neck from side to side to find any unnoticed path she could use later to escape.

Before she could form a plan, however, her mind filled with the Maker's presence. Taken aback, she emptied her mind of all thought and waited for him to speak to her.

Ari, don't try to make any plans of your own. Wait for my leading.

But, Maker, I've got to find my Gran and take her out of here!

Let me guide you through your next challenges. It's such a time as this that you need me the most, faithful Ari. Trust in me. Will you?

Bowing her head, she cried softly trying to ignore the stabbing pains she was now feeling from Wuz' shoulder digging into her stomach. Finally, she agreed to follow the

Maker's plan and let go of the desperate ideas she had begun forming.

Maker, I will trust in you. Use me as you need to. I place Gran's life and my life in your hands.

Even as she said this, all trace of anxiety left and she could actually feel a peace settle over her. Looking up, she was surprised she didn't notice that they were climbing steps to the entrance of the stone castle.

Fear returned at the thought of what awaited her inside the stony walls.

Putting her down roughly at the castle's entrance, Wuz turned around and looked terrifying.

Growling and screaming at the mass of strange Outcasts who had congregated at the first steps to the castle, he snarled, "Watch out you filthy beasts! This one is for the high queen herself! None of you is to approach her! Any one of you who does not follow these commands, will find themselves without a head!"

Despite the instant grumbling and ignoring the shouted protests, Wuz turned back around and shoved her roughly toward the huge stone doors that blocked their entrance.

In a booming voice, he called up to the guards peering through the turrets and demanded entrance.

She realized Wuz must be an influential member of the evil queen's court. Without any questions, the doors opened, revealing a sight she was not prepared for.

Castle Surprises

Expecting crumbling walls to match the outside view of the castle, she gasped at the opulence she found.

Golden walls and extravagant chandeliers hung from ceilings that made her catch her breath. Pictures she had seen in school of the humans' Vatican City instantly came to mind as her eyes grazed over breathtaking embellishments that decorated the ceilings.

The walls adorned with several quite large and exquisite paintings of lush green country sides featuring men and women dressed in royal robes in statuesque jovial poses.

Their happy moods leant to the air of a leisurely life within the castle walls. Before she could take anything else in, a tall gilded door cracked open releasing two seemingly harmless lizard-like creatures.

Standing straight and glistening with wet skin they walked briskly toward her and Wuz.

They were all black and as one of them turned slightly she could see a red stripe running down its back and tail.

She jumped when Wuz stepped in front of her with one quick movement.

"She's not for the two of you to interrogate," he snarled.

Peeking around Wuz' arm, she could see the twin Outcasts register his statement with shock. One recovered first and said with a leer, "Since when do you decide what we do?"

"I *said,* that this one is not to be touched," he repeated with a snarl.

With a sinister smile, the other lizard said, "Queen does not mind if we weaken her enemies a bit, before she begins her questioning."

"A bit? More like leave them for dead," Wuz said quietly. "Queen barely gets a word out of them after you two are finished."

Shrugging, the first Outcast said, "We tell her what they told us. As will this one. She'll tell us everything we need to know."

Shivering, Ari shrieked when she backed into a studded wall. Looking over her shoulder, she froze when she saw what she ran into. A towering Outcast who resembled a rhinoceros with horns jutting out all over its body.

Not moving, it ignored her as she backed slowly away to where Wuz was standing.

Turning around, she faced the trio arguing over her.

Scowling, the two evil creatures looked at her as Wuz finished his argument.

"So, she will *not* be going with you, and that order, as I just said, comes directly from the Queen herself."

Without looking at her, he grabbed her arm and began walking down a long expansive hallway.

He set a fast pace as they walked and she hardly had time to study anything else she passed. She did spot several more rhino-Outcasts along the way guarding more doors.

The hall seemed to stretch endlessly and her legs were beginning to tire with Wuz' long strides. As she slowed down, Wuz grabbed her arm and dragged her back to his tireless pace.

"Wu..." she began.

Shaking her, he warned her gruffly, "You walk or I will carry you."

Realizing she had almost given his nickname away, she tucked her chin into her chest and tried to keep up.

"Where are we going?" she asked wondering how much longer she could walk like this.

"None of your business!" he yelled just as they approached another rhino-outcast.

She heard a throat clearing and realized it was the rhino they were now passing. She saw Wuz glare at it and walk by more quickly.

This rhino seemed to be following her with his eyes. She wondered why. All of the other rhinos had completely ignored her.

Now breathing heavily, she saw that Wuz was heading toward a solid black massive double door. They practically jumped out at her since she's only seen gold doors and solid gold walls.

Wuz stopped. His brow furrowed and he stood staring at the door.

Barely moving his lips he said, "Say nothing, I'll take care of the rest. Say *nothing*," he repeated grimly.

With that command he pushed open the great doors and they walked into a magnificent throne room.

Her attention was riveted on the woman sitting in an exquisite chair, which Ari realized was the throne. She could hardly see the woman as her throne lent off a brilliance that made her eyes water as she tried to look at it.

As they walked closer, she realized the throne was covered in decadent stones. Jewels of all colors and sizes surrounded a woman who was by far, the most beautiful woman she had ever seen.

Ari wondered cynically if the Queen had transformed herself that way or if she had been born this gorgeous.

Hair like corn silk fell past her waist, gracing a figure that put Ari's own short dimensions to complete shame.

Eyes the color of emerald green returned her stare. It was disconcerting to be studied, but she refused to break her stare.

Suddenly memories of the past year filled her mind. Anger clouded her vision as she looked at the queen with revulsion.

When she had first found her grandmother gone, she had felt this same fury take over.

And the reason was sitting right in front of her perched on that ridiculous chair.

In a fit of sarcasm, she decided to name her, Queenie. Ari was doing everything she could to not jump at the woman's slender throat. 'One little name wouldn't do a bit of damage, but it made her feel better nonetheless,' she thought.

Trembling slightly at the anger coursing through her she struggled to suppress her inner fury from showing.

After a few tense moments she resolved to follow Wuz's directions. She would not say or respond to anything this woman had to say.

With a satisfied look on her face the evil queen said, "I suppose you are wondering why I brought you here, Arella."

When she did not respond, the queen continued, "Well, I guess not then. You are going to try to ignore me then?"

Everything in her screamed to ask where her grandmother was, but she held herself in check.

The Queen tapped her slender finger on her cheek and turned a questioning gaze at Wuz.

"Bear, tell me why you thought it so necessary to attack the spies who captured this girl."

"Because I don't like them. They deserve a little tossing around. Their arrogance has gone unchecked for far too long," he answered brusquely.

Grinning with amusement at Wuz, she returned her gaze back to Ari. Her voice rising, she asked Wuz, "And my two devoted servants have informed me you interfered with their excellent mode of questioning. Pray, tell me why."

Looking a bit uneasy, he explained quietly, "You told me before I left to be sure she was not harmed. And I doubt she would have survived those two. She is but a child."

Trying not to squirm under the queen's direct perusal, she watched their exchange.

Heat flared in her chest when she realized what Wuz had just said. She was not a child. She was an adult. She bit her tongue to prevent herself from retorting from his last comment.

Seeming to agree with Ari, the queen replied, "She doesn't look like a child to me, Bear, and I think we are underestimating this little Dream Weaver. She has a strength I haven't seen in quite some time."

Folding her hands together and resting her chin on them, she then said slowly, "I think we should let the Twins have a stab at her, don't you?"

Looking over at Wuz, Ari could see his eyes narrow slightly, then nod curtly.

Satisfied with his response, she looked over at him saying, "She doesn't really leave me much choice. Since she won't speak to me, let's see if she's more cooperative after the Twin's interrogation."

"Now, Mistress?" Wuz asked.

"Let's give her the night to rest. I'd like her to be fresh and ready tomorrow for my little pets," she responded.

Bowing, Wuz firmly grabbed her arm and wheeled her around as he led her back out the doors.

Running to catch up, Ari tried looking up at him to analyze his expression.

It looked grim, and so must be her situation, she thought with a sinking heart.

Taking her directly to the rhino guard who had watched her earlier, Wuz ordered him to take her to a cell.

"Inform me immediately of where she is placed," he said.

And without another look in her direction, he left her alone with the monstrous Outcast.

As she craned her head to look up at him, he grunted at her and pointed his spear in the direction he wanted her to go.

Feeling morose at Wuz leaving her so suddenly, she bolstered her courage. And not wanting to anger the horned beast, she quickly obeyed.

After following several hallways and two sets of stairs, she found herself in a desolate part of the castle.

Guessing this must be the area where she would find her cell, she looked around at the rows of doors that lined each side of the halls.

Wanting to pound on each door to find Gran, she started toward one when the rhino guard blocked her with his arm.

"This isn't the time for such action," he said in a deep voice.

Surprised he had spoken to her, she looked up at him and was shocked to see a gentle expression in his eyes.

Wanting to question him, he shook his head at her and pointed to a door at the end of the hall.

"That's your cell, lil' one," he said softly.

Looking down at his arm, she decided to try what Wuz had taught her. She brushed his outstretched arm as she walked by and reached out with her mind. She was met with an overwhelming sense of peace.

Walking in, she turned around to look at him. Shyly, she said, "Thank you, you have been most kind."

His eyes crinkled a bit. He acknowledged her thanks by nodding and closed the door firmly.

As the lock clicked in place, she turned around to view her room.

It was small and held little. There was a stone ledge protruding from the wall, which she guessed was the bed as it was covered with a thin mattress and even thinner blanket.

"She really knows how to make you feel at home, doesn't she?" she spoke out loud as she eyed the small sink and toilet in the corner.

Walking over to the stone ledge, she sank down onto the mattress.

The day had proven to be the most tiring one of her life. Lying down on her side, she curled into a ball and tried not to think about the Twins and their plans for her.

She thought instead of her interview with Queenie. She wished the woman had at least mentioned her Gran during her time in the throne room.

Unable to relive any more, she closed her eyes to the darkness her heart could hardly bear, welcoming the oblivion of sleep.

Finally

A kaleidoscope of grays and blacks swirled into her vision as she closed her eyes, sucking her into a vortex of dark emotion.

Before she could succumb to the despair of nightmarish thoughts, however she heard a voice, breathing out in relief.

"Ari, Ari, where have you been?!"

Looking around the dismal colors that took over her mind, she searched for the source of that beautiful voice.

"Find me, Ari, look hard, I'm here, *find me*."

Her soul crying out to penetrate the darkness surrounding her, she searched for color, for life.

"I won't leave you, I *won't* let you go, didn't I tell you that?" the voice said, laughing softly.

A sliver of light penetrated the dark fog, breaking through. Keeping her eyes focused on the light, she said tentatively, "Del? Del, is that you?" Tears clogging up her voice, she struggled to speak.

"Yes! Ari! Keep talking to me, I won't leave you, you know that. Trust that light, it's me, trying to break through. Concentrate, Ari. You can do it," he said with a determined voice.

Summoning all of her strength, she willed that light to get stronger, to drive away the rest of the darkness. And for the first time, she wanted him in her dreams.

But, she was struggling to penetrate the despair she was feeling. It seemed to cloud her vision.

With an angry voice, Del said, "Ari, I love you. I will fight to get you in here, and I'll fight dirty, I told you that too."

"What do you mean?" she asked, surprise taking over.

"Oh, I don't know, this *is* a dream, I could tell you I have someone else over here with me."

Her temper flared and she barely noticed more light streaming around her.

"Like, who?" she asked icily.

"I guess I could imagine up a Lacey Starwick."

Barely noticing the rest of the light crashing through to her, red completely took over her vision.

Red and orange swirled around her as she trembled in fury.

Finally noticing she was in a room, she searched for Del and his *friend*.

Strong hands suddenly gripped her shoulders from behind. Jumping with the sudden contact, she turned around with one thing on her mind.

She hit him as hard as she could.

Recovering quickly, Del gave Ari an astonished but amused look.

"Where is she?" she asked, seething.

He said laughing, "Ah, there she is. Did you miss me?"

Ignoring his question, she looked around and said testily, "So where is Lacey? And since when did you take a liking to blond Dream Weavers?"

His eyes twinkled and he said, "I told you I wouldn't fight fair, Ari. And you weren't even pushing back that darkness. I can't let you just become an Outcast, can I?"

Switching topics he gripped her shoulders tightly and asked, "*What* made you leave me, Ari? Do you realize what I have been through these past twenty-four hours?! Do you even know where I am right now?!"

She realized they were in her dream and he could be anywhere. Fearing for his safety, she cried out, "No! Where are you?"

He shook his head curtly and replied, "That's actually not important, what *is* important is that I am in a safe place to Catch with you."

Ari looked around and hoped no one else was in her dream. Relieved she didn't see anyone else besides Del, she returned her attention to him.

"Del, can they find out we are Dream Catching right now? I mean, can they sense this? Will they find you because of me?!"

He shook his head and said, "Don't worry, your dreams are safe, they can't penetrate and see or hear this. But, they might find out you are Dream Catching and try to wake you up."

She tried to argue, but he covered her mouth with his hand and said, "Let me finish, Ms. Questions. Your Gran caught my dream already to tell me you are being protected by someone reliable, so we can talk for a few minutes."

"Someone on our side? Over here?"

Smiling at her warmly, he said, "Yes, I've been talking with Gran for some time now, she's been keeping tabs on you through me. And she's been a busy granny. She's been recruiting."

"Recruiting?"

"Yes, she's been quietly turning Outcasts back into good Dream Weavers."

Amused at Gran's propensity to save anything lost or hurting, she asked him, "That doesn't surprise me, does it surprise you?"

Smiling back, he answered, "No, it really doesn't."

Thinking of the rhino Outcast who had helped her into her room, she asked, "So, Outcasts like Wuzzy are changing their ways and switching sides, but incognito?"

Nodding, he answered, "Yes, many are turning back and contacting the Dream Maker again. And he is asking some of them to remain here."

Confused, Ari asked, "For whose benefit?"

Cocking his head to the side, he studied her with a tolerant expression on his face.

Puzzled over why she would get such a reaction, she ran her question over in her mind again. A light dawned when she suddenly figured out the answer.

Fear clinging to her throat, she could hardly ask, "Please tell me why these reformed Outcasts stay in such a hedonistic place?"

With understanding in his eyes, he rubbed her arms comforting her, "For you, Ari. You should have known that."

He drew her into a hug, rested his cheek on her head and continued, "They have never seen what true goodness looks like. Gran has shown them that. And to truly love is to follow the Dream Maker, allowing him to guide them along his plan, not theirs. They've tried so hard to make their own way of things. Many of them here realize they have made an awful mess of their lives."

Holding her at arm's length, he continued, "Your Gran has said so many wonderful things about you, they couldn't let you stay here without protection."

"And the Maker approves?" she squeaked out again. Her throat felt like a punching bag. She could hardly believe these former Outcasts would have any interest in her whatsoever. Let alone risk their lives to protect her.

"Of course." Looking at her with concern, he squeezed her arms and asked, "Ari, are you ok with all of this?"

"I'm honored and thankful for them," she answered with feeling.

Stepping into his arms, she rested her head on his chest. She was so happy to be here with Del, finally. Overwhelmed with the information he was giving her, she could not believe people cared for her so much to stay in such a place.

And she couldn't imagine a better scenario right now than being in Del's arms.

Seeming to notice a change in the atmosphere, Del breathed deeply, and slowly slid his hands up her arms to softly cup her face.

Afraid to meet his eyes, she looked away. Her heart crashed in her chest, and she could barely hear what he was saying to her.

"Ari, I've missed you, would you mind if I..."

She answered by reaching up and pulling his head down so their lips could meet.

Feeling his soft kiss, she could hardly believe she had left this all behind.

A sob came up her throat and she broke away crying softly onto chest.

"Oh, Del, I've been so stupid. I left you, for this. How could I? What was I thinking?"

Continuing to hold her tightly, he said, "Ari, I disagree. You are meant to be where you are."

She hit his chest and cried, "Del, I'm not even Dream Weaving yet! That's all I've been trained to do, and I haven't even started yet!"

Grabbing her fists with his large hands, he stopped her and said, "The Maker has this all in mind, Ari. Trust him and his guidance! You don't think the Maker knows you are frustrated? Don't worry, he will give you someone to Dream Weave with. And it will be at the right time, in His time."

Comforted, she rested her head on his chest and said, "I'll wait. I just wish I knew how to Catch with you, when I want to."

He cupped her face gently and drew it up again.

She looked up into a beaming smile.

Speaking warmly, he said, "Ari, it will happen. Your bond feels the same as when you left. I can't believe you left without me, but thankfully nothing has changed between us since then. Eventually you'll be able to Catch my dreams," he promised.

Her heart constricted painfully when she thought of leaving him. "Will you Dream Catch with me every night I'm here?" she asked with a tremor in her voice.

Folding her into a warm hug, he answered, "Are you kidding? I wouldn't miss getting punched by a beautiful vixen for anything." Then continuing lightly said, "And maybe, you'll be surprised to find an Outcast with an awful lot of my mannerisms where you are."

She felt a crazy hope and she jumped happily. "Are you going to be here, really? Del! But, how?" Leaning away from him, she searched his eyes for answers.

He answered grimly, "I'm not so crazy about this idea, but for you, I'll do it."

"Do what? I don't understand. What, in our dreams, you mean?"

Patiently, he looked at her waiting for her to come up with another answer.

The answer dawned on her. "Del, are you going to pretend to be an Outcast?"

Laughing, she hugged him and said into his chest. "You really would do anything for me, wouldn't you?"

"Yes, I would. Unfortunately, I have to do this revolting thing and protect you from yourself. And there are a few more of us, too. Do you remember Cy?"When she nodded, he said, "There are others too. Try to find us."

"Where will you be? How will I find you? And what if you're hurt, because of me? I couldn't imagine it if...."

Hooking his finger under her chin, he kissed her cheek and said warmly, "You need me, Ari. I won't leave you here to fend for yourself. I have to know you are ok. I don't want to imagine my life without you."

Moving his lips over, he kissed her again tenderly. "That was for good measure."

Breathing deeply, he hugged her again saying, "Please, take care of yourself. Don't do anything rash. Those two lizard-things will try to reach you, but don't worry. We have plenty of us to protect you. Remember to use your sensory abilities to judge who is good from evil before you trust anyone."

Trying not to worry, Ari rested as he held her. Suddenly thinking of something, she pulled away quickly and asked, "Del, how do we know they don't do the same thing to us? Sense our intentions?"

"Ari, what do you have to worry about? They already know you aren't evil. They expect the goodness in you."

"Del, what about you though? You think I'm not going to worry about you disguising yourself?"

His eyes hardening, he looked away saying, "Look, if they can penetrate our village by disguising themselves, I certainly can. It won't be difficult to pretend to hate everyone here."

Concerned with the force of his feelings, she tried to calm down, so he couldn't sense her worry. If Del let these kind of feelings take over, he could be very vulnerable here.

She didn't want him to rescue her only to join the Outcast ranks.

Touching his arm lightly, she entreated, "Del, you've got to let these feelings go. Give the bitterness and anger over to the Maker. He's told me before not to hang onto them. They can end our relationship with him. Don't do that to yourself."

Closing his eyes briefly, he hung his head and with a strained voice, said, "I know. He's already told me that." Running his fists through his hair, he said, "I just can't seem to help it, Ari. If I had found those two who had betrayed you," he said, his eyes darkening with anger, "I think I would have hurt them."

Alarmed, she said, "But, Del, the Maker didn't allow for me to get hurt! Wuz came and found me in time. And, He's given you time to calm down, too. It' like that quote we heard in school, you know, that human actress, Carrie Fisher, said, 'Bitterness against someone is like drinking poison and expecting the other person to die.'"

Reaching for his hands still clenched in his hair, she held them and kissed his knuckles until he relaxed his fists.

Looking sorrowfully at her, he rasped, "Ari, I can't describe to you how it felt to know you were gone, only to find out later you were taken against your will." Hanging his head, he rested it on their joined hands. "I thought I was going out of my mind."

Tears dropping onto their clasped fingers, she said, "Del, I know. I saw you walk by me in the bushes. I could feel your anguish. I've never known such pain before."

Both crying, Del wrapped her in a fierce hug and said into her hair. "I'll be right there, ok? I *won't* leave you alone. I'll be with you...always."

Nodding, she said, "And you will let go of this bitterness? You'll try to? It's not safe for you here if you hang onto it, Del. The Maker will be here with us, as he always is."

Making sure he was looking at her, she continued, "And remember what he said, Del. If he is for us, who could be against us?"

Reluctantly, it seemed, he moved her to arm's length. "I will have another talk with Him. I'll have to let it go." Pausing, he said as he studied her, "Now, you need to get your rest. The Maker may need you to Dream Weave."

"What?! Now? In the middle of all of this? There's no way..."

"Ari, He sometimes uses us in the midst of trouble to be of help to others, that includes humans. Just be prepared, ok?"

Disbelieving, she nodded.

"I love you," he said quietly.

Surprised, she looked up. "Even after what I'm putting you through?"

Nodding, he smiled. "Even after we are done breathing, I'll love you, my Ari. And don't you go forgetting it, either."

"How could I forget such devotion?" she asked, feeling ecstatic.

Pulling her to him, he said, "Say it back, you little vixen. Tell me what I know you feel."

Watching his flashing eyes, her breath left in a rush when she said, "I love you, Delius. I can't believe I fell in love with my best friend, but I did."

With a triumphant look, he closed the little distance there was and kissed her. Wrapping her arms around him, Ari wished she wouldn't think of goodbyes.

As a tear escaped, she finally pulled away to let out the sob caught in her throat. She wanted to hold on to him and fervently wished she had never gone on this journey.

Letting go of her thoughts, she said, feeling broken, "I'm being selfish, I know I am. But, I don't want you to leave, Del. I wish you were right here. Not in this dream. Not in my imagination."

Fiercely grabbing her arms, he said, "Don't think for one minute I'm not with you. We are connected. And now that we are so close, I can feel your emotions again. When you wake up, you'll be able to feel mine. It's a connection no one else can intercept.

I'm the only one you can reach out and sense. They won't be able to sense what we have. Bonded Dream Weavers can always sense one another when they are close."

Relieved, she bowed her head and said quietly, "Thank you, Maker, for giving me such a wonderful guy."

"That's what I want to hear, my Ari. And now, keep dreaming. Sweet dreams. I hope to be there by the time you wake up. Remember, I love you."

She knew that when she looked up, he would be gone. The air was cold and empty without him. But she felt a warmth within that heated her heart in a more and more familiar way.

Looking up, she saw she was alone in a room she kind of recognized.

She realized it was a nursery with small toys and colorful rugs covering the hard-packed earth floor. Her eye caught a toy she hadn't seen in a long while. Reaching down, she picked it up as memories flooded back to her.

It was Del's old playroom and these were his playthings. He brought her to a place he knew she would recognize.

This serves him well, she thought with humor. He's reminding me of our history, even placing her old favorite toys in the room. Giving himself some brownie points, she thought, smugly.

Feeling a love for Del pour out of her, she understood this room was his memory. A memory meant to calm her, a memory they shared as small children.

Closing her eyes, she hoped Del could feel the love she was feeling right now. Smiling and half awake, she reached out to see if she could sense Del's emotions.

Feeling a powerful love engulf her, she went back to sleep thinking her heart would burst if she felt much more.

"Thank you, Maker," she breathed as the restful darkness finally claimed her mind.

"Ari," a voice said, claiming her mind.

"Yes?" she said sleepily.

"Ari, stay asleep, do not wake up. You are to Dream Weave. There is a little girl who needs you. Pay attention to me."

Unsure of who was talking to her this time, she asked, *"Maker?"*

"Yes, Ari. This is your time. Stay in the Dream World. You are going to reach out with your mind and find a small girl who is very scared to dream. Her name is Alicia Savani. Comfort her by shielding her dreams from the Outcasts. They've caused some damage and I am concerned."

Forcing herself to relax so she could stay asleep, she knew she needed to stay in a lucid dreamstate. Where she would be sleeping but retain control of her dream.

She asked, "How do I shield her?"

"Remember your Dream Weaving lessons, Ari. By blocking your mind against the fallen Dream Weavers."

"And vice versa? If they were to reach her first, they would shield her against me?" she asked.

She was just about to see for herself the Outcasts' dirty work. Anger began to build against forces of evil she had only read about.

"They can try," the Maker responded. *"By serving me, however, your light will force their darkness away. If you speak aloud anything I have told you, they will leave."*

"Gone? Just like that?" she asked.

"As quickly as light brightening a room."

"So, I'm a light," she said awestruck. *"But, do I begin now, in the middle of this place?*

I'm afraid I won't be able to do my best," she asked trying to mask her uncertainty.

"It may not seem the best time, but it is sometimes in the most difficult times that you are most useful to me."

"And this little girl needs me," she said, remembering the child who needed comforting.

"I'll certainly relate with her," she thought to herself.

"That's my thought, too," the Maker replied. *"Remember, miracles can happen. And I need you to dream a miracle."*

"A miracle?" she asked, unsure if she was capable of such performance.

"Help her to dream a dream she wants to stay in. Pull her happy memories together and weave those moments together in a setting she would love imagining. Remember, you want her to think her imagination came up with her dreams. Never let her know of your presence."

"She'll never know about me, Maker. I will do everything I can to protect this girl and to help her."

131

"I know you will, Ari. She is not sleeping and without your help, she could become very sick."

Steeling her mind, she said, "Ok, I'm ready." She tried to prepare herself for a dream with a small girl she's never met.

She knew from her classes this was as much a dream for her as it was for the little girl. She would feel as rested when she awoke as if she had simply dreamt on her own.

Noticing darkness speckled with flickering lights, she traveled toward it, reaching out her mind for a little girl named Alicia, who was too scared to dream.

Alicia

"Ok, time for a miracle," Ari breathed as she searched many minds for a familiarity she had been told she would recognize at once.

The Maker put this little girl on her heart and her heart would react once she found her.

Since this was her first time Dream Weaving, she didn't know what to expect. But Gran had once described the feeling as a breath-stopping experience.

Scanning all around her, she was beginning to lose hope. Not sure she would find her Alicia, she continued to search when her heart suddenly felt like it had dropped out of her like a rock.

As if it were in someone's death grip, her heart wrenched viciously when she heard a gut-wrenching scream. She immediately pinpointed the area where she knew she would find her terrified little girl.

She almost woke up, but she struggled to stay asleep and keep dreaming. She was surprised such a little presence could speak to her heart so strongly.

Rushing her mind toward her stricken child, she was ready to face any Outcast, Queenie herself, and tear them away from their treatment of Alicia.

Not truly understanding how she knew where her child was, she continued on until she came upon a brilliant little light.

She remembered from her classes, when she Dream Weaved she wouldn't ever encounter a human face-to-face. She would approach them completely by thought. And the Maker was the key to finding Alicia. Since he

133

planted this little girl on her heart, Ari would have no problem sensing Alicia's mind.

The Outcasts, on the other hand, found victims randomly. The Maker will not assign children to Outcasts. By refusing contact with the Maker, they have lost the ability to find a child more than once.

But they left such ugliness behind, the children would remember the nightmares and sometimes dream them many times.

As she watched Alicia's light flicker and wave, she understood Alicia was in the middle of a nightmare.

An Outcast could be feeding the nightmare, or it could be her remembering a past nightmare.

She prepared herself for the worst and hoped for the best when she breathed a quick prayer to the Maker. Fervently, she prayed, "Maker, be with me. Give me peace and strength for whatever I will face. Help me to help Alicia."

Bracing herself, she plunged into the brightness. Looking around, she could hardly make sense of her dream.

She watched as a dark hallway sped past her vision. Several viewpoints of the same hallway sat around her. Confused as to why these images could produce such terror in Alicia, she stayed still trying to absorb its meaning.

She had studied dreams in Dream Weaver School. A hallway was almost always associated with rooms. But, why would Alicia be afraid of a hallway? Did it hold a room she was scared of? She remembered rooms without exits invoked nightmares. But the hallway was an exit from what she could see. Or was it?

Studying the hallway, she searched it for clues. The only light she could see was a lone light at the very end of the long passageway. Several doors graced the quiet scene.

They were all closed, but elegantly decorated with pretty handles. This hallway was decorated with a woman's touch, Ari thought. Was this Alicia's home?

She hoped not, since Alicia was so scared of this image.

Wanting to change this scene as quickly as she could, she focused all of her attention on the brightness around her.

Ignoring the quiet hallway, she searched Alicia's memories for other happier ones.

The bright aura she held was beautiful and translucent. Every human possessed one and Ari was amazed at the beauty of it.

She marveled at the shimmering colors it emitted. Imagining she was walking inside it, she pictured herself reaching out and grazing the tips of several sparkling gold and red tendrils with her hand.

As soon as she did, she was blinded for a moment. Several images began to shape.

'These must be Alicia's memories.'

Focusing her attention on one memory, she was looking at a field of daisies. Vibrant yellows and bright whites littered the field. She could easily see why this was a memory Alicia would keep.

She hoped the child would not revolt at a sudden change in dream images. Dream Weavers need to make smooth transitions from one dream to the next. All traces of a nightmare needed to be erased completely. If the job wasn't seamless, the change in dreams could wake the dreamer. Such action would also wake the Dream Weaver, and the sequence of Dream Weaving would have to begin again.

Ari did not want the child to revolt at a sudden dream change. So, delicately holding the gold tendril that held the memory of the field of daisies in her hand, Ari slowly began to move it.

She carefully drew it over to the hallway scene and replaced the dismal scene with the bright field.

She hoped Alicia would not panic. Ari waited for a few moments, and when the field remained in place, she knew that Alicia had accepted the change.

Ari was relieved and pleased at the sight of the peaceful image. She grazed the aura's tendrils to find more memories for Alicia's new dream.

A Dream Weaver hopes that by making a human's dream happy, the human would begin drawing from their own imagination and add to the dream. Together, a human and a Dream Weaver could make a dream both satisfying and restful. Ari was to teach Alicia how to dream peacefully. Eventually, Alicia would need to create her own sequence of illusions, or dreams. But, until then, Ari would help by finding Alicia's most beautiful memories and replacing the nightmares or creating new dreams.

'It's not that difficult,' Ari thought to herself as she slid over an image of Alicia holding a butterfly.

Now, the dream held a mirage of images, butterflies fluttering over many of the flowers and dancing over to play in Alicia's hair.

Alicia looked up and laughed. Ari was surprised when she heard the high-pitched giggle.

It reverberated all around her, like the scream earlier had done. She must really be laughing, Ari thought happily.

Looking around, she quickly found other memories, details she had missed earlier about the pretty field and added them to the dream sequence.

Wooden fences bordered the field in every direction. Alicia then took over the memory as she climbed over the rails and dropped into the neighboring giant sunflower field.

More yellows spurred her on as Alicia raced through the rows of towering flowers. Laughing harder this time, Ari laughed with Alicia as the little girl ran on.

Alicia began spinning wildly her arms catching the wind currents and Ari thought her heart would burst with pride. The lack of reservation this beautiful child was showing was just what she was hoping for.

Blonde and blue-eyed, she was the face of innocence. Ari's heart flamed with anger knowing what was responsible for this sweet girl's nightly anguish. Trying to keep her attention focused on the dream, she watched the dancing, frolicking girl in the sunflower field and smiled to herself.

Ari reached for the aura's tendrils around her and found some wonderful additions to the dreams of picture-book fawns and rabbits. Ari rested when she saw that Alicia took to these new memories by adding the new friends to her play right away.

Feeling greatly relieved Alicia was happy and content, Ari knew she could stop Dream Weaving.

Her night was successful, Alicia was happy and dreaming.

Surprising News

Ari rested her eyes from Alicia's playful scene and within moments was out of Alicia's world.

Before waking, she adjusted to the feel of being back in her body. 'Dream Weaving is a sensation I'll just have to get adjusted to,' she thought. Stretching tight muscles, she froze when she heard someone humming.

Cracking her eye open, a blurred face came into view just as a voice said, "Well, look at that. It's about time my lil' Ari woke up."

Popping both eyes open, she inhaled loudly as she found herself looking up at Gran. Disoriented, but wild with excitement, tears sprang from her eyes and she asked, "Gran? Is it really you?"

"Well, what do you think, lil' one? That some Outcast copied me from a child's nightmare? Now, let me ask you, what child would ever be afraid of me?"

And looking at her Gran's happy face, Ari threw her arms around her hugging and crying as she answered, "No one could ever have a nightmare of my Gran!"

After holding each other for a few moments, Gran whispered into her hair, "I've missed you, do you know that?"

Sobbing quietly, "Gran, I've missed you, so much. I didn't think I would ever get over the pain of losing you."

"Now, come on lil' one, you need to get up, we have work to do. No more of this crying and tomfoolery. Let's wipe our eyes and get down to business," she said as she used the hem of her dress to wipe her own tears.

Getting up, Ari looked Gran over, inspecting Gran's treasured face as she sat there beaming at her.

"My Ari, you haven't changed a bit, have you? Well, we have no time to exchange pleasantries, not right now anyway. You have company coming, and you need to be ready."

"Who, those lizards?" Ari asked, fear clogging her throat.

"No, my child. You have several visitors coming. Your friend, Del, will be arriving, in who knows what get-up," she sighed rolling her eyes. "I swear, the things that boy will do for you, is endless," she said smiling affectionately. "You know you have a keeper, don't you?" she asked with a sidelong glance.

"Yes, Gran, Yes! Of course, I know that. Who are the others, Gran? Will Del be here first?"

"Calm those horses missy, but, no I'm not sure. I've got a good idea I know who's coming right now though."

Taking a deep breath, Gran's deep green weathered eyes stared into Ari's for some time before Ari finally asked, "Gran, what news do you have? Why are you giving me that look? If I know you, and I do, you have something big to say, so please, just say it."

Ari's heart was nearly bursting when Gran finally decided to share what was on her mind.

"Sweetie, I know this will come as a mighty shock to you, but, I've gotta tell you. Your momma is alive. I've found her, or she found me. Took me is more like it," she added underneath her breath. "But, nevertheless, the Queen is on her way."

"Queenie? What does she have anything to do with my mother?" Ari asked hotly.

Gran's knowing eyes filled with wordless tears. Ari's horror echoed in a scream as the entire room began to spin.

Catching herself on her hard cot, Ari hung her head shaking her head at the dizziness, just as there was knocking at her door.

"Her imperious Highness is wanting to speak to the prisoner, Arella Moira," a voice boomed from outside her door.

Just then the door opened and her eyes met with cold, slightly wavering stare from the Queen of the Outcasts.

Drawing in a shaky breath, Ari managed to ground out a greeting.

"Well, hello, Mother. Fancy meeting you here."

Part Two

Del

Planning

Running his hands over his eyes, Del stayed in bed trying to ease the fear out of his chest. The effort was useless, the feeling still gripped him. Memories of the terrorizing nightmare that plagued Alec, the child he was assigned to, haunted him even now. Remembering he was home and not Dream Weaving, he sighed heavily and did the only thing he could do, he got up.

Leaving his room in a rush, he hoped Cy hadn't left yet. Grunting in surprise, he had to stop suddenly when he nearly ran over a graceful figure who was about to fall behind a large load of clean laundry.

"Mom!" he cried, "So sorry, here let me help you." He reached for a large portion of the clothes and jumped when her hidden voice said quietly, "First, I nearly get run over for doing *your* laundry, son, then you wrinkle nearly every garment I just ironed."

Sighing, she reached for his hold on the bundle and took it back from him.

"You sure are jumpy, running out the room like that," she remarked her worried eyes looking him over.

Shrugging his shoulders, he agreed. "It's not only Ari I'm concerned about," he admitted.

He walked with her as she continued her walk down the short hall. His voice shaking, he voiced his concerns about his human assignment, "It's Alec too. I'm having trouble coaxing any kind of normalcy into his dream state."

"Del," she sighed, "how many times do I need to tell you that your version of normalcy and a child's may be vastly different? He has a need to hold onto those memories, for some reason," she cautioned. Laying her hand on his arm, she looked up at him saying softly, "You were the best choice for guardianship of his dreams, but he's not ready to let go of those memories, yet. And don't force him," she added hastily, "He needs to be ready to move on from that attack when he, and he alone, is ready."

He decided he needed this advice for his feelings for Ari, too. Lifting his eyes to hers, he asked a hard question, "And with Ari, am I supposed to just let her rot in that castle too? Should I pursue her when she hid her plan from me, even when she knew how I felt for her?"

With a sad smile, his mom put down her load and straightening, reached up to gently hold his unshaved face in her hands saying softly, "Now that's a question for you, the Maker and your little Ari to go over."

Then patting his face she picked up her load of laundry again and continued, "Go on, go see what trouble you can involve yourself in. I have work to finish, work you can't help me with," she added as she quickly scooted by him.

Watching her round the corner, Del battled frustration saying under his breath, "I don't have to look far, I can see you don't want my help either."

He had learned when he was Dream Catching with Gran that Ari went looking for the Outcasts. Despite what he had told her, he still felt hurt and betrayed she had not confided in him before she had left.

She had had plenty of opportunities to tell him. Thinking back to their last kiss under the moonlight, he cringed. He knew her moonlight kiss for what it was now, she was saying goodbye.

But, had she expected him to come rescue her, he wondered? She must have known the consequences would be terrible if she got caught. And by him rescuing her from her imprisonment, his would be far worse.

Steeling himself, he was willing to face those consequences and far worse. It was Ari they could be torturing, and he meant to find her.

Shaking his head, he breathed out another frustrated sigh, he couldn't get to her fast enough.

His bond with her has been conspicuously silent these days, something he wasn't used to. He has been able to feel her emotions for a year now, every day it had grown stronger until finally he knew he had completed his year bond cycle. Now, it was up to her whether she would love him in return.

The thought she may end up rejecting him hit him like a punch. He wasn't sure what he would do only that he would always love her. He had to trust her love will continue to strengthen. He had to get her out of that castle. The rest will follow, he was sure of it.

Knowing his thoughts were disjointed, he collected his thoughts and returned his attention to searching for her in the bond that tied him to her.

The absence of not feeling it was unsettling. It had become natural to feel the dance of her cyclic emotions.

He missed it. Sighing, he knew he just missed her. He knew it was a silence serum that was the reason for it, but we was still concerned with his trouble of sensing Ari.

He couldn't help but recall bitterly the day the silence serum had taken hold of her emotions. It was a day he would never forget. Knowing he passed within inches of her without knowing it still tormented him. The serum had blinded him to their bond. He worried that he still couldn't feel her emotions.

How did the Outcasts invent a potion interrupting a bond between two Dream Weavers? That was a significant danger. The Guardians should know about this new potion. A full scale war could erupt between the Outcasts and the rest of Oneiro should the Dream Weaver Guardians find out.

The ability to hold a bond with another Dream Weaver helped them protect each other, and he knew it was a centuries-old tradition they would want to protect. But, right now, it was Ari that needed to be rescued and a full-fledged war could harm her position in the castle.

He was hoping when he did reach Ari, that one touch would erase the effects of the serum. And he would know immediately if the saying, 'Absence makes the heart grow stronger', was true.

He desperately hoped so; his thoughts were hard enough right now, he didn't need to think that he may be loving someone he might lose forever.

But, thinking about their dreams together encouraged him. The dreams were different. In their dreams, he could feel her emotions. The night before, when he had Caught her dream, he could still feel her emotions and they were just as he remembered, sweet and binding.

She loved him still, but he knew that could change. She could still find someone else and change her feelings toward him. It made the need to see her that much more important.

He doubted there was anyone there at the castle who could possibly interrupt his bond with her, but he wasn't taking any chances. Ari was never one to even like troublemakers. The thought that she would fall in love with an Outcast was enough to make him laugh. It just wasn't her.

He needed to be careful when he he converted to an Outcast, that she not see him in his disguise. It would ruin his mission. She could give him away accidentally. It was better for her to not know those details. He just had to be careful if he fell asleep as a man and not a bear. He was still unsure of his decision, however to have him and a crew convert to Outcast shapes during their rescue mission.

His thoughts went back to his mom's advice about Alec and frowned wondering if his knowledgeable mother was right about that as well.

Swinging open the door that led to the small common room, he walked out and to find out if Cy was still having breakfast.

He had sought out his reclusive friend when Ari first disappeared. He knew he would need the fellow Dream Catcher's help. Thankfully, Cy had agreed to help him recover Ari from the Outcast castle. They had discovered her whereabouts when they had happened upon Ari's kidnappers who were tied up in the forest, Franz and Helga.

Cy had enjoyed getting Ari's location out of them as much as Del had. After turning the couple in to the Guardian Dream Catchers, a small but very skilled task force in charge of Maone's security, Cy and Del went to work gathering their own task force to get Ari home.

They had an elaborate plan and Del was ready to continue planning in order to get his mind off his recent dream and Ari and whoever was meant to be her bondmate.

Cy was drinking coffee at the table and when Cy looked at up at him with understanding in his eyes, Del's shoulders slumped.

Turning away, he continued to feel the weight of Cy's concern. Suddenly he felt a great weariness settle on him. He hadn't rescued Ari and despite his best efforts, Alec continued having nightmares. A week's worth of weaving and the child was still experiencing the same awful images.

"What's wrong?" Cy asked bringing Del out of his dark thoughts for a minute. "The kid still having the same dream?" he asked.

Reluctant to answer, Del murmered, "Yes. I haven't been able to help him shake it."

Disappointed with his failings, he tried to talk instead about the day ahead.

"Is it the bear again?" Cy asked, not allowing them to switch topics.

Frustrated, he answered, "Yes. And to think, I have to become that *thing* to save Ari."

Ari's captors kept a tight but simple defense system. If you weren't an Outcast, you would not be trusted or welcome. He needed to get into the castle's defenses and the easiest way to do that was to take a shape from Alec's nightmare, which was a giant black bear.

"Well, since you were just in his nightmare," Cy reasoned, "You should be able to transform pretty easily. Can you picture the bear now?"

Glaring at him, he answered, "Yes. But, it still feels very wrong."

Transforming into Alec's worst nightmare was not going to be easy. If it was a matter of concentration, he knew he could make the change. But, it was the guilt he would have a hard time looking past as he made the atrocious change. It felt like a betrayal to the boy if he became that memory that haunted his dreams nightly.

Del knew he was good at handling difficult situations, however. He had plenty of proof for that. Secretly training to become a Guardian Dream Catcher was one, not to mention the year he had spent hiding his feelings from Ari. It had been hard enough dealing with dreaming of her, but she also needed to be comforted. Remembering being that close to her and not sharing his feelings for her was still a torture.

Shaking his head of the memories, he looked over at Cy who was wearing a strange expression. Returning the look steadily, he asked, "What?"

"You haven't heard a thing I've said. You're thinking about Ari, *again*?" he stated. Cy shook his head.

Biting back anger, Del returned, "Look, when you've bonded and can understand, you let me know. Ari is out there in the worst Outcamp there is, with just her stubbornness as protection."

"She is being protected," Cy disagreed. "She has her grandmother and all of her Outcast converts watching over the two of them. So," he said, "Stop worrying.

Remember, with us becoming six of those blasted Outcasts, she'll have even more protection."

The Tracking Twins, along with Jack and Philippe, were all were coming with them to help them find Ari. They were all great guys to have in a fight or a hunt, as this was both. They each boasted different skills and Del was grateful to have them.

Nodding reluctantly, Del still struggled to contain his frustration. The thought of knowing Ari was in danger was maddening.

Remembering the converts at the castle Ari's grandmother had converted, he asked Cy, "Those Outcasts who have supposedly converted," Del asked Cy, "what do you know about them?"

Shrugging, Cy propped his feet on the nearest chair and answered, "Not much. I met someone once who had changed back from being an Outcast."

"And," Del motioned impatiently for Cy to finish.

'I don't know, it was like they were refreshed with life, like they were..."

"Renewed?" Del finished.

Surprised registered in Cy's eyes, and he nodded. "Do you know what that is about?" Cy asked uncertainly.

Smiling, Del nodded. "It's like when you first discover the Maker's presence," Del began. "You realize he's real and can be a part of your life. It's a discovery that surpasses every expectation, every reality you've ever known," shaking his head, his smile widened and he finished by saying, "There really isn't anything else like it. Nothing can compare to it. It's like you're reborn. You're whole life starts over, man."

His heart soared again as he remembered the time he had made the heart-stopping realization that the Maker wanted to be a part of his life, his every moment. And he had made the decision not to dismiss that gift. It was a gift he treasured and he felt humbled to have it.

Breaking into his thoughts, Cy chuckled darkly saying sarcastically, "Well, now that that's cleared up, can we move on to our plans for this prison break we are planning?"

Giving Cy his full attention, Del remarked, "Cy, if you don't understand what I'm saying, just say it. You don't need to hide behind your comments all the time."

"Well, you know me, I can't back off from a good joke," Cy retorted, his eyes closed off to any further talking.

Del's heart saddened and he suddenly felt sorry for the young tracker sitting with him. "Well, that is what happens, whether you choose to believe it. Why would I make that up?" Del questioned.

"I don't know, why would you?" Cy retorted halfway opening his eyes.

"I didn't. You're just gonna have to believe me." Running his hands through his hair, Del turned around from Cy's now curious look and decided the conversation went as far as it could. His thoughts went back to Ari but panic began crowding his airway to the point where he exclaimed, "If only I can be sure she is alright!" slamming his hand down on the table next to him.

"You know," Del said turning back around to Cy he exclaimed, "Visiting her in dreams is not going to save her if there were an actual physical threat."

"Will you just listen to yourself?" Cy demanded. "You are underestimating not only Ari, but that grandmother of hers. She is one of the most talented Dream Catchers out there. She is with a legend, man. So, get a grip and transform into Yogi Bear already and stop complaining."

Del couldn't help grinning. Cy was right, he did need to stop complaining. Ari was too important for him to waste time like this.

His heart was lighter now that he had made his decision and Del couldn't help remarking, "Yogi, huh? Can't wait to see what your get-up is. Are you going to tell me what I will be working next to for the next few days?"

Leaning back in his chair, Cy answered with a smile, "Nope, but you'll see it soon enough."

Cy's answer was typical for him, so Del decided to drop the questioning and went into his bedroom to check over his bag.

Remembering the rest of the team's arrival who were coming this morning, he called out into the room to where Cy was sitting, "Is everything set for the rest of the guys today?"

"As set as it will ever be," Cy replied. "They'll be here soon enough."

Everything was in place and it was time. Dream Weaving was not going so well, but he knew with the Maker's help, it would eventually right itself out. Everything else that happens, happens. He was strong enough to handle it, he hoped.

Day Two

Ok, so things weren't going as easy as he thought.

It was the second day of living as an Outcast and he was starting to feel sorry for those traitors.

How do you get used to being a nightmare?

He certainly couldn't. Very quickly he learned to stay behind when he and his team approached a house or any Dream Weaver in that case. Terror was an emotion he did not like directed at him. It made Del wonder why it was something the fallen Dream Weavers enjoyed.

Looking at his group, he also wondered why none of the others had changed. Del started to wonder if he had lost the ability to lead. He was happy to have the crew he had, but he hoped he had made the right choices. He had handpicked all of them; he knew their strengths and weaknesses and wondered if he had judged correctly. He needed the best team possible, for this could very well become a one-way mission.

Everyone in his group were risk-takers, but this was obviously not going to be easy. They were all tough guys, each having proved themselves valuable in the past.

He's known them since DW school and he knew they each excelled in at least one area.

Dream Weaver classes not only studied the dream state but trained for defense against Outcasts as well. Dream Weaving had been an easy subject for him, up until young Alec, at least. But his real love was learning strategy and combat, which could be said for everyone in his group. Training had been their focus and they were all just as eager as he was to put their knowledge to good use.

Looking over at his motley group as they walked under a forest canopy, he knew he had selected well.

Ron and Ronnie, twins who looked and acted completely opposite, made the perfect tracking pair. Ron was by far the best hunter Del had met and Ronnie was top in the class as a tracker. Together, nothing got away once they were on its trail.

Philippe, the tallest of the group, stood at 6'3. At school he had excelled at hand-to-hand combat, but Del knew Philippe's tall height and strength pushed his advantage over other opponents. He had nearly beaten Del a few times in scrimmages, but not quite.

Del had been one of the best in his class, he didn't go down easily. Philippe's battle strength, however, was not his passion. The tall fighter was also a thinker, a philosopher. To him, books were as important as air was to breathe. Even now, Del watched as Philippe moved his heavy bag full of books to his other shoulder. Chuckling, Del knew he probably kept up his workouts just so he could tote around his precious literature.

Jack, on the other hand, was widely known for his toughness. Nicknamed by some, Rip, after a disgusting human named Jack the Ripper, Jack's nature could get nasty when provoked. It was understood by all to just not mess with him when his mood was up. But, somehow people did. Jack was involved in more fights than anyone he knew. As annoying as that was to be around, it was always a good fight to watch. Jack thrived on finding his opponents' weaknesses and then finishing them off easily. It was like watching a choreographed show; Jack made fighting look good. Yes, he definitely needed him around in this fight.

Jack, of course, had been the most enthusiastic about joining the group, but that had faded quickly when he heard they had to go under cover.

Thinking about their transformations again made Del grimace. His had not been fun.

And the worst was, no one else had joined him. He kept asking them when they were going to transform, but they each had one excuse or another. The fact was, he could not get used to his body being covered in hair, or fur. It was itchy, he thought irritably.

And, he asked himself, again, why was he the only one to change so far? Irritated, he looked over at Cy and scowled.

Noticing the attention, Cy growled, "Stop looking at me like that, you'll make me think you might like me."

That was it. Del's anger exploded. One minute Cy was standing there with that stupid smile on his face, the next minute he was sporting a fat lip.

"What was that for, you stupid bear!" Cy yelled, sprawled out on the ground.

"You picked on the wrong Outcast, Cy, so back off," Del said in a dangerous voice.

The fight had stopped the group in their tracks, all wore shocked expressions on their faces, except for Jack who looked like a kid in a candy store.

Drawing his knee up looking more like he was lounging on the ground, Cy asked in a languid tone, "What happened, Del, did I hit a furry nerve?"

Roaring, Del jumped on him or tried to. Cy, anticipating the attack, rolled over just in time for Del to knock his head on the ground right where Cy was laying.

The threat of a concussion got the others to move quickly. Philippe got to Del first, rolling him over to check his head.

Del, still angry, managed to mutter, "Get your book-lovin' paws off me."

With a small smile, Philippe answered, "My friend, I think you are forgetting, you are the one with the paws. Are you sure your head is not injured?"

Frustrated, Del sighed and stopped trying to get up. Laying down, he looked up at the faces crowded around him, "Can someone please tell me why I am the only Dream Weaver who looks like an Outcast?"

Ronnie covered his mouth and coughed to hide a laugh as he answered, "Not sure you want the answer to that just yet, bro. Why don't you rest for a minute," he asked.

Glaring at the twin, Del felt a surge of anger at the group, so grabbing the nearest person to him, he ripped Ron's ankle upending his balance.

Laying flat on his back, Ron cried out, "What are you doing?" Scrambling up quickly, he yelled out, "We didn't know you were gonna go grizzly on us so soon. You do realize we aren't even close to that castle right?"

Philippe ran over putting himself as a barrier between Ron and Del. "This is not a good idea, guys," he consoled.

Sighing, Del got up from the ground and looked down at himself. Looking at his fur-covered arms, he grumbled, " I feel like Goldilocks is going to come around the corner any second."

Philippe barked out a laugh just as they noticed Jack running toward them quickly coming around a bend in the road.

Calling out to them excitedly, Jack said out of breath, "There's a camp up ahead, it may be an Outcast camp."

Del got up as quickly as he could. The others all nearly choked when he almost fell over.

Jack's expression turned into stone. "What joke did I just miss out on," he asked dangerously quiet.

Not able to resist, Del said dryly, "Well, we were just waiting for Goldilocks to join us and here you are. Is this a coincidence, Jack? With your yellow hair, you could look the part."

Jack's eyes hardened slightly, and putting his pack down, he stood with an loose stance. "Del, if you would like to continue this great conversation, and I promise you this is a great conversation for a great fight, then by all means, let's continue. But, as I respect your leadership, Grizzly," he said sarcastically, "You may want to reconsider talking about me like that. Because I will be only happy to skin the fur off your sorry, love-sick hide."

With a gleam in his eye, he waited for Del to respond. A few snickers from the group was the only noise in the forest. Even the birds hiding in the trees seemed to be waiting on the result of this testosterone-charged moment.

Del looked away, and his gaze fell on Philippe who stood nearby.

"Who would want to fight on a fine day like this one, but then again," Philippe said with a broad smile, "If you were looking for another fight, Jack would be the perfect one to irritate." He turned and walked away shrugging on his heavy pack.

Considering the situation, Del knew he had been looking for a fight; his temper had been simmering quietly all day. It raged even now, but breathing deeply, he tried to control his fury. He wasn't mad at Jack, he was angry at the group as a whole. So, reaching over, he held out his hand, and said, "Sorry, Jack, my fight is not with you. We good?"

Jack, of all the guys in their group, seemed to understand Del's mood the best. Del thought it may be because Jack dealt with anger daily. He tested Del's temper probably to measure Del's common sense. To fight with his entire crew on one of their first days on the trail is not good leadership. More fighting will come if Del was not able control his temper.

Studying him quietly, Jack finally answered by shaking Del's hand, "Yeah, we're good. No problem."

Looking ahead at the trail, Del said firmly, "Let's go. We don't want night to catch up on us. How about we pay a visit to this camp Jack mentioned? We could all use a rest."

Del only hoped rest was going to be on the agenda. They were all going to break if tensions became too tight again.

Day Two and a Half

Hiding behind a large bush, Del took a look at the rest of his team as they crouched behind large trees or bushes. Exhaling quietly, he breathed out slowly as he checked his weapons. Grimly patting his hunting knife in its sheath, he hoped it wouldn't be needed.

He recalled the last count he had made with his arrows, but he dismissed that immediately. The only time for arrows was wartime in his opinion.

He put his hands around his mouth and made a bird call. Getting his team's attention, he hand signed that their bows were not to be used. Seeing their agreements, he looked on as Ron and Ronnie both reluctantly put theirs away.

They both had stunning accuracy with their bows and he knew they did not appreciate that order. He knew they could maim and not kill, but the treatment for getting an arrow out for even an Outcast was too much.

Looking back at the camp, Del still wasn't sure which side the camp called itself. He hadn't seen anyone come out of the large tents, so he and his crew had been forced to wait. Because of his Outcast appearance, he had wanted them to wait to see if they were Outcasts. Normally, he would send in one of the others without this wait, but something gave him the feeling this may be an Outcast camp. The game would change if that was the case.

If these are Outcast tents, then the rest would have to change into their Outcast shapes and attempt to join these traitors. The thought still turned his stomach. Reminders of Franz of Helga immediately stopped his uneasy feelings. If they could fool his people into believing they were Dream Weavers, he could make this camp believe he was an Outcast, he resolved. Anger surged through him as he remembered how they had fooled everyone in the village that they were simple bakers, even the Dream Weaver Guardians. He calmed his anger with the thought that they were jailed within the hidden walls of the Guardian jail cells. There was no chance of other Outcasts breaking them out. Only very trusted members of the Guardian knew the jail's location.

Thinking back to their current situation, he focused again on the quiet camp in front of him. If the campers turned out to be fellow Dream Weavers, he would send in Ron and Ronnie, his best diplomats. They seemed the most harmless out of all of them.

When Del had made the decision, Philippe had grumbled claiming he was the best choice since he read detailed accounts of proper diplomacy. Holding back a sarcastic comment had been hard, but Del had succeeded in not laughing. In his opinion, there was no such thing as "proper diplomacy" and book knowledge doesn't help when everything goes south. Not wanting to start a fight with another member of his group, he had kept quiet but stuck with his choice.

Pulling out his stunner, he cocked the trigger and released it without the ammunition. He didn't want to accidentally fire a shot announcing their presence. And without the medium-sized rubber ball in place it was harmless and quiet.

Studying the tents for any sign of movement, he tried ignoring his uneasy feeling. This camp was too quiet. Looking over his favorite weapon again, he nodded to the twins when he saw they had exchanged their bows for their stunners.

This was his strongest weapon because of his excellent aim, but he knew they were uncomfortable putting their bows away. A situation like this called for a weapon you were comfortable with. And he had practiced enough hours with it to be good at it. And he liked that it could incapacitate someone without really doing a lot of damage. Well, it could shatter some bones if shot too close, but that's what happens if an enemy did try to get too close. Recovery from a broken bone was better than losing a life, he reasoned.

Tensing suddenly, he heard something in the brush. It wasn't any of his guys, he thought quickly. Everyone was still in position. Looking over at them, he knew they had all heard it too. Scrutinizing the area he had heard the noise, he glanced back at the camp. The same lamps were on outside of the tents, swinging in the slight breeze.

Frustrated, he motioned for Jack and Cy to go into the dense undercover to check out the noise. If it was an animal, he would have them hunt it and bring it back to the camp.

Strange though, it was approaching dusk and he couldn't smell any signs of dinner and the quiet grated on his nerves. Hoping they hadn't gotten too close to the camp, Del watched uneasily as the brush covered his toughest fighters and he lost sight of them completely.

Watching where they had disappeared, he jumped up when he heard a shout and metal clashing. Running quickly in that direction, he was stopped suddenly by a row of arrows pointing at his chest. Stopping on his toes, he had to keep his balance as Philippe and the twins ran into his back.

The arrows didn't move and he shouted at the twins to back off as Philippe's weight pushed him into the arrows' tips.

The twins recovered first and Philippe was able to take a step back. Moving slowly away, Del stopped when a voice commanded, "Take one more step, Outcast and we will be happy to discharge these arrows and end your very pitiful life."

Cold fear washed through him as he remembered his stunner was without ammunition.

"And drop that pitiful weapon, Outcast. We have more weapons, and you are outnumbered," the voice said.

Looking beyond the arrows, an older Dream Weaver, most likely a Catcher, held his weapon easily and with a practiced ease.

Knowing not to make any sudden movements, he dropped his stunner and kept his hands away from his sides where his attackers could see them.

Still not sure if he was facing an Outcast or a legitimate Dream Weaver, he asked carefully, "My friends seemed in trouble, can you tell me where they are?"

Frustrated, he knew that looking like a huge bear was not helping him right now.

Outcasts were completely self-motivated and were ruthless and cunning. Del knew he needed to be careful he didn't come off that way with this man, obviously the camp's leader.

The man replied in a deceptively friendly voice, "Now that's a first, an Outcast showing concern for his group. And another first," he continued as he spoke to two others standing next to him, "is an Outcast who is in his freak shape, but the others retaining their Dream Weaver look. It's a new tactic, but one we can resolve as efficiently as the others who have tried to break our camp."

Del's heart sunk, his tactic to show compassion had backfired on him. Grabbed from behind, several hands gripped his arms and began dragging him away from the now busy camp. Men piled out of the tents with an occasional woman poking their heads out to witness their capture.

Looking behind him, he could see Philippe and the twins being dragged with him.

Praying he hadn't already led Cy and Jack to their deaths, he breathed a fervent prayer to the Maker to rescue them all.

Trying to think quickly about who this group could be, he started to judge his guard's strengths to see if he could overpower them. Unable to get good handle on his guards, he decided not to fight. He would have to talk their way out of this. They came to a clearing with large posts stuck in the ground. Not sure if they were normally used for weapon practice or to tie up their captives, Del began to get very worried. But, a firm resolve quickly took its place.

He was not going to die. He would get his friends out of this. They were Dream Weavers, he just needed to convince them of it. For all he knew these Dream Weavers and Catchers were renegades who took it upon themselves to get rid of any Outcast they could get their hands on. Some did not trust the Guardians effectiveness, which he didn't necessarily blame.

Wincing at the ropes being wrapped tight against his thick arms, Del thought the Guardians should recruit this camp of fighters. They were taking it upon themselves to locate and desist Outcasts, which wasn't a bad idea, but they weren't in a revolution.

They fought the Outcasts in the Dream World, not in Oneiro. He had heard of camps like these, but had yet to see one for himself. Angrily, he wondered why it had happened while he was disguised as an Outcast.

As he watched the rest of his team being tied up to other poles, Del watched as the leader walked slowly over to them. His weapons were in his pack digging into his back.

He thought he could reach his hand into a side pocket, and grab a small knife stashed there. There was no way to reach anything else tied up this way.

Before the leader made it over, he tried reaching his bag, but his hands were too firmly tied together. Wriggling his wrists, his thoughts became frantic. Why hadn't these commancho Dream Weavers taken away their weapons first, he wondered. There really was only one reason. They didn't expect him to live long enough to escape.

And looking up, he found himself staring right into the double barrel of a shotgun. How he didn't hear them approach, he didn't know. But, he needed to talk fast.

"Look," he began quickly, "My name is Delius Forgrove, I live in Maone about 10 miles east of your camp. You can send a messenger, they will verify I am a novice Catcher on a journey to find my..." he paused, hesitating to bring up the details of his relationship with Ari.

"Girlfriend," Philippe finished. "He's quite in love with her."

Glaring at Philippe, Del returned his attention to the man holding the shotgun. "Ari, her name is Arella Moira and she is in trouble. I, we, are trying to rescue her from Lucia, leader of the Outcasts. She has been kidnapped by two traitors who had claimed to be Dream Weavers. They've taken her to the Outcast castle. I've disguised myself as an Outcast in case we came upon any of them. We are trying to go undercover in their castle so we can rescue Ari. Please, listen to me about this. I can give you any details you want...."

Before he could finish, the leader said curtly, "What did you say her name was?"

Watching the gun lower, Del tried not to be too hopeful, but for some reason, Ari's name seemed to be important.

"Arella Moira," he repeated, "And she's in trouble."

"Well, son," the leader said a smile slowly taking over his weathered face, "Trouble is my middle name." Then staring intently at Del, he said to Del, "I'll free you, for now. It seems you may have an interesting story after all."

Ties

As the leader stood back and watched carefully, Del felt the tight restraints slipping off his arms. Bringing his hands into his lap, he rubbed feeling back into his stretched limbs.

Trying to keep the fear out of his voice, he asked, "And my friends?" He asked, "Two of my friends who fought some of you in the bush, have they been taken?"

"Full of questions, aren't you?" the man asked leaning back against a tree.

"You know, I just find this so strange, to have a civilized conversation with a converted Dream Weaver. And, I'm not so sure I believe this outlandish story you are spinning. But, I have to say, this name, Moira, intrigues me."

Del's eyes hardened but tried to keep his expression neutral. This man seemed friendly now, but Del could see there was a fierceness behind the man's gaze.

Wondering what this man's interest in Ari was and whether he needed to protect her identity, he asked, "So, you know Ari?"

His voice hardening, he answered, "Don't expect answers, son, since there aren't any to give." Looking away, Del thought he saw a flash of pain cross the man's face. Masking his expression, he looked back at Del saying, "Tell me all you know. Let's just say, you have my attention and I want to help. But, if I find out you are lying to me, it will be the last deceitful act you do."

Studying the man's careful expression, Del decided he needed to give a few more details, but he wouldn't trust this man with Ari's life. All he knew now was an assassin wanted to know more about Ari. That thought did not sit well with Del.

Reaching down for his pack, Del quickly stopped, when the leader stopped him.

"I suggest you keep your hands away from that pack of yours," he said lightly.

"Look," Del said trying not to sound irritated, "We have no intention of hurting any Dream Weaver, except the Outcasts," Del responded firmly. "I have a lot to explain. I am not an Outcast. I've gone undercover, and..."

Before he could say more, the leader interrupted and asked dryly, "So far, what I can see is an Outcast looking for a young Dream Weaver, whose Grandmother is a very well known Catcher. How can do I know this isn't an attempt to use the granddaughter to get to the grandmother?"

"Why would an Outcast sneak into its own castle to get a Dream Weaver already captured? That makes no sense," Del answered trying to speak calmly.

Hoping he wasn't giving away too much information, he continued, "Besides, her grandmother is already captured."

Not missing the alarm passing over his captor's face Del asked, "Are you alright?"

Anger replaced the alarm, however, and in an instant the now, furious leader reached over to grab Del's shirt front and roughly questioned, "You better, if you know what's good for you, tell me everything you know. If you are a stinking Outcast, I want to know now, because if I found it out later, you will regret it to your last tortured breath."

Shaking him, he ground out, "Tell me, who are you? And how do you know Celeste, Ari's grandmother?" Shaking him again, he yelled, "Tell me!"

Moved that he seemed to know Gran, Del answered quickly, "Look, I told you, my name is Delius Forgrove, I am a friend of the family. I've known the Moira's my whole life.

And Gran, I mean, Celeste, disappeared before Ari did and I am just trying to find the two of them."

Letting him go, the leader turned away to talk to one of the Dream Weavers standing close by. No sooner had he spoken and the man ran off quickly rounding up several more Dream Weavers.

Turning back around, he said composing himself, "We see strange things, and this is definitely one of them," the man answered. "Now, I have questions. But, before we talk, why don't you put your weapons over there at the base of that tree," he said gesturing toward a tree about thirty feet away.

Del's hope sunk quickly, he had hoped they were to be trusted more quickly. He wasn't sure if he trusted this volatile renegade leader,and with the information he gave, he had hoped to have been given better privileges.

Viewing the tree from where he stood, he weighed his options. There weren't many.

The tree was too far to quickly grab their weapons, but close enough to tease him with their nearness. Making his decision, he looked over at Ron and Ronnie, giving them a hard glare. He could see they were itching to fight, but he thought negotiations could still be salvaged. They had gotten this far, weapons shouldn't be needed.

Walking to the tree with arrows still aimed at them, Del knew any wrong move, even innocent would be punished. Reaching the massive trunk, he faced it so he couldn't be seen talking, and said lowly, "This guy's a nut, but I think we can get out of this without fighting. Put your weapons down."

Philippe, ducking his head as he reluctantly put his pack down, said, "I want to believe you, my friend, but this does not look good. Are you sure?"

Loyally, the twins both said in unison, "He's sure." Then, looking at each other smiling, Ron dropped his pack to the ground and other weapons he had hidden saying, "Let's go. I have a feeling we can trust this man. And Del wouldn't do anything stupid enough to get us killed."

Relieved Del dropped his own pack and hunting knife to the ground, and replied, "No, I wouldn't and thanks, Ron. That was confidence I heard, not sarcasm, right?"

Smiling again, Ron answered, "Time will tell, fearless leader. Now, make us proud and get us out of this mess."

Bolstered he had Ron's verbal vote of confidence, he stepped away from the tree and led them to the renegades. Whether he was leading them to their rescue or their doom, Del couldn't be positive, but he had it in his gut that this leader wasn't out to kill. Del kept his arms well away from his body as he walked back, however, because he was positive he could and would maim.

All the while remembering something the Maker said to him some time back. It was a promise he was holding onto right now, that all things worked together for the good of those who loved Him, the Maker.

Feeling reassured, he hurried to meet the man who had, at the moment, seemed an enemy, but was sure was soon to be a great asset.

Campfire Illusions

A roaring fire lit the faces of the camp of men they had no choice but to join. Mindful of their hardened expressions, Del could see they all radiated distrust. Cy and Jack leaned back disinterested in their glares but watchful. Philippe, Ron and Ronnie all looked uncomfortable under their study.

He had been thankful when Cy and Jack appeared, relatively unharmed. Besides a cut on Cy's face, the two actually looked refreshed after their capture. Danger fueled the two fighters like dry air fed a fire.

Grinning, he glanced among the men seated around the campfire, but his mirth was gone when his gaze stopped on the man who had captured them. Known as the General, Del had overheard his true name spoken earlier when someone called him General Tom.

Studying him, something played on Del's intuition that there was more to him than met the eye. He needed to figure out what his interest was in their rescue mission. He had a feeling it was more than a hunt for more Outcasts.

He would have to watch him closely and keep his ears open for anything that would explain his sudden interest in their plans.

The General had allowed them to camp with them as free men tonight, but didn't make any promises for the future. He had promised they would be watched closely until he decided what to do with them and with their mission. First, he said, he needed to think over all that Del and Cy had explained concerning Ari's situation.

They had negotiated on the field for the Cy and Jack's release and their freedom to leave the camp to find Ari.

The General still didn't seem to completely believe their story. Del had nothing to hide, so he kept repeating the truth until the General stopped his interrogation.

He hadn't liked the General's final words to them, "I could torture you to tell me more, but I'm not sure I would get any more truth out of you. I'm going to trust my gut and wait to torture you later if I see or hear anything that tells me you've been lying."

With that, he had turned and walked away leaving instructions to allow Del and the rest of them to join their camp.

Hours later, they now sat around this campfire, the tension palpable as he could see everyone eyeing them with sneers.

Shaking his head, he refused to back down from the glares. He was not going to change back into his Dream Weaver state just to appease some renegades. By backing down, it would be a direct admission of guilt.

Besides that fact, it had not been easy to transform into the bear of Alec's nightmare. When you changed into a dream image, good or bad, it has to be a process you completely believed in and wanted. And since he's been opposed to this change, his conversion had been uncomfortable, to say the least. Pain had wracked through his body because his mind kept rejecting the changes. It had taken time and these campfire glares weren't enough for him to experience the anguish of changing back and forth from man to bear.

Ari was his only incentive to change back. She couldn't see him as a bear when he Caught her dreams. It

171

would devastate their rescue plans. If she recognized him at the castle and gave away his cover, he would be captured and be killed as a spy.

He wasn't about to let that happen. He wanted a life with Ari, and he meant to protect it by protecting her.

Leaning back, he picked at the meager dinner he shared with his camp mates. Everyone was going to suffer from an empty stomach tonight. Because of their appearance, there wasn't enough meat to fill the camps' empty stomachs. Which wasn't making his presence any more welcome, he thought grimacing.

Staring into the flames, his eyes unfocused as watched the fire's rhythmic dance. Remembering Ari's temper, he imagined her staring at him through the fiery depths.

Mesmerized, he let his mind wander back to when Gran was still living in the cottage with Ari.

She was fifteen , he had just turned sixteen. He had gone searching for her and remembered how he had found her. He had followed the turn in the path, and he could still feel his breath leave his chest.

When he saw her watching a waterfall standing at the water's edge, it was like time stamped on his heart. He would never forget that moment.

It was his first memory of loving Ari. Her hair fell to her waist in waves then, and she stood there in a beautiful quiet. She didn't notice his approach and he smiled as he remembered. He had always been able to sneak up on her and at the moment he had relished that ability. She wore a yellow sun dress that played with her calves as the wind caught it and he couldn't help but notice the woman she was becoming.

He remembered how he didn't know how to stop his heart stop from racing. He was so afraid she would hear its frantic rhythm. But, miraculously she hadn't. A quail finally interrupted the scene as it made its way across his path.

Irritated it had disrupted this quiet moment, he had blushed furiously when he realized he might begin to form a bond with her. Just then, he had looked up.

She was looking at him strangely too, and his breath caught in his throat for a minute until she laughed, its lovely sound breaking the tension. But, the hold she had over him from that moment never changed.

From that moment, his bond with her began its effect. Like Ari's bond with him, it had begun in small doses.

Feeling her strongest emotions at first, it took great restraint to keep the discovery of his feelings a secret.

When he would feel her in great anger or pain, it took creativity to come up with reasons to chance upon her to learn if she was alright.

He learned she hid her feelings very well, because when he would find her, none of her outward appearance told how she had really been feeling.

But, he was afraid of telling her about his bond with her. He had hoped she would feel the same as he did and they could experience the beginnings of their bond together.

So, when they would take lessons together at school or walk through their backyard paths, he would study her feelings and expressions for any change.

But, when he didn't notice anything for a few months, he had realized he was going to have to tell her. And he almost had had his chance.

Gran's disappearance, however, changed everything. He could still remember the evening Ari discovered Gran was gone. He was going to tell Ari that night about his bond with her, when he had suddenly felt a crushing blow to Ari's feelings.

He had ran over to her as fast he could and had found her on the steps to her cottage crying hysterically. It was raw agony feeling her pain and not being able to help her.

After searching for Gran with the initial search team and later on his own, he had done the only thing he could do for Ari. Be her friend.

The rest of the year, there wasn't any chance of telling her about the state of his heart when hers was broken over losing Gran.

So, his bond had quietly grown stronger until he finally reached a point when he could feel her every emotion and the Maker came to visit him in a dream.

The dream had started with a blinding light, so bright he wasn't able to focus his eyes completely to the brilliance. But, awe filled his mind and heart as he realized he was in the company of the Maker, the author of dreams and dream making.

The Maker had said, "I see your heart has bonded, Delius Forgrove."

"Yes," he had replied painfully, his head bowed.

"You have done right by keeping it from Ari. Her heart was not yet ready for your revelation."

His head still bowed, he had replied quietly, "Yes, and I thank you, Maker, for allowing me to be a friend to her."

"You've taken very good care of your friendship to her. Now that you have bonded with Ari, do you promise to take care of her heart should she bond with you?" the Maker questioned with authority.

"Yes, Maker, I do. I've always loved Ari. This only turns my love for her from friendship to something deeper," feeling every word cut deeply into his soul permanently binding himself to his best friend, now bond-mate, Ari.

"Do you promise to wait for her decision then, Delius?"

"Yes, Maker. She is grieving. I will wait," he had promised.

And so he had waited. It nearly killed him, but he did it because of the fear of possibly losing her.

Ari has been his friend since his first memories. There were millions of memories forever tied with Ari.

Soon after that conversation with the Maker, he had hoped those memories would help his chances, so he would interject those memories to Ari every chance he could. He also studied her in a new light waiting for his chance to reveal his feelings.

But, the chance didn't come until much later. He smiled as he remembered how he had finally resorted to Catching her dreams to help her notice him as more than a friend.

He wondered now how he could have changed the course of events that led to her capture, however.

Admonishing himself again, he remembered how he had confused her anger at Gran's abductors for determination to find them herself.

He wouldn't be sitting here as a stupid bear if he had known the difference, but he would be with her helping her find Gran.

Shaking his head of the memories, he could only move on from here on out. And he was looking forward to going to sleep tonight so he could find her in her dreams.

Dream Catching was an art form that he had immediately understood, even at a young age. He used to play around as a kid dancing through the dreams of his friends. It had been fun then, but now he couldn't escape the fact he was hopelessly addicted to seeing Ari.

And if dreams were the only way, then so be it. Until she was safely in his arms, he wouldn't lose her in her dreams. No one could tear him away.

He was torn away from his thoughts when a voice quietly spoke, "She must be something to behold for you to have such a look upon your face."

Looking over at who just spoke, he tried not to jump when he saw the General sitting next to him.

Uncomfortable in his presence he also couldn't shake the feeling he had met this man before. Something about him was familiar.

He also couldn't forget that with one command he could kill his chances to free Ari. By forcing them to stay with their camp, it would stall his chance to free Ari since he would have to plan an escape.

With this in mind, Del took one more glance at the General while he studied the fire.

Not able to read his expression, Del decided to answer honestly, "Yes. She's something, alright."

"Tell me about this girl," the General commanded.

Looking over at him again, Del wondered his reason in wanting to know more about Ari.

He didn't want to answer that question. Not wanting to reveal more about Ari than he already had, he watched as the General waited for his answer. His unwavering gaze swept over Del's friends seeming to measure them with a glance.

Turning to Del, he pinned him with a hard look and spoke with derision, "I won't have you and your friends putting a young girl into further danger by your inexperience. You will have more company on this journey of yours. I will be accompanying you."

Exploding, Del yelled, "Inexperience?! What do you know? We were doing fine, before you stepped in! We could have been at the castle by now if it wasn't for your interference," he finished.

Responding quickly in a cold voice, the General said, "How were you planning to do that, when you allowed yourself to be captured? And very easily too, by the way? No. You will have an escort. And I am taking over this mission," he announced. "You will now follow my orders."

Rage built inside Del. Closing his eyes, he tried calming his anger. Breathing deeply, he was surprised when a calm washed over him and a voice whispered, *"Pride comes before a fall."*

"Maker," Del spoke in his mind after thinking over the Maker's words, "Your guidance couldn't come at a better time. But, at this price? I value Ari over anything in this world, and to let someone dictate the direction of this mission...it seems too costly," he admitted.

"Trust in me," said the Maker.

177

Del's heart clinched tightly as he bowed his head surrendering his will, his pride.

Putting his head in his hands, he begged, "Renew a steadfast spirit in me, Maker. I don't want to let you down. Please take this sick pride from me. I need help, I can't do this alone," he finished shaking his head.

As he sat waiting for the Maker's help, he realized pride had a tight grip on him. Closing his eyes, he began to release his fears of the trip, his desperation to find Ari, his need for absolute control, all the things that may be blocking the Maker's help.

Looking up at the General, he felt a renewed sense of purpose wash over him.

Speaking calmly, he said, "I don't suppose you will have a contingent of men with us as well."

If the General was surprised by Del's change of attitude, he disguised it well by pausing for a moment before answering gravely, "No."

Relieved, Del released his breath he had held as he had waited for his answer. "Good," he responded, "Because that would have been like blaring trumpets at the castle announcing we were coming."

The General raised his eyebrows and nodded. "I will have two of my most trusted men with me, as help." Upon Del's silence, he continued, "Once we reach a close proximity to the castle, they will return to camp and we will continue into the castle under cover."

"Under cover?" Del questioned incredulously. "You are planning on transforming into an Outcast?" Del barked out a laugh, unable to disguise it into a cough, which he tried.

The General glared at Del, responding, "No. Not all Outcasts go into other forms. But, of course, you must have known that," crossing his arms waiting for an answer.

A blank surprise crossed over Del's expression, and he said, "Well, I guess I had just assumed they all would transform."

"Some don't have to," the General said grimly. "They have enough hatred in them to terrify anyone." Standing up suddenly, he said to Del, "Have your camp ready by the morning, we leave at first light."

Del watched as he walked quickly away barking orders at the rest of the camp to put out their fires and put in for the night.

A warmth spread over his chest as he remembered it was almost time to connect with Ari through a dream.

But, first, little Alec still needed his help. Before he found Ari, he needed to find Alec's dream and try to weave as much peace into the poor child's nightmare.

Anticipating a long night, he barked out a command for his teammates to get some rest. He watched them make their way to their tents.

Three tents housed all of them, the lightweight material made it possible for them to have the luxury of their protection from the elements.

Striding over to his tent and his waiting bedroll, he was glad he had set it up before dinner. He wouldn't have had the energy to get it all ready now. Laying down, he had barely closed his eyes when, in his mind, he flew toward the mind of a terrified young kid.

Run, then Walk

He wasn't hard to find, literally. In young Alec's memory, he was hiding from a terror he had only heard about, but now had to face. He was crying, and hoping it didn't hear him. He trembled from head to toe shaking the leaves surrounding him.

It was hopeless. There was no way the giant brown bear didn't hear his desperate hiding place. He was too close, too close to hide out from this real nightmare.

Trying not to get pulled into this memory, Del paused the dream. Breathing deeply, he calmed his own present fears for the boy. Even as a Catcher he only had a few moments and it was difficult to stop a dream in sequence.

The fear was real, images too visible for this child. Del has been battling this sequence over and over, he knew what happened next. Alec needed his full attention for them to conquer this nightly terror.

The memory of a chase through the woods by a 700 pound grizzly bear was not an easy thing to forget. Del knew Alec was healing from wounds inflicted by the beast, which he was never going to recover from if he didn't stop thrashing and moving violently in his bed as he dreamed.

Concern for Alec's mental state from this traumatizing experience also steeled a determination in Del to make a change from the devastating effects of this dream.

The difficult thing about this dream was that this is not a conjured event, this was real. And this memory was hard to battle. He wanted to wipe this entire experience out of Alec's memory. Del had to force himself to not resort to this tempting tactic.

Memories were never to be permanently altered. The first thing you learned about Dream Weaving was to leave a true memory alone.

A memory was part of a person's history. Changing the memory changed their entire life's sequence. If a Weaver robbed a human of a memory, the effects were devastating. No matter how good your intentions were, memories were to be left alone.

But Del knew what he had to do. He could remind Alec of the safety of the rescue team who had confronted and killed the bear saving Alec's life. There was also the memory of his mother's comfort, her encouraging words throughout his recovery.

Del knew the story of Alec's miraculous recovery would help his healing ultimately. He just needed to help poor Alec recover from the pain of his memories. It's taken too long, though. He needed to make this Dream Weave count.

The bear had chased Alec through the woods, but Alec saved himself when he heard the search party's voices calling him through the woods.

He had ran toward the voices, concentrating on breathing so he could run full speed through the small trail he had found. Unfortunately, when he had left his small hiding place and decided to run, he didn't know that was just what the bear wanted.

He came crashing behind him through the undergrowth. This 700 pound bear who could surprisingly enough run very fast, did catch up to the small boy.

Del remembers the attack as Alec relives the horrific memories. Alec had not allowed surprise to dictate his speed; he knew he needed to speed up not slow down. Dodging branches, jumping over roots, he had almost been there, almost reached safety when the pounding feet of the bear was suddenly too close.

He had turned as he ran, looking behind him. Instinct had made him block his stomach when he had seen the huge paw swiping at him.

That was it. Almost in slow motion, he watched as the whole forest went past him. His small body flew through the air crashing into a tree, it's branches catching his fall.

In a rage, the bear roared and came after him again determined to finish off its attack and possible meal.

Not high enough in the tree for height to protect him from another attack, Alec knew this was his last chance to alert the rescue team.

Screaming, his breath had been cut off as the bear stood up. It's massive size was a terror in itself.

He had closed his eyes, as he expected his life to end right then. When he hadn't felt another crushing blow, he had opened his eyes when several gun shots rang out. The bullets had stopped the bear mid-swing. The attack was over at that point. Man had conquered beast once again.

Unable to hang onto the branches any longer, Alec had let go of the saving tree falling to the ground next to the prone bear.

Terror had filled his heart once more when he thought the bear would move again.

Mercifully, darkness had claimed his traumatized mind and he had fallen into a deep sleep.

Del knew the danger hadn't been over, however. Once the rescue team had reached the young Alec, they had discovered his arm and shoulder a mangled mess. If Alec hadn't protected his side and stomach, the outcome of his rescue would have been much different. Alec most likely wouldn't have made a recovery.

But, now the sequence of the memories were robbing him of life and recovery. By day, life seemed bearable. Del could see through his memories the beautiful vision of his concerned mother diligently and lovingly taking care of the young boy.

It was as he slept that he was robbed of much needed rest. The disturbing memories continued to surface. Del knew it wouldn't be long before Alec's restless sleep took over his young mind.

Sleep was necessary for his full recovery, mentally and physically. Del wasn't about to allow the darkness claim Alec's young mind. He had a full life to live and it was about time for him to start living it again. Alec was in his second month of recovery. The first month was spent in and out of a controlled coma. Doctors needed his bones to heal properly and Alec's terror-filled dreams made it impossible for them to keep his arm still.

This second month his days have been filled with physical therapy exhausting his limited energy supply. For Alec to have full use of his arm again, he needed to sleep and be able to rest.

And Del was ready to help make a change in this depleting pattern of repeating the same dream over and over.

Unpausing the dream, Del went to work. Immediately he found the memories he was looking for. Casting them in front of the next part of the sequence, Del prayed for Alec to latch onto the new memories.

Beautiful memories of his mom brushing his shoulder-length hair as he laid in bed when he first woke up at the hospital. He had been unconscious when he had been flown in. Doctors had been forced to put him under heavy anesthesia to begin surgery immediately.

But waking up to her eyes filled with happy tears as she smiled down at him was the vision he needed.

Del coaxed a new memory into his dream sequence. Del prayed Alec would latch onto this lifeline and hold onto it. It was Alec's sense of safety as his mom held him, crying.

Holding his breath, Del waited. Instead of Alec ignoring the memories Del was sending him, the boy paused the vision of the attack. His attention became riveted on his mother's tears dropping onto his hospital nightgown disappearing into the fabric.

The memory continued to play, as Alec remembered watching the tears and feeling some drop onto his uninjured arm.

Suddenly, the realization he was safe and in his mother's arms was more than he could bear and he released his own torrent of emotions.

Del smiled as he watched the disturbing memory of Alec's attack recede in the light of this beautiful and healing memory.

"Maker, thank you," Del thought gratefully. He knew there was still work to be done, but this was the first time he had been able to help in any way.

Del retreated from the safer images that were now flooding Alec's mind. Happier, safer times were the images he was focusing on, times he had spent with his mom.

Ballparks, beach stays, late-night ice cream trips, early morning donut stops, the memories came one at a time, but each one were cherished.

Alec had only known his mom's care. She was all he had, he never knew his father. But, his bond with his mom was close and he was at peace with their life. She was at peace also, and that made Alec happy. Del knew that Alec thought he was being a little selfish, but Alec couldn't help that he liked having her undivided attention.

Del left Alec to his now new, tranquil thoughts and returned his own thoughts back to his bedroll. Laying still, he rested as he thought of young Alec and the rescue of his attack and now dreams.

Knowing he had had the Maker's help in reminding Alec of the one memory he would latch onto, Del took a minute to thank Him for his intervention.

"Thank you, Maker, I was beginning to think that poor kid would always be tormented by those memories."

"Always. It is not over, he will continue to need your assistance. I've chosen you for a reason."

Nodding, Del committed his help once again, "I will continue to do my best, Maker. I want to help him overcome his fear of that terrible memory."

"Well done, good and faithful servant."

Not able to help the next question from reaching his mind, he decided to just ask instead of ignoring it.

"Maker, will Ari choose me like I've chosen her? What will I do if she chooses another?"

"Son, ignore the enemy's call to give up. I know you. And I will never abandon you."

"Who is this enemy, Maker?"

"There is an evil force always at work to discourage, trip and trick you into thinking you will fail. Ignore these beings. Remember, my words are truth. Now go to Ari, your bondmate."

Feeling himself again alone in his thoughts, Del thought back to the enemy the Maker had mentioned.

He had known this enemy was at work, but teachers at DW would never elaborate on that teaching, but to only trust the Maker's voice.

Did that mean, he wondered, when a thought reached his mind that destroyed his confidence or like the Maker said, tricked or tripped him up, it was that other force at work?

Wondering too, if his world had mistakingly neglected to teach their young how to defend themselves from this evil force.

Stretching, he was always surprised when he woke up from a Dream Weaving session refreshed and energetic. It was a blessing since now he needed to Catch Ari's dream.

Smiling, he knew she was going to be furious. The night was half over. She's probably been waiting for him. The doubt crept in that she might not be waiting.

Ignoring that feeling, he tried picturing where she would be right now. He could never tell with that girl, he thought, amusement replacing his worries.

Knowing he needed to begin his transformation, he fought the urge to delay it. It was painful and uncomfortable, but he couldn't let Ari see his Outcast cover.

He tried relaxing his thoughts knowing his body would follow making the change easier.

A combination of pinpricks and heat began the transformation, in small increments at first until it escalated. The heat multiplying by more than a hundred degrees and the small pinpricks began stabbing everywhere.

He knew that it only took a few minutes after this happened, but it didn't make tolerating the pain any easier.

Knowing why he was doing this made this a little easier, but the urge to stop took over his thoughts. He fought them, however.

This always happened, and now he knew those thoughts for what they were. They must be from the enemy the Maker had told him about.

Remembering he needed to focus on the Maker's words, not anything else, he recalled what the Maker said to him, repeating them in his mind until his transformation finished.

Shaking from the exertion of transforming back to his human form, he raised his hand to be sure it had happened.

Sure enough, his fingers greeted him as he waved his hand. Breathing a sigh of relief, he waited a few minutes until his shakes had quieted down.

As soon as he felt himself again, anticipation filled him. Joy filled him since he knew he was going to see his Ari.

Without waiting another minute, he closed his eyes diving into the darkness sparkling with light.

Remember Me?

Finding himself in a grey room, he looked around for the girl of his dreams. Glancing past the grey slab that must be her bed, he turned around only to find her with a furious expression on her face and her hands on both hips.

Trying to find his voice, he was having a hard time of it, since she looked so beautiful standing there. Her hair seemed to float around her face creating a curly halo effect.

She looked like an angel. But, if looks could kill, he'd be dead.

"Del, I don't even know what to say to you right now," she said as her petite form trembled with fury.

All he wanted to do was hold her to calm the tremors that seemed to be taking control of all her rational thought.

"I can explain," he said instead in a calming voice.

"How can you can explain the fact that you have been M.I.A., all night! Where have you been?" she finished in a whisper wringing her hands together.

Worried for her, Del hoped she didn't suspect he had been caught and held against his will.

Reaching for her, she backed off, demanding, "Del, I am a little upset right now, and I have every right to know why you are just now stepping into my dream. I've been waking up every hour stressing that you weren't here, yet."

Walking over to him, she looked him over and asked, "Have you been hurt? Would I be able to tell if you had? What's going on, Del? Are you here in the castle, yet? I deserve to know!"

Not able to help himself, Del laughed loving her torrent of questions. "Take a breath, why don't ya'? Man, you really are mad!"

Her eyes flashed and she put her hands on her hips again.

"Whoa, whoa," holding his hands up, saying quickly, "I only said that because when you get mad, you never take a breath. I'm only trying to tell you to breathe," he said trying to diffuse the situation.

Releasing a pent-up breath, she said, "Don't try to sweet talk me now, Del." Walking over to the stone bench, she sat down, her head in her hands. "This has just been an exhausting night."

He had been so relieved to find her, he didn't notice how tired she looked. Her shoulders were slumped and there were dark circles under her eyes.

"Ari, I'm sorry." Not wanting to alarm her with his situation, but wanting to give her hope, he said, "Everything is fine. I'll be here soon to come and get you."

He knew he was being selfish, but he needed to hear she had missed him, so he asked her, "So, you couldn't wait to see me?"

Standing up suddenly, she advanced over to him pointing a finger in his face, asking him, "You wanted me to miss you, Del? Is that was this was about? Fine. I can do that. I can leave this dream and then see if you can find me."

Just noticing he hadn't felt their bond come to life, alarmed, he realized he had to do something. So, he closed the distance between them. Pulling her to him, he bent his head closer to hers saying against her lips, "Ari, you even think of doing that, I will..."

Loving her blue-green eyes, her temper, he gave into the moment and kissed her wanting to remind her how much he loved her game, her dance through life. Pulling away, he drank in the image of her flushed cheeks, which reddened as he watched.

But, he was floored when she said, talking softly, "I didn't miss you, you jerk, I was worried about you, and there is a big difference. And you think one kiss will make me forget that?"

Del reeled under her cold treatment, and he knew he needed to step back and wait out her temper. Once it started, he should know better than to let her get it out until she had released all of it.

So, Del stepped back, folded his arms and agreed. He'd agree to anything she'd say right now.

"How about asking me the difference between being worried and missing you?" she asked her glare slicing through him.

Not waiting for an answer, she said, placing her hands back on her hips, "Because, when I worry, I get mad, and lately, all I've been is mad at you. I mean," she exclaimed as she began to pace, "You haven't been here all night. And the last time you came, it was without any information at all. I need to know what to expect here. Do you realize I am stuck in this castle with a witch for a mother and some crazy loons walking around her day and night?"

Pacing, she resumed her tirade, "And you expect me to just melt under one kiss? I am telling you, Del, I need answers. Are you in the castle?"

Feeling guilty he hadn't gotten her out of there yet, he looked up quickly when something she said suddenly registered.

"What do you mean, a witch for a mother?" his worries increasing.

"Oh! Didn't you know?," she asked with throwing her arms up in the air, "I have a mother now. And, my mom, the one who disappeared when I was two, has been busy! All of her time has been taken up raising up an Outcast army." Shaking her head, she said suddenly looking deflated, "She's Queenie, the Queen of the Outcasts. Oh, Del, what am I going to do? I thought I hated her, but how can I hate my own mother?" she asked, her anger deflated, despair edging into her voice.

Del looked down at the floor trying to register her words.

"Ari, are you sure? How do you know?"

"Gran came here looking for her. She had a suspicion my mom was here, but even she was surprised to find her their leader."

Wondering how to comfort her, he found himself speechless. He had had every intention of killing the Outcast leader if he ever had an open shot, but this definitely complicated things.

"What are you going to do?" he asked.

"Try to convert her, I guess," she answered. "What else can I do?"

Not expecting that answer, Del tried to reign in his temper, saying quietly, "Ari. You can't do the impossible."

"It's not impossible, Del. The Maker said, 'Nothing is impossible to those who believe.'

And I do believe," she insisted. "It took some soul searching for me to get to this point, believe me. But, being stuck in a room by myself all day will do that to you."

Looking down, she played with her fingers for some time before she said, "Believe me, I was not happy to find that Queenie is my long-lost mother. But, I can't just leave her here, lost, as an Outcast."

"Queenie?" he asked with understanding in his smile.

Smiling softly she said, "That's just a nickname I first gave her, and it's kind of stuck."

Wanting to say something that could ease her pain, he stopped when he was suddenly stormed with her emotions. Crushing his hands against his chest, he looked up at her searching her expression for the anguished feelings he felt her feeling.

Her head was still down, and so using his finger to gently coax her chin up, he could see tears leaving trails down her soft cheeks.

Wiping them away carefully, he pulled her to him where she gave vent to her all her emotions.

As she cried softly, he relished feeling her in his arms. Her grief reminded him of the many times she wept on his chest when Gran had disappeared.

Resting his cheek on her soft hair, he asked hoping it wouldn't open a sore wound, "Gran came searching for Queenie, er, your mom? She wasn't kidnapped?"

"Well," Ari answered wiping the rest of her tears away as she sat up, "She was home resting in her chair when she saw an Outcast looking through her window."

At Del's raised eyebrows, she went on, "Wuz is quick, but Gran is quicker, even at her age she still managed to catch him so she could question him."

"Gran?" Del asked incredulously.

"Well, let's say she pulled a Catcher trick on him and he was no match for her."

Shaking his head, he said, "You are going to have to tell me more than that." He just couldn't believe Gran could take on a healthy Outcast.

"She put him under a deep sleep then tied him up so she could talk to him," she answered.

"I'm surprised he allowed her," as he feasted on her beautiful blue-green eyes, distracting himself from the conversation.

"He was curious, so he allowed her questions and answered them," her eyes laughing for a moment.

Bringing her focus back to him where his fiercest hope was that it would stay with him forever, he kissed her lips softly.

"Mmmm, that's nice," she whispered hugging him.

As he held her, he decided to question a nagging thought that had just occurred to him.

"Are you curious, Ari?"

"About what?" she answered sleepily.

"About that life, is there any enticement at all to be a part of it, to know more about it, them, maybe Wuz," he finally asked wanting to hear a fiery denial.

Her body stiffened in his taking with it the answer he had hoped to hear.

"No," she finally said. "Well, in some ways, I want to understand them, their choices. To find out, why."

"Why, what?"

"Why they would give away a beautiful life and a beautiful hope and become something ugly, something the Maker never created," as she relaxed once again in his arms as she worked out her thoughts.

He'd take this over anything, he thought, hugging her tightly to him.

"Ari, I love you," he said against her ear.

Looking up at him, she answered her eyes taking that shine to them, he had only seen in the moonlight the last night they were together. "I love you too, Del. I miss you. I can see forever happening, just give me time to be ready for it." Hope stood gleaming in her eyes and with that answer he would promise her anything.

"You know I'll wait forever, my sleep angel, if I need to. Just don't go giving your heart away, ok? It's a very valuable thing to me, one I would be sure to keep precious."

He could see her heart shining through her eyes when she nodded at him. He knew it was time to go, but before he could start saying goodbye, she put her finger on his lips.

"Don't you say it, Delius, you will not leave me here just yet. I'm not ready to say good..." her voice cracking into sob as she buried her face into his chest weeping softly.

"Shh, shh, shh," he whispered in her hair, as he hugged her tightly and swayed her gently.

"I't's going to be fine, Ari, I'm here, I won't leave you," he said softly.

"Yea, but you will have to leave soon," she said looking up at him.

Gazing down into the depths of her watery eyes, he lost himself in the moment, saying before he kissed her again, "Then let's make every minute we are together count, ok?"

The next minute, he held her tightly as he relished her in his arms.

He looked down at her again and was glad to see she liked their kiss when he noticed her blush come back.

Wanting to prolong the time they had, he asked, "Do you know what one of your most adorable features are?" When she shook her head, he answered running his thumb across her cheek, "Your freckles. They are one of my most favorite decorations on your face."

He resisted kissing each one. "I miss seeing them. I've missed you, Ari." Not able to help responding to the impulse to kiss two of them, he moved his lips over each one promising himself again, he would do whatever he could for them to be together, awake and asleep.

Not wanting things to go too far, he forced himself to pull back resting his forehead on hers and said, "If you can promise this kind of treatment every time you get mad at me, I'll start more fights in the future."

"I can get mad at you if I want to," she said softly.

"Is that a promise?" he asked smiling.

They stood silent for a moment and he wondered how he was going to be able to let go this time.

"Hello? Remember me?" she asked.

Smiling down at her, he responded, "How could I forget?"

"I hope you never do."

Looking at her trying to hide the intensity of how much he felt for her, he answered, "Don't make promises my sleep angel, unless you intend to keep them."

With the same intensity, she held his face in her hands, saying, "Del, I do promise. Just come and get me, please. I need you."

With that he knew the morning was coming, nearly there, so he regretfully began to fade out, as he told Ari, "Don't worry, I am coming, I'm on my way. Hold on a little while longer, I'm coming."

The next moment he jerked awake, still feeling his heart beating wildly for a girl he would always love. He didn't regret forming the bond early. He really didn't have much choice. She had captured his heart a long time ago, really he held out as long as he could before the bond finally completed, on his end.

He hoped and prayed he would one day feel that she loved him, enough to spend a lifetime with only him.

The realization that is was dawn finally hit him, and he looked around to see if anyone had noticed his transformation.

Four pairs of eyes were staring at him, several accompanied with open mouths incredulously looking him over.

Jack was the first to comment. "Finally, the real Del steps forth!"

Cy quipped, "And it's about time. Got tired of looking at that hairy back side of ya."

With that they all began laughing, including Del.

One thing was certain, he could never get bored with this bunch. He thanked the Maker for each of their presences and hoped their mission could be over so he could enjoy them, with Ari by his side.

"All right, boys, enough fun stuff, we've got my girl to save, so let's get to work."

Reminders

General Tom barged into Del's tent clapping his hands demanding they all get to their feet.

Groggy, Del climbed to his feet hoping he could keep his temper. He could see the agreement he made with the General was going to be hard to keep.

Grimacing at the sunlight streaming through the open tent flap, he resisted covering his ears with all the shouting. Cy would not roll out of bed fast enough and the General was getting angry.

Del hoped Cy would cooperate with the older hunter. When Cy did get up, Del watched a face off begin. He knew he needed to ask the Maker for help, but he couldn't get his thoughts together fast enough. He did manage to quickly ask the Maker to feel his intentions, however. He did not want to lose Cy from his group. He had a bad feeling the General was wanting to make an example of someone and he wished Cy would wipe off the resentful glare he was emanating.

Cy had had a hard life, with hardly any breaks. But the General wouldn't know that and Del had a feeling he wouldn't allow it to hinder his orders anyway.

Just as he feared, the General widened his stance parking himself in front of Cy.

"Is there a problem son?" he barked at him.

Cy seemed calm, but Del knew he wasn't. The problem was he also had a feeling the General was just as testy.

Cy visibly tensed and lowly growled, "I am not your son."

"I wouldn't mind discussing a complaint this morning," the General said with a smirk.

"You've got one," Cy replied his voice shaking.

"Good," the General smiled sizing Cy up. Standing tall, taller than Cy's medium height, he lowered his face into Cy's and Del groaned.

"Keep your opinion to yourself, loverboy," the General said in Del's direction. "This isn't your concern."

This visible battle of wills was enough to wake the group. Del actually heard a snicker coming from the back of the tent. Stifling a sigh, he promised he would deal with Jack later.

The rest grimly watched the scene unfold between Cy and the General.

"I am pretty sure I am going to have a problem with you, boy," the older man said putting his hands on his hips as he glared down at him. "And I don't think that will work."

"Why would I care if that happened?" Cy asked with a hard edge to his voice. "You are not in control of this group." Turning to Del, he asked in a low voice, "Or did that change?"

Del cringed hating that he hadn't told the group what the General had ordered last night at the fire pit.

The General spun around, put his hands comfortably behind his back and said, "Well, it's about time you did, Delius." Steeling his eyes at Del, the General waited for him to make the announcement.

Clearing his throat, he began with an apology.

"Sorry, guys, I should have told you this, but as of last night the General is taking over our group until we find Ari."

Tensing his shoulders, he waited for the group to curse rain angry comments on him. He was surprised to hear only a couple, coming from Cy's direction.

Looking up, his suspicion was confirmed as Cy came striding toward him. Rolling his shoulders, he prepared himself for a fight.

Stopping just short of reaching distance, Cy asked in hard voice, "When were you planning on telling me I wasn't going to follow a weak, lazy leader anymore?"

Del steadied his breathing to control the tremors racing through him. He needed to fight back, but not with his fists.

"I never knew you to deal low blows, Cy," Del said in a low voice.

"The same could be said for you," Cy retorted. "I've had my share of having to listen to tyrants. I have a choice. Don't I?" he asked deliberately directing the question to Del.

Without taking his eyes off of Cy's, he answered grimly, "Yes, you do."

Looking first at Del then at the General, Cy stretched his arms out, almost casually.

"Then, I'm out," he announced.

Striding over to his bunk to grab his bag, he left the tent without another glance in anyone's direction.

Del knew he had just made an enemy out of a friend. How much damage he had just caused, he didn't know, only the Maker did.

Their friendship was one Cy had finally agreed to and Del felt terrible he had lost it this quickly. Knowing he could do nothing to change the situation or Cy's mind, he gave up and breathed an appeal to the Maker for a chance to regain Cy's trust.

Shaking his head, he directed his attention to the seasoned leader currently sizing up the rest of his team.

Cy

Ambushed

Cy walked into the forest with a red haze meeting everything he saw. He walked without listening for a while wanting to diffuse the ticking time bomb he knew lay inside his chest.

He was ready to explode with frustration. Having General Tom take over the group was the last straw he could take. What was that expression, the straw that broke the camel's back? Well, that was him, but instead of broken he was angry, fighting angry.

He hadn't wanted to hurt any of his team mates, so he had left to nurse very old wounds and this fresh one alone.

General Tom was just like his father he thought bitterly. Always forcing his authority by throwing his weight around. The General may not use his fists like his father had, but he had the venom to make his words just as destructible.

Right now, he needed a good fight. He looked around finally noticing his surroundings, which was unusual for him. He always took stock of where he was, and was always on the lookout for anything out of character. But, now he was craving to find danger and what better way than to find an Outcast or two to give it to.

Looking around, he scanned the area willing something for him to give chase to. Not knowing why, he almost expected something to come at him. Maybe it was his sixth sense, but whatever it was, he was ready.

He half wondered if the Maker was finally giving him some help, some intuition. But, as quickly as that thought came, he dismissed the notion. The Maker had time only for other Weavers, that much had been clear his whole life.

Forcing the bitterness aside, he concentrated on the air around him. Crouching low into a high fern, he hid his body from any view. Testing the air with all his senses he tried to figure out what it was he knew was out there.

Something waited for him and he wanted to turn the tables. Before he could think another thought, a voice carried through his mind stopping him abruptly.

"Run Cymeus, and fight with all you have."

Looking around wildly, he tried to see who spoke to him. Jumping out of the ferns, he could see the reason for the warning when two large shadows cast over the forest floor.

Searching the skies and seeing nothing but the tops of tall pine trees and patches of blue and white sky, he waited.

"Run, son, run!"

Taking the faceless advice that reverberated through his mind, he took off on a sprint dodging trees and an enemy he knew was hunting him.

He ducked when he heard a piercing screech from above and just missed two large talons hooking onto his shirt.

Changing directions, he feared the huge bird would try to grab him again. Fiercely wanting to live, he zigzagged through the forest jumping over fallen logs. Running as fast as he could without tripping over the forest growth, he tried finding his way back to camp.

He knew when he didn't see the bird's shadow that it was behind him. A loud caw filled the air, and he realized the bird may not be acting alone. Pulling his short sword free as he ran, he decided if those talons came close again, the bird would be short one foot. He wasn't going to be some giant bird's meal.

Feeling a draft of air rush behind him, he tucked his sword into his stomach and rolled onto the ground. Jumping up as soon as he got back onto his feet, he looked up and saw he had just narrowly missed being captured again.

"What do you want?" he yelled at the creature. He was sure it was an Outcast, disguised as a giant bird. He tried to look behind him as he kept up his mad run. He needed to see if another one lurked behind to catch him off guard.

Barely missing a tree trunk, he heaved several breaths knowing this race would be over if he could just make it back to camp. Looking ahead, he could just see the break of forest cover. He knew though that the open sky would be his greatest threat. The birds would have an even clearer shot at him.

Slowing down, he knew he needed a plan. Just as he was thinking through how to call for help to the General's camp, he was jolted upward with two clawed feet that felt like manacles around his shoulders. Yelling as loud as he could, he screamed for help. Frustration coursing through him, he kicked his feet trying to break free from the iron grip the bird had on him.

He realized he still held onto his short sword, and just as his hand reached backward to thrust the sword into the bird, it gave him a big shake surprising him.

He could only watch as his sword dropped to the ground below. The surprise of the bird's defensive move made him forget to grip his only weapon. High up by now, he could see the General outside of Del's camp with his team as they shouted and took crossbows out to shoot down his captor.

With an even more sinking feeling, he knew if they were successful, he would fall with the birds. He resigned himself to face whatever was ahead of him.

He had wanted a fight, and it looked like he had gotten one and lost miserably.

Hanging on to the clawed feet he thought about where he was being taken. He wondered if he would be a meal or possibly taken to the Outcast castle. The only good part of the castle option was Ari was there.

Maybe he could help her escape and finally get to know the girl whose face has been haunting his dreams lately.

He tried to ignore the guilt he felt that she was Del's girl. Del had become the closest friend he had ever had. Well, he thought, he deserved a chance too. Why should Del get the girl? Del has had everything handed to him his whole life, he thought bitterly.

It was time for him to get something he wanted. And if Ari was willing, he would take that chance. Life was only about chances and what-if's, he had discovered. Ari was one chance he was willing to take.

"Cymeus."

Not knowing what else to say, he answered simply, "Yes?"

"You are masking your fear with anger, let it go, Cymeus."

"Maker?"

"By recognizing my voice, you know the answer. Forgive Delius my son, you need your concentration to be right in the days ahead."

Not masking his sorrow, Cy replied, "What more can happen Maker that hasn't already happened? What more can I take?"

"My son, let go of your past. Give it to me, I will take your burdens.

Bitterness clawed at Del's throat. He wondered where was the Maker when he was a child. The abuse he had suffered could have been prevented, why hadn't it?

Instead of voicing his anger, however, he kept silent.

Let the Maker have a taste of the silent treatment like he's gotten from him all of these years.

He's just now going to hear from the esteemed Maker? Well, he fumed, it was too late. Swallowing, he narrowed his eyes and memorized the flight path the birds were taking him. He intended on leaving the castle and having Ari with him.

Resentment continued to boil inside him. By now, it was a familiar feeling. It joined with the anger he always felt.

Anger, it was one emotion he could trust. It has always been that way and it looked like it would stay that way.

Ari

Prisons

'Where can he be?' thought Ari as she looked out her prison window for quite possibly the millionth time. Placing her hand on the thick cold window, deep set into the stone wall, she searched her mind for the last time she had seen him, really seen him.

It had been weeks since she last saw his grinning face and warm brown eyes melted into delicious intent when he looked at her. The dreams were real enough, but she couldn't help but crave really seeing him, holding him, and just experiencing Del.

Sighing, she turned from the window after seeing nothing but the same camps scattered around the castle. Wondering why they didn't build more permanent residences for themselves, she stopped herself.

They may not have truly bought into this evil existence, she thought. The Outcasts may consider this evil life temporary and want to return to Dream Weaving again. She could only hope that as she returned her gaze out the small glass window.

It was possible, she repeated to herself, but unfortunately, until they accepted the Maker, the truth was obvious. They would remain Outcasts until they die. Maybe if they witnessed true hope they would want to leave this decrepit life.

That was where she came in, she reasoned. She hadn't had many chances to talk to any Outcasts about the Maker because of her confinement. But as soon as she could find some freedom, she would get to work letting Outcasts know the Maker is not someone to fear or despise, but to love.

Wuz and her grandmother have been sheltering her to protect her from the attentions of the leeches, she liked to call the disgusting lizards who loved to torture their victims. She shuddered and was disgusted that her mother would allow them to have victims in the first place.

She had been following a strict schedule her mother had agreed to, so she could be trained and hone her powers. Every morning for two hours Gran and Wuz drilled her relentlessly as they trained her to reach dreams faster, see them clearer, not miss any detail of a memory she may have missed.

Dream Catching was remarkably easy for her, which Wuz was happy about since he said they had much more to learn once they got the basics of Catching down. Ari always referred his compliments to Del's training, since she would have known nothing if it hadn't been for Del's patient instructions. Gran had been impressed with Del's teachings also, but hadn't been surprised that he had succumbed to Ari's pleading to teach her himself.

Gran thought he should have insisted on formal training for her granddaughter.

"He insisted Gran, but my begging eventually paid off," Ari had told her happily.

Gran had sighed grumbling, "I'm sure he enjoyed every minute of your attention too." Ari smiled now at the memory, just as she had done then, loving the rush of love filling her when she thought of those past moments. Looking back, she now knew he had sealed his bond with her before those lessons had ever happened.

How could she have been so blind, she asked herself, again. She felt a sharp pang of remorse as she thought of how much it must have hurt him to hold that secret for so long. It was part of what made her love him so much. He sacrificed so much so he wouldn't scare her or threaten their friendship with his intentions.

Shaking her head, she held her hand close to her heart, wondering if he could feel her love for him right then. Hoping he could, she didn't know how she was going to stand being away from him much longer. Of course, he may be in the castle now, she thought, since he would be rescuing her dressed as an Outcast. She just may not know it.

The thought gave her a strength that was surprising. She would survive this castle stay and she and Del would be that much stronger for it, she resolved. She didn't doubt he would come for her, it was just a matter of time when he did.

Hugging herself, she tried containing her strong feelings, her heart seemed to want to fly out of her chest. Laughing at her sudden giddiness, she held her arms out and spun around.

She twirled slowly at first, then faster and faster until she was breathlessly laughing. Dizzy, she fell on the floor.

Not having heard the door open, she almost jumped to her feet when Wuz said with a grave expression, "And I thought I had seen it all. Yet, you continue to surprise me, little Ari."

"You scared me, Wuz," she complained.

His eyes hardened, "How many times do I need to remind you not to call me that? You could lose my cover."

Slapping her mouth, she cringed into her hand whispering, "Oh no, did anyone hear?" Trying not to look obvious, she looked behind him.

When she didn't see anyone in the hall, she stumbled over to her stone bench falling onto its hard perch thinking she was never going to learn. One of these days she was going to give his or another converted Outcast's identity away if she wasn't careful. That was a regret she didn't want.

The thought of such an accident wrenched pain throughout her body. Hoping Del couldn't feel these painful feelings, she didn't want him to misinterpret them thinking she was being hurt, so she worked on calming her feelings.

"He's bonded with you, hasn't he?" Wuz asked quietly. Looking down at her, he had walked over to her and the look in his eyes seemed sympathetic and something else, disturbed maybe.

Wondering why he would be upset by Del's bond with her, she studied his expression until he finally looked away wiping his face clean of any clues.

Surprised he closed himself off to her as quickly as he did, she reprimanded herself. Of course he knows how to close himself off, he was one of her mother's favorite students, she thought, angry at her lack of insight. He needed to be good at that technique to survive around here.

Suddenly curious, she asked Wuz in a small voice, not understanding her boldness, but she suddenly wanted to know, "What do you really look like, if you don't mind me asking?"

Turning back to her, Wuz' eyes sparkled as he grinned at her question. "You may be too curious for your own good, little lady." Laughing, he grabbed her hand pulling her up from her seat on the bench, pulling her into a dance spin that both surprised and delighted her.

She felt herself spin out away from him, then just as quickly he pulled her back spinning along his arm. Stopping suddenly, she found herself tucked into his arm.

Giggling, she looked up at him, but stopped when she saw his eyes. An intent look had replaced his dancing and before she could think what that look might mean, Wuz' friendly look replaced the other more confusing ones.

"Before any more thoughts come into that pretty little head of yours, I'm afraid I'm going to have to disappoint you. I won't be showing you my tempting good looks here, lil' Ari." Speechless, Ari searched for something to say, when he rescued her from a response.

Letting go of her hands, he moved away from her sighing, "I can't risk showing my true form in this place. I have too many enemies for that."

Realizing something, she whispered suddenly fearful for him, "It's because when you leave this Outcast life, you don't want to be recognized. You know, I'm afraid for you," she admitted. She had grown close to Wuz in this crazy environment, and didn't want anything happening to such a good soul.

Smiling softly, Wuz said, "Don't be lil' one, I'm a survivor. I've been surviving here a long time now."

"You aren't scared?" she asked suddenly curious again who that person was behind that mask.

His eyes were blue, she just noticed, when they hardened again. "For the first time in a long time, I'm afraid now."

"Why?" she asked.

"I'm terrified for you," he admitted quietly. "But," he said his voice strengthening, "I won't let them have you, you are safe here, Arella."

Surprised he didn't use her nickname, she responded, "I don't think I'll be here much longer." Walking over the window, she crossed her arms as if she could lock inside the crazy hope that soared through her whenever she thought of Del.

"What makes you say that?" Wuz asked.

"It's just a feeling I have," she said with a quiet certainty. "Del is coming, he is trying to get here as fast as he can."

"Ahhh," Wuz replied changing the topic completely, "You are starting to return his bond, then."

Bewildered, she answered, "Yes."

"But, it's not happened yet," he stated.

Astonished, she whispered furiously, "How do you know that?"

With his blank mask back on, he replied, "I can just tell." His eyes betraying nothing, he turned to the window when a loud commotion outside drew their attention to see what was going on.

One of the vultures that had carried her and Wuz to the castle was flying low through the Outcast camp. All the Outcasts were jumping and trying to grab whoever the vulture was carrying. It seemed to her like the vulture was trying to terrorize whoever it brought to the castle.

Her heart lurched when the vulture nearly dropped its burden, then screeching, almost laughing, it pulled up just when an Outcast on the ground tried raking the poor Weaver's leg.

She had a feeling he was not an Outcast but another prisoner, like her. Grabbing Wuz' arm, she begged, "Please help him, Wuz. I can't stand the thought of those lizards hurting anyone."

"Please don't call me that," he said quietly his eyes on the vulture's human load. He seemed to consider his next words carefully before he spoke. "My name is not Wuz."

Her curiosity was piqued at the mystery of Wuz' identity.

"What is it then?" she asked.

"Alex," he answered his blue eyes intent on hers. For a moment she could almost see handsome features staring down at her face, but when she blinked she stood looking at Wuz, not Alex.

"Alex," she said, trying it out to see if it matched the handsome face he allowed her a glimpse.

Changing the subject, he asked lightly, "Do you know this Weaver?" his eyes flashing that indiscernible look again, but just as quickly as it came, it was gone.

Not sure about his tone and before she could decipher the look, she answered honestly, "I can't tell from this distance."

Wuz stood silent and seemed to be thinking. Not knowing what to do for the poor person the vulture had by this time brought to the castle steps, she reached and touched Wuz' arm.

He jerked at her touch saying softly, "Or course I will help him. That's what I do here, remember?" Turning in her direction, he said chucking her softly under her chin, "I'm in the business of saving people. Even those who need saving from themselves."

At that, he diffused the light in his eyes, replacing it with the fearsome creature she had seen her first day at the castle and several times since.

Moving quickly to the door, he turned, nodded in her direction and just like that was gone.

Queenie

The Queen

'Every time Beak and Eagle bring me something, they always overdo it,' the Queen sighed as she watched their amusing display.

She was delighted when the beasts' burden revealed it was Cymeus Roman. She was pleased he hadn't screamed or appeared scared, but looked angry instead. That was perfect, she needed him to be strong, not dim-witted or easily scared.

Things were progressing nicer than she thought possible as she reflected over her handiwork. Cy, her chosen leader, had been dreaming of Ari on his own for quite some time now. She hadn't had to slide Ari's images into his dreams for several weeks.

It has almost been too easy, she complained to herself. 'I hope he isn't too easy to manage,' she said to herself thinking Ari will never accept or fall in love with a push-over.

'Not my daughter,' she thought proudly as the great doors to her throne room were pushed open.

As she waited and watched her Rhinos push and force Cy into the center of the room, her thoughts traveled to Ari's father. What would he think about this boy for their daughter, she wondered. His intuition had always been his best strength.

It was how he knew early in their marriage, she was attracted to power over goodness, which was the darker side of Maone. He had tried to curb her tendencies. But when he threatened to leave her if she didn't believe in the Maker's promises, she decided to leave him first. She didn't get far before he caught up to her. She hadn't learned yet how to seal their bond from each other.

Funny that she would remember that night now. She cringed. But, memories don't always stop when you want them to.

The decision to leave Ari had been hard, harder than anything she's experienced, even here. It had been easier to leave Ari's father at the time because she had been angry.

She still remembered how he had found her easily since she couldn't outrun him, so she had faced him in the path. The memory was crystal clear, even now.

'So, you were just going to leave, then,' he had stated without a question in his voice his eyes burning with intensity, whether it was pain or anger, she couldn't tell.

'Yes,' she had answered, holding onto her hate so strongly she didn't know how he wasn't showing the pain of feeling it.

She had projected her feelings so strongly then, just to end it quickly between them, when he had interrupted her and sent such a transfusion of anguished love, pure and sweet into her being.

It had made her speechless, but she had realized his ploy and hated him even more for trying to guilt her with his feelings.

"You won't force me into returning home," she had said in a strong voice.

217

"Who's forcing you, Lucia?" he had asked his arms reaching out to her only to hang limply at his side.

Just like his feelings, she could still remember when he finally let go of her.

Even more angry, she had yelled, "You, you forced me into this life Tommy, by forcing my hand to choose. When I only had questions, you made them into what they are now, a mission to discover the truth." With that she had walked away taking with her his broken heart.

She could still feel his emotions, to this day. He had never learned how to block them from her. Either that, or he wanted her to always remember him. It was a sentence she would always have to endure. She had bonded with him at the same time he did and it's been almost twenty years since it happened. Their anniversary was approaching soon, she wondered what trinket would make its way to her.

Every year, at their anniversary, Tommy would send her a reminder of their former marriage. Either by message from a returned Outcast he had captured and given back to her, or some reminder from their past would be presented to her in her court.

She hated how he kept sending her reminders of their past relationship, but it amused her in a strange way that he refused to forget her.

He also didn't forget who and where she was now. He had not kept it secret from her that he has made it his mission to hunt her kind down. Not able to hear his thoughts only his emotions, she knew from Outcasts he had captured that he was on the warpath. He meant to obliterate her army and she wondered what he would do with her if it ever came to that.

Shaking her head from these thoughts, she trained her gaze on this Cy who stood waiting in front of her.

She had once hoped Ari would choose never to bond with anyone, unlike herself. But, when she had discovered Ari's recent conversations with Del and that she had begun the bonding process, she knew she needed to intervene.

Del would never accept this life, she understood his character. He was too much like Ari's father. So, she had had to find a better partner for Ari, someone who would accept this life, and one day lure Ari to rule it with him.

As she studied the young man in front of her, she was pleased once again by his strength. He wasn't backing down and didn't seem to look the least bit threatened by the large forms guarding him on either side.

She knew Ari admired strength, she had found it appealing in her friend, Del.

Comparing the two in her mind, she could see the two were different in looks and temperament, which was good. It wouldn't be good for one to resemble the other. It wouldn't be good to give Ari any reminders of Del.

This Cy would need to win her over completely on his own. Cy had good looks, which was in his favor. Ari will notice, she was sure. Dark hair, dark eyes, tall and strong, yes, it was time for Ari to meet her future.

Saying nothing to Cy, she spoke instead to her head guard. "Throw him in the upper dungeons, next to our other prisoner."

As he walked away with her two guards, she grinned. Her plans were steadily advancing just how she liked them. She only hoped Cy could steal Ari's heart. Del didn't belong here, Cy and her daughter did.

Ari

Dream Invasion

Ari flopped down on the bed exhausted from her morning lessons. She was learning quite a bit. Her favorite lesson was the sleep inducer. It would be a great weapon whenever she escaped. Wuz said she was a natural at putting a Weaver to sleep.

She had been tempted to slip into his dream to see his true shape. But then he had surprised her when he invited her to try inducing him to sleep. It was almost too easy. She thought she would get a glimpse of who he looked like, but in Gran's instruction this morning, she learned some Weavers or Catchers can choose any shape in their dream. If Alex had that talent, then she would never discover his true identity.

She accepted Wuz' invitation, but it didn't feel like much of a dream invasion since he was so willing.

Promising to make it hard for her however they continued the lesson. As part of his self-defense, he had told her, he formed blocks in his mind preventing inducements. Yet, he had had a teasing smile after his warning and the look in his eyes was almost a challenge. It was if he dared her to try to find him in his dream. Not sure if she had imagined that meaning, she ignored it. She wondered if he knew she wanted to catch a glimpse of his Weaver self, not as Wuz but as Alex. She hoped he hadn't guessed the truth, as a warm blush had crept over her face.

Once it had come time to put him to sleep, that smile had stayed on his face until he had finally fallen asleep. She then ventured into his mind, despite being tired beyond her limits from breaking down the barriers he had indeed constructed. But, she had reached into her last reserves of energy and penetrated the walls he had told her he erected. Painstakingly finding the cracks, she slipped in and watched as he stood on the edge a cliff bearing himself with ease even as a harsh wind tore through and around him.

He had a breathtaking view of a violent ocean roaring below him. He didn't seem to mind the wind buffeting him, which displayed a strength she had witnessed many times and could now admire. But, with a pang of regret stronger than she should have felt, she didn't see Alex on that cliff, but Wuz.

She had been a little too disappointed that he kept his Wuz shape in his dreams.

When she had retreated from his dream, Gran had tried to encourage her. She insisted she did well even getting to the cliff in Wuz' dream. His blocks are very difficult to get through, Gran had emphasized. Not wanting to admit the reason for her disappointment, she accepted Gran's praise.

Gran's presence was the best part of this disastrous time at the castle. She softened the blow of her mother's evil position as well as taking her under her wing in her training. Truly thinking about it, however, she realized Alex has helped in that way too.

Her mind, exhausted from her lessons, began to wander and she thought back to his last comment. What did she need saving from? Herself? What could she be involved with that she needed saving from? Del? At that thought, she stopped. He wouldn't care about her and Del bonding, would he? He shouldn't, she thought.

Their training was going so well, she would hate to have to stop it, if she became uncomfortable with Alex. Except, it wasn't an unwelcome feeling to have Alex interested in her. For some reason, if he did care for her that idea felt kind of nice. But, she couldn't return the feeling. Sighing, she knew she couldn't care for Alex that way because she loved Del or was starting to. And she wasn't the type to love two guys, so she was sticking with her first choice, Del.

Deciding to banish her crazy curiosity and continue on with her life, she attempted to sleep.

She felt guilty because of her lingering thoughts of Wuz. She was completely devoted to Del, so it felt wrong to wonder about Alex. It was a betrayal to be interested in someone else. But, if she had to be honest, the root of her curiosity was she was charmed. Charmed with the idea that a handsome Weaver resided under all of that fur. Thinking of Wuz as a Weaver and not an animal, was disconcerting. And he seemed to think well of her too.

She had always wondered what it would be like to be loved by someone else, but on one hand it was Wuz she was thinking about. On the other hand, Wuz and Alex, who were one and the same was not a standard Weaver or Catcher. His skills far exceeded that of Del's. But, she rallied, the only reason Del didn't have as many abilities, was that he had not had as much training or the experience of battle, like Alex.

Banishing all memory of Alex and his stupid dreams, she groaned in frustration. Having not heard from Del in a couple of days, Ari was growing restless to leave the castle and thinking more and more of trying to leave.

She had not seen her mother either, which was always positive. As much as she wanted to see her mother embrace the Maker's way, she couldn't see herself being the one to initiate that conversation. As soon as her mother entered the room for their weekly visits, Ari could see and feel her mother's eyes measuring her strengths and always seemed to be testing her patience.

Almost as if on cue, a knock sounded on her door. An imperious voice followed, "Open the door nitwit, I do not need to knock on my own daughter's door. Now move!"

By this time, she had sat up waiting for her mother's grand entrance. The door opened and her mother stormed in. Even angry, her mother was beautiful. She carried herself with easy grace. But, her next command couldn't have surprised Ari more.

"It's time you met your neighbor, Ari." Stunned, Ari realized she hadn't thought about him since his noticeable arrival. She hoped he was alright and was surprised to find his room was apparently close to hers. Suspicious of her mother's intent, she reluctantly agreed. She thought she would have had to sneak a visit to ensure he had things he needed. Having done that for several prisoners, she had made sure they were brought dinners and had necessary items.

With a guarded look, she led the way to her door saying simply, "After you, Mother."

Wondering what her mother had in store for her next, she tried to prepare herself for whatever surprise her mother had for her. She breathed a quick prayer to the Maker for strength and guidance and followed her mother out the door.

Mind over Matter

Walking into the hallway after her mother, she watched the guards scrambling away from her neighbor's door to allow her and her mother inside.

Still confused of her mother's purpose in arranging this meeting, Ari guarded herself as well as she could before she entered the Weaver's room. Not knowing who was behind the door, she strengthened her defenses and prepared herself for any kind of attack, like Alecx and Gran had taught.

Who she saw however made her stop in her tracks and she couldn't stop her gasp of surprise. Cy from her hometown sat on his bed watching their entrance. He didn't seem surprised to see her, so she hurried to draw her defenses back up. She learned to suspect everything and everyone, so she defended herself like she had been taught and looked at Cy with caution. For all she knew, he may be on her mother's side and she didn't want to fall under any kind of spell.

Not having seen him since school days and most recently at her and Del's graduation party, she guarded herself.

He continued to watch her and her mother with a careful look in his eyes. First he glared at her mother, who returned it with equal measure, then he turned it to her. His eyes were black as night, dark pools that seemed to take in every detail.

With her however, his glare changed. He gave her a slow, measured look that made her nervous. No, she changed her mind. It was more like she was on display. She seemed to know immediately that he was not one of her mother's puppets. For one thing, he disliked her mother too much.

Interrupting their silent appraisals, her mother broke the silence, "Ari, dear, I thought you could use a partner for your defense lessons. So, I've brought you, Cymeus Roman."

Ari was surprised at being given more lessons and at the disclosure of Cy's full name, it was something he protected when he was younger. She didn't have time to question it however when Cy whipped his head in her mother's direction.

"How did you know that was my name? And why would I be a good teacher?"

In a frosty tone, her mother answered, "I know a lot of things, darling, and as far as your defense skills, that was quite easy. You put up quite a fight when they brought you to our camp. You demonstrated quite a few techniques my men lack, by the look of the ones who received your attentions. So, I would like you to teach them to my daughter. In fact, I insist. Or, I can make your stay much less accommodating. But, she is not to be hurt. If she is, you will be given the same treatment you give her times a thousand."

He seemed to process her mother's orders and Ari's breath caught in her throat. She had learned that getting on her mother's bad side could be very bad for Cy. Her demands were strange, she had to admit. But, it wouldn't hurt him to train her. She could get hurt, but her mother just fixed that problem. Teaching her defense moves may not be a bad idea. He could be convinced to help her escape.

As he processed her mother's threat, he glanced over to her. Imperceptibly, his eyes softened. It was a quick look, but one she caught. As tense as he looked, she was surprised his eyes could look so warm, even if it was for a moment. When he turned to her mother and nodded saying quietly, "I'll do it", she wasn't sure why her heart jumped.

Her mom watched her for a moment, then announced, "Training will begin as soon as possible. How about tomorrow, my dear?" A gleam filled her eyes as she smiled.

Ari jumped. "What? Mother," she said, her voice shaking, "Cy just got here, I'm sure he needs some rest and would rather start later than tomorrow."

"That is not my concern. You are. And your skills are sorely lacking. This young man is going to help you in that area. Aren't you?" she asked turning her attention back to Cy.

Bowing his head slightly in agreement, Ari couldn't believe she was about to train with Cy Roman. From what she remembered, he had a father who turned him into a dark, sad youth. Looking at him she saw he hadn't changed much.

Her mother barked an order and the guards yanked Cy off the bed forcing him to stand. He was tall, she noticed, taller than Del. He looked strong which helped in his handsome looks.

She tried to be indifferent in her assessment. But, she couldn't help comparing him with Del. She saw easily that his looks were darker than Del's. He had dark hair with a wave to it that almost covered his eyes and those dark eyes seemed to see right through her. Cy was night where Del was day. Why she was thinking about that and not training her mind on Del was a question she'd rather not think about. It was like she needed a good reminder of the man she loved.

Right then, he frowned over her study of him, and she couldn't help but smile. In that expression, she could see the little boy she remembered. She recalled he frowned more than he smiled.

Something about Cy's expression attracted her attention but she found herself unwilling to study him anymore than she had already. She looked down at the floor but she could feel that he continued to watch her.

Her mother stayed and Ari had a feeling she was enjoying the strange tension in the air. Ari wanted to leave, but she had a feeling her mother expected her to say something, so she looked back up at her mother's new prisoner and found Cy was watching her. He was looking at her with a softness she knew didn't reach his eyes often.

"Thank you," Ari said wondering why he looked at her that way. Unsure about her new teacher, she stammered, "I appreciate your help."

In a low, sure voice, he replied, "You're welcome Ari. It's nice to see you; it's been a while."

Ari's eyes raised. Interesting conversation for a prisoner. And it had been a while, but only a couple of weeks since the party.

"Well, now that we have introductions over," her mother announced, "It's time you both discussed your training. Guards," she commanded. "Leave."

She half expected Cy to say something sarcastic, like he would of back in school days to the teacher. Bracing herself for what he might say to her mother, she cocked her head to the side and waited. But, even upon her mother's silent exit, his eyes remained on hers with his

227

lips curved in a small smile. It was unnerving, he didn't seem to mind his new job at all.

Well, she did, as she sighed to herself. It would take time to teach her the level of fighting her mother wanted, she realized with a sinking feeling. She knew next to nothing about the art of fighting. Del had always gave her excuses when she had asked him to teach her what he was learning. He had assured her he would always protect her. When she asked how he would know when she needed help, she remembered he had looked at her warmly and said he would just know. She knew now, his bond with her would have alerted him to any feelings she may have had during an attack. What he didn't expect was her leaving on her own free will.

Swallowing thickly, she looked at the last guy she would have thought would teach her the art of defense and said what was on her mind, "Well, I never would have guessed this."

"Mm, hmmm," he murmured, his head bowed and hands on his hips. It was like he was waiting to start already.

Well, she wasn't ready. Starting to ramble, but not being able to help her nervousness, she continued, "I mean as kids you were always the toughest out of all the boys, so I guess I'm in very good hands."

Blushing, she looked up embarrassed at her nervous ramblings. He stood there quietly, his eyes burning into hers before he said, "Yes, you are."

Wishing more than anything that Del were here so she could blame the butterflies in her stomach on him, she realized what had been in the back of her mind since her mother explained Cy's presence. Defense lessons would require time together and they would be very close to each other. With those thoughts in her mind, her throat seemed to close up completely. Suddenly, he looked up at her with a light in his eyes as if he knew something she didn't.

"Sorry," she found herself saying, "I'm just nervous for some reason."

Surprisingly, he cracked a small smile saying softly, "That's the most promising thing you've said today, Ari."

Breathing out the air she had been holding in, she shook her head.

Even if Cy was exceptionally beautiful, Del was even more so, and the sooner she remembered that, the better. Taking a deep breath, she repeated in her mind, 'Mind over matter, mind over matter, mind over matter.'

"Yeah well, I am sure whatever you decide to do tomorrow will be good start and," she stammered, "I will try to be a quick learner. So, on that note, I am going back to my room."

Not looking back and leaving the room as quickly as she could, Ari put distance between herself and Cymeus Roman. That was one Roman she could do without. Yanking on his cell door with more force than was necessary, she forced herself to close it quietly.

This was crazy. Her emotions were all over the place. Feelings like this could not be normal, she yelled at herself as she walked the short distance back to her room. Was it normal to be attracted to another Catcher when she was already starting a bond with Del? She needed to talk to someone about this. Her first thought was to talk to Alex, but she abandoned that idea as quickly as it came.

And then it struck her who she can ask, Gran. As uncomfortable as it was talking about love and attraction with her Grandmother, she was the perfect choice.

Gran

Her palms were sweating by the time she reached Gran's room. Wiping them off on her pants, she drew a deep breath. This conversation was going to be the life of her. In fact, Ari wasn't sure she wanted to travel down this romance-talk road, especially with her Grandmother. She wished she had known more about bonds before Gran had disappeared, but what was done was done. It was the intimate details she did not want to get into.

Gran had never had the conversation with her about the relationship between a man and woman, which Ari had been fine with. Hearing those details from a fellow classmate sitting next to her in the lunchroom had been one time too many. Blushing even now, the memory resurfaced exactly how it had happened when she was nine-years-old.

It had been lunch hour in her fourth year of school. Ari was in the back of the room eating her lunch, when she had looked up into the crowded room and noticed an buzz traveling around the long tables. She knew it had to be some secret, she remembered thinking, because the lunchroom had never been so quiet then loud as the secret was passed to the next person. It didn't take long for her neighbor to turn to her.

Still standing in front of Gran's room, she was glad Gran wouldn't be describing that process, but wished she could have been prepared with how a bond happens. At least then, maybe she would have recognized some of Del's first signs before his bond had been completed.

231

Instantly remorseful for that thought, Ari hung her head. She wanted Del's happiness to be complete, but she wasn't sure which direction her happiness would take her. Would it be with Del, who completely loved her and was everything good, true and right? Or would it be with someone like Cy?

She thought of her kisses shared with Del and the memories of their last dream embraces sent shivers through her heart. But with Del she needed to be careful, a bond was permanent and she did not want to live with the consequence of making the wrong choice.

Ready for some much-needed advice, she knocked loudly on Gran's door.

The door creaked opened to Wuz' smiling face. "Well, look who came calling Gran, your Little Red Riding Hood, who is trying to save you from the Big Bad Castle."

Tamping down her frustration, she tried forgetting Wuz and hers' recent dance in her room. She did not need another guy confusing things that were already confusing enough.

She looked into Wuz' eyes and asked the first question she has been wanting to know. "Why won't you show yourself to me, Alex? Am I really that distrustful?"

His eyes went from a twinkling brown to a deep black pinning her with his glare. "You are not ready," he finally said. "And I'm not either." Pulling the door open, he brushed past her and strode down the hall at a pace she dared not follow.

"Well," a beloved voice crooned from the doorway as Ari watched Wuz disappear around a corner, "what's happening here, my little Ari?"

"Nothing, really, nothing at all," Ari said, believing every word.

Gently taking hold of Ari's arm, Gran pulled her into her room. She seemed to choose her words carefully and said slowly, "You know, Wuz reminds me of your father so much." She looked over Ari's shoulder as if she could see the long-ago days.

"Your father was admired by everyone, and with good reason, too." She paused collecting her thoughts, "There was nothing he couldn't do and wouldn't try, meeting with success at every venture. But, as with a lot of things in this life his successes weren't good enough. As a young man, he wanted adventure. And he found it, in the arms of my daughter, your mother."

"Gran!"

Shaking her head at Ari, Gran continued, "Not like that, my star, not at first. I tried to focus my daughter's pursuits of adventure into healthier avenues. I, unfortunately, taught her the secrets to dream weaving hardly any Catcher knows." Sighing heavily, she continued. "I thought she would see the unfortunate humans dreaming their terrible memories and she would want to help. Instead, it showed her a world she wanted to control, not make better."

Shaking her head, she continued, "Your mother had become quite a beauty at that point, and attracted the notice of Tommy, your father."

Ari's heart sunk, knowing her fate, but said, "Couldn't he see, Gran, what she had become?"

"An Outcast?" Gran said for her.

Ari nodded, a tear sliding down her face.

"Sadly, yes, he saw. But, he thought he could change her; show her the excitement of life, not try to control life, but to live it to the fullest."

"How do you know all of this, Gran? How do you know what he was thinking?"

"He came to talk to me a lot in those days," she said. Sighing heavily, she said, " He wanted to know your mother better, since she wouldn't let him in emotionally."

"Gran," Ari said tentatively, "You've explained what drew my father to my mother, but what drew her to him? A bond has to grow and seal for both of them, so how did he attract her interest?"

Smiling softly, Gran said, "I've already explained that part. Just as I saw him rise to the top in this village, so did she. She notices everything and everyone. She saw power in him and she was attracted to that, unfortunately."

Shaking her head, Ari tried to envision what was indelibly burned into Grandmother's mind. "Attracted to power more than love," Ari reflected sadly. "How sad."

"But, did she ever love *him*, Gran? I have to believe that, over the alternative."

Taking Ari's hand with her softer, older one, Gran captured Ari's attention and said, "My star, you were a product of their early love. Your mother was drawn to him, much like a moth to a flame. But, once she felt the power of his love, she wanted more and more of that heady feeling. Tommy knew the obsession of power, too. He had craved that at one point, but, you, my dear was what curbed that insatiable thirst."

"Me?" Ari whispered, so engrossed in this tale, the story of her beginnings, she almost forgot she was a part of it. Running her wrinkled hand over Ari's smooth one, she looked at Ari with loving, tear-filled eyes and nodded.

"When you were born, something changed in him. Every desire, every craving for adventure had stopped as if a plug was pulled. He looked at you that first time with such a loving, tender gaze it stopped my very breath. After holding you close in the softest embrace, he turned to everyone in the room and said in a tearful promise, 'This child, my little star, will never know danger. Not for as long as I live in this world will she know fear.'

Sniffing loudly, she wiped her tears. Ari watched Gran collect herself before she continued. "Then, he turned to your mother lying in the bed and told her, 'Our lives will be different, Lucia. No more risk. Our child is a part of our new adventure. And we will keep her safe.'

Hanging her head, Gran stopped and whispered, "I'll remember that vow to my dying day, little star. To my dying day."

Squeezing her hand inside Gran's, Ari encouraged her to go on, "Gran did my mother say anything, what did she do?" Ari had to know the whole story, what happened to make them disappear from her life nearly forever.

Gran looked far away again, with a pained expression. "To my utter despair, little star, I watched her say nothing, then do nothing."

"Nothing?"

235

"Nothing," Gran repeated. "She seemed to get lost in herself. I thought it was the baby depression. Many Dream Weavers and Catchers will find themselves in weeks of blue feelings after a birth, much like humans do."

"Ari," Gran said raising her tearful eyes to hers, "I thought it was the best thing to do. It was what I needed when I had your mother. When I had the baby depression, I just needed time to get used to the idea of having a baby. My husband, your grandfather, took such good care of your mother during that time. Maybe, that's why she was closer to him than me...it's hard to say what happened," she said sighing heavily again.

"And Mother, she did the same thing you did?" Ari asked trying to make sense of this part of her story she had never heard.

"It seemed like she did," Gran answered. "She wanted time, she had said, time to herself. So, I advised Tommy to give her what she wanted, that she would come around. But, we found out later, she wasn't resting. She was planning."

"Planning what?" Ari asked as her heart broke.

"Planning an upstage of the current Outcast leader. And her plans for how she would run things."

"But," Ari questioned, "I thought she left when I was two. You make it sound like she left a lot earlier."

"Her body was with you and your father, but her mind and dreams were, literally, out of this world. She learned how to conceal her true feelings from Tommy, so when it came time for her make her move against the Outcast leader, she took it. Tommy didn't know what hit him when she left. He left you in my care and followed her, finding her easily."

Shaking her head, Gran continued, "She silenced her end of their bond thinking he would never find her, but she didn't know Tommy as well as she thought. Tommy can find anyone and anything he has a mind to. He is one of the best trackers I have ever known."

"What happened after that, Gran?" Ari croaked, closing her eyes and throat to prevent the tears from falling just yet.

"Ari," Gran said cupping her face tenderly, "I don't know what was said, thank the Maker because truthfully I don't want to know. But, your father came home alone that night. He went straight to your bed and sat for hours looking at you."

"Why?" Ari asked knowing the answer in her heart. She could almost feel his sad eyes on her as he said his goodbye.

When Gran didn't answer, Ari answered her own question. It looked like it was too difficult of a question for Gran to answer anyway. "He has been looking for her ever since, hasn't he?"

"And looking after you," Gran whispered.

"What? How has he...wait, has he been the one to bring us game and food when we were near starving? When all this time, I thought it was friends helping us, it was my father?"

At Gran's curt nod, Ari asked again. "Why?" This time her tears broke free and she cried, "Why did he never show himself to me? All this time, he's been in my life and I didn't even know..." Her sentence went unfinished as she buried her face in her hands and cried.

"Ari, my love, he had every intention of coming back into your life, but then your mother got her darkest wish and became leader of this place. He made it his mission to hunt her kind down and destroy this castle from the inside out. If she had no one to lead, he thought, then maybe he could save her...and you."

Picking her head up, Ari said, her voice quivering, "I see how it would save her, but how does it save me?"

"My darling, you are the next piece of her puzzle. If she can have you join her, with both of your powers combined, there would be no stopping her plans. Your father is protecting you by attacking her men and keeping her distracted from you."

"But, I'm here. How did he protect me from a kidnapping, how is he protecting me now?"

"You may be here, darling, but Wuz protected you from terrible danger when he came with you. Your father knows Wuz, he is the one who found Wuz as a wild Outcast, showed him the Maker's kindness, which tamed his dangerous ways and sent him to me. But, not after extensively training him in the ways of battle."

"To protect you?"

Smiling, Gran said, lovingly putting a stray piece of hair behind Ari's ear, "No, my little star, to protect you."

Her heart crashing, Ari's heart stopped. Forgetting to breathe, she suddenly recalled Alex's words, 'I'm in the business of saving people. Even those who need saving from themselves.'

"Gran," she squeaked, "He hasn't bonded with..."

"You?" Gran answered chuckling. "He isn't that easy to catch, dear. But, should you like to go down that route, good luck!"

Ari watched as Gran's chuckling turned into laughing and Ari couldn't help but giggle as Gran's laughing brought tears down her cheeks. It only took a moment before Ari was as worse off as Gran and they were both holding their stomachs from laughing so hard.

As Ari lay on Gran's bed, giggling with her Grandmother, she realized hard circumstances can bring a person to their knees, but a laugh like Gran's can bring you to the floor too, but happily.

She was so glad she had Gran to share times like these even if the times were confusing.

Quieting down, Gran spoke to Ari's heart as she said, "That boy, Alex, reminds me of your father, but in a way, so does that friend of yours, Delius."

"Del has bonded with me, Gran. I have started returning it, but suddenly with Cy here, it's been kind of confusing."

Hooting with laughter, Gran managed to say, "And, Wuz has caught your eye too? Girl, how do you keep them straight?"

"I never said I liked Wuz," Ari grumbled, "I am just curious as to what he looks like, Gran."

"Hasn't anyone ever told you curiosity killed the cat, dear?"

Ari smiled and said sweetly, "Yes, but with nine lives, I'll live this time."

"You are one sassy girl! Who ever said you were sweet," Gran grumbled good-naturedly.

"Problem is, I care too much what they think."

Switching to a serious tone, Gran advised, "All that matters is the one you love, sweetie. Don't try to catch too many bees with all that honey. You'll just get stung for the effort."

Ari smiled and couldn't agree more. "Yes, Gran. I won't. I'm not looking to get hurt, just to fall in love...with the right guy."

"It'll happen, dear. All in good time, the right boy will reveal his true intentions and it will happen. It's like the Maker says, 'Don't rush love, wait for the right time and it will be the perfect time.'

Surrendering her strong will and desire for selfish answers, Ari silently agreed to take Gran's and the Maker's advice. She didn't want to live with the consequences of a rushed decision for her or her bondmate. Ari wanted happiness. And for that she knew she would need the Maker's help.

Walking over to Gran's door, Ari turned around and blowing Gran a kiss, said, "Gran, I love you and thank you for always steering me in the right direction."

Gran nodded and Ari left with a heart much lighter than when she walked in Gran's room.

Stepping into the hallway, she walked the short distance to her room and decided to have a heartfelt prayer to the Maker for her life and Gran's, her mother's life and now her father's, who she very much wanted to meet but would pray for his much-needed protection.

Honesty

Cy began her lessons the next morning by testing her skills and range of motion. Thankfully, he did not ask her to engage in hand-to-hand combat. She was too rattled to even try.

Cy either seemed to sense her jitters or decided to go easy on her, as all he did was test her flexibility and asked her to perform some basic defense moves against the air. Thankfully, she didn't need to get close to him.

All in all, she did fair, she thought as she walked back to her room.

Now, she lay in her bed willing herself to sleep and not think about the guy next door. Flustered, she sighed and rolled over to a more comfortable position. What is it with her and the whole guy-next-door-thing? She needed to get a grip, she admonished herself.

She felt right in loving Del. Not that she loved Cy or even Alex, but they both had gotten under her skin and she didn't like that.

She wasn't the type to string along guys' emotions. And if she was going to complete her bond with Del, she needed to be one hundred percent committed to him only. Del deserved nothing less. She loved him too much to see him hurt, especially by her.

Relaxing as she thought of being in Del's arms, she really wanted to see him. Sitting up quickly, she had an idea. One she could not believe she hadn't thought of until now.

She was a Dream Catcher, so she could catch his dream. Elated, she cast through her memories trying to

241

remember what she had been taught. There had been that course in Grade school introducing the subject. They taught the essentials and more advanced courses in DC school. Frowning, she realized what she knew wasn't much. Would a preliminary course be enough for her to Catch Del's dream? True, she had been tempted to look into Wuz' dream, but to become a part of it was another thing entirely. It required a different amount of concentration and skill. She had the focus, but she had never actually walked into another Catcher's dreams.

Was Del even asleep, she questioned? Resolving herself, she had to at least try. She was excited at the thought of seeing Del within moments. Instead of the anxious and tense feelings she felt all day with Cy and before that with Wuz, she relaxed in this new warmth. She hoped Del could sense her feelings blossoming through her right now. She wanted it to give him assurance that she still loved him.

Her decision was made, she was going to find Del. No more waiting for him to find her. Guessing she could Catch a dream standing up or lying down, Ari decided on the latter. Lying flat on her bunk, she breathed in through her nose and out her mouth allowing a peaceful warmth to slowly saturate her mind and body.

Closing her eyes, she calmed her growing excitement about seeing Del soon and concentrated on this challenge. She needed to find his brilliant light amongst thousands.

Her breathing slowly steadied. She trained her mind on finding Del until she saw dark purple streaking through her vision in dazzling rays of beauty. As she swirled in a vortex of stunning magenta colors, she recalled from her training that she needed to ignore that initial sensation and move through it quickly. Closing her mind to its dizzying effects, she passed through it finding it relatively harmless.

Looking around, she took in a breathtaking scene. Lights surrounded her, as though she were floating in another universe. Which, she supposed she was, but the sheer enormity of it awed and cowed her. How was she supposed to find her Del in a cosmos of this size? Desperately, she searched through the different sparks that twinkled around her simultaneously.

She remembered their bond and wondered if it could help her find him. Ari allowed herself to feel what Del might be experiencing. Feeling drawn toward one direction, she turned around. A light drew her heart like none of the others did. Holding herself still, she wouldn't take her eyes from the one light that called to her from thousands. She slowly approached it and soaked in its heat, familiarizing herself with the beauty of its aura. It seemed to be reaching out pulling her in. It must be Del, she thought, her heart singing with joy. Giving in to its call, she sped towards it, throwing herself into its cosmic arms.

A blinding white light blinded her for a moment, but then a room spun around her causing her to swoon. Squeezing her eyes shut, she waited for the dizziness to pass, wondering how Del could jump in and out of dreams so easily. Thinking of Del, her heart jumped and she opened her eyes hoping to see him. As her sight began to clear, she took in a vague outline of a man standing over her. Her heart soaring, she whispered, "Del!"

Except the voice that spoke was not Del's.

The Wrong Catch

"Not exactly," the man answered grimly.

"What is going on?" she asked hoarsely wondering what happened to Del's voice because this man had to be Del. Hadn't she just found her bondmate, she questioned herself, and feeling confused asked the only question she could, 'Why aren't you Del?'

This man's light had spoken to her, had reached her in such a way that she couldn't deny she had been undeniably drawn to him.

She must have been lying down because the figure kneeled next to her.

"Don't worry, your vision will come back," he reassured her in a soothing voice, "Give it a second."

Panic began creeping in as she tried to place the baritone voice. Squinting her eyes, she willed them to focus.

"This must be your first Catch," he said. And just then, she could clearly see the face that went with the voice.

Her heart stopped. Dark eyes, the color of night, were watching her with a guarded expression. Leaning over her, dark hair that usually fell over those arresting eyes was hanging close to her face. "Cy," she barely whispered. She was horrified. She didn't know how to react. Panicking, she scrambled up, ignoring the sick feeling in her stomach and bolted away from this nightmare, because that was all it could be. She was looking for Del, she screamed in her mind as she ran toward a door.

Hearing footsteps too late, she screamed as a hand clamped over her mouth and another hand spun her around tucking her into a broad chest.

Trembling, she began to cry. Having nowhere to go, she could only lean herself into the one holding her captive and pretend to relax. Breathing in and out as tears fell uselessly, Cy's arms continued to squeeze her, never giving her a chance to break his hold.

Giving up, despair took over and she went limp in his arms. Turning her head resting her cheek on Cy's chest, she tried to ignore his rapidly beating heartbeat. Turning her head so she couldn't listen to his distracting heart and wonder what it meant, she said a little breathlessly, "Can you let me go now?"

His arm gentling but not moving, he said casually and a little carefully, "I'd rather not. But, as long as you stay I will. None of those moves I showed you earlier, either. Besides," he added with a smile in his voice. "You might hurt yourself."

Blood boiled inside her head, but she tried to calm herself down.

"Fine," she finally said, just wanting to leave his warm embrace. These were *not* the arms she imagined herself in tonight.

Slowly releasing her, he stepped back, watching her carefully.

"Can you please explain how I ended up here?" she asked, seething.

His eyebrows raised and he casually crossed his arms as if her whole world hadn't just crashed down on her.

"You are stepping into my dream, Sugar, so maybe you can explain it to me. I am very interested in knowing myself."

Refusing to allow him any satisfaction in knowing the answer, and desperate to hide the truth, she closed her mouth and stood stubbornly silent.

Stepping closer, he asked, "I wonder, if maybe you went looking for someone else and found me?" Pausing for a moment, he then asked in a tight voice, "Didn't they train you to study a Weaver's or Catcher's light pattern before you went looking for a particular one?"

Advancing again, he was as close to her as when he had held her moments before. Not knowing why, she held very still.

In a hushed voice, he asked, "Do you know how beautiful your eyes are? Even now, they captivate me, I can't seem to look away. Their blue is so deep I could drown myself in them." Softly he ran the back of his hand down her cheek.

She didn't know what to do, but collecting her good sense she did step back. Needing to know the real reason he was in the castle, she realized she had been wanting to know that since he first appeared there.

"What are you doing here at the castle, Cy?" she asked, her voice shaking.

Dropping his hand, he turned on his heel, walking toward a window in his cell.

She finally recognized where she was and wondered if she could walk back into her cell and find herself sleeping. She turned her attention to Cy when he answered her.

"I have no idea why I was brought here," he answered in a tight voice. Turning around, he explained almost as if he was telling her his secret, "You know, I have been searching for you for quite some time."

Alarm coursed through her when she remembered the last time she saw him.

"My party?" she asked her voice cracking.

Smiling sadly, he said, "Yes, I went looking for you."

"And you found me with Del."

Nodding, he turned again looking out the window.

Not knowing what to say, she stood silently.

"You were a vision that night," he said softly still not looking at her. "Then you disappeared and even lover boy's bond couldn't trace you, so I decided to help find you."

"You left Maone to try and find me?" she asked in a small voice.

Turning around, a hard look came in his eyes as he studied her, then it left just as quickly. "You can say that," he said. "I kept to myself and then those crazy birds found me and now here I am."

Knowing there was much more to his story than he was saying, Ari shook her head trying to make sense of everything. She could not come up with an explanation that made any sense. There was so much he was hiding, she could feel it.

Deciding to get right to the point, she asked the one question she needed answered, "Cy, why am I in your dream? Why with you?"

With a small smile, he answered cryptically, "Could it be fate?"

"No, my dears," a voice interjected behind her, a voice that froze Ari's muscles. "Fate is not as brilliant as I am."

Finally able to move, Ari spun around and glared at her mother she was having a hard time loving.

"Ari, dear, meet your future husband, Cymeus. I have decided he is perfect for you."

All of her breath left her as she turned to face Cy.

He looked as surprised as she did. "Husband?" he asked in low voice.

"Oh, yes. It has all been arranged. I've just decided that you two will be married in two days time," the Queen said, her icy stare daring either one to argue.

"And if I say, 'No?'" Cy asked, his voice barely controlled.

"Then you will die," she answered without any hesitation.

Ari's body had been numb from shock, but now heat fueled her limbs and she straightened asking in a hard voice, "Mother, have you gone crazy? I will not agree to a wedding! And since when do you choose my bondmate? Even you can't do that! The Maker is the only One capable of sealing our bonds."

Laughing quietly, the Queen looked at Ari affectionately. "You'll spend enough time together, darling, and it will happen. You've already started it. Just look where you ended up when you went searching for your Catcher," she said with contempt. "In Cy's arms, not your precious Del's, and that, " she promised, "will leave an impression."

Burying her face in her hands, Ari wondered if this was some kind of horrible dream. Then raising her head,

Ari laughed softly. It was a dream, which she could leave anytime she wanted. She was so out of this nightmare.

Glaring first at Cy then at her mother, she said icily, "I have a choice about my future. It's mine to make, not either one of yours."

Disagreeing, her mother said in a threatening voice, "The only choice you have, Arella, is whether this man lives or dies. You will marry him, or he will have an untimely death."

Horror choked Ari until she could hardly breathe. Horrified that her mother needed to exert so much control over her life that she would arrange her marriage. Ari stood silently shaking with barely suppressed fury. This unbelievable situation was testing her sanity.

Interjecting for her, Cy asked, "Why me? Why am I the lucky winner of your daughter's hand?"

Smiling maliciously, Ari's mother answered, "Because you are the perfect one to rule by Ari's side in this kingdom I have created. You will be her King."

At that Ari finally lost the fragile control she had on reality and welcomed the pressure that had been slowly building in her head. Giving in to the darkness that had been hovering on the edges of her vision, she sank into an oblivion where she could escape and forget.

Laughter is the Best Medicine

Waking up in Cy's room was not what she expected to find when she came out of her first Catch. It was actually the very last place she wanted to find herself. And she especially did not want to be in his bed. But, coming out of such a disastrous dream sequence had her feeling disorientated and she didn't trust her body if she moved just yet.

Groaning, she turned her head and caught sight of a brooding face watching her with an almost careful expression.

'Why would he need to be cautious,' she asked herself, 'what was he afraid of? Was he afraid she would jump up and bite him?'

Her tired mind couldn't handle that image and she suddenly found the idea funny. Her queasy stomach forgotten, she welcomed the giggles that erupted.

A bemused but somewhat irritated expression crossed Cy's face when he asked, "Why are you laughing? What about any of this is funny?"

His aggravation made this, their arranged marriage, even funnier. Giggling harder, Ari tried to take a breath as she laughed at her precarious situation. She held her aching middle as tears filled her eyes. Trying to see the person tangled up in this mess with her was difficult. Her tears prevented her vision to clear. Giving into the madness of her mother's plan was out of the question, but she could laugh at it. And it felt good, really good to reject it. And that was what she was going to do.

Rejection was the only option for her and this stranger sitting next to her.

Her eyes were closed when she started to sober and stop laughing.

Speaking her heart, hoping he took her seriously after her laughing fit, she spoke earnestly, "You realize we have to leave, escape from this place." As tears clogged her throat she whispered, "My mother is crazy."

"Is this something you are just now noticing?" he asked his voice rising with his temper.

Frowning sadly, she sat up slowly. Not sure why she bared her feelings, she spoke quietly, "My whole life, I wondered about my parents. Why they disappeared. What happened to them."

Different tears filled her eyes now, tears of grief. Drawing her knees to her chest, she tried to cover her breaking heart. She hadn't wanted to admit this to herself, but she couldn't help it. She only wanted a family to love her, a mother who would love her for herself, not for her strengths and potential powers.

Hiding her face, she cried quietly, lost in her grief.

Arms came around her picking her up without any effort. She stiffened and tried to move out of an embrace she shouldn't want and couldn't.

"Shhhh, I am here. Let me hold the reason for my possible death." Cy chuckled and his arms tightened around her. Ari couldn't think past her anger. She could only feel the pain in her heart that pumped its course through her numb body.

In her mind, she screamed about the injustice of it all. Outwardly she stayed still. She felt she owed it to this man who has been sucked into her mother's schemes that much. Tears slipping down her cheeks, she knew she needed to begin planning. Planning their escape since she couldn't allow this insane marriage to take place. She desperately tried to think of a way she could ferret Cy out of the castle.

Beginning to panic, her heart was pumping a frantic rhythm she needed help calming down. She needed the Maker and his ever present reminder that he was with her, in every moment, even now.

Desperately trying to slow down her thoughts, she breathed deeply then said in her mind, *'Maker, help me, help us. Show us the way,'* she begged, *'Help me and Cy learn Your plan, Your way. May it be Father as You will.'*

At her words, peace enveloped her, cocooning her in its warmth. A clarity she knew could only from the Maker filled her mind and her heart. Relishing its serenity, she breathed deeply, thanking the Maker for His constant Presence. She knew whatever happened, He would lead her to the right path, guiding her to make the right choices. Thankful beyond words, she lifted her face.

She stopped when she slammed into Cy's deep stare. He must have been waiting for her to talk to him, she reasoned, her senses confused at their closeness. Wanting to share her calming peace, she leaned back as far as she could in Cy's arms. Even then, their noses were nearly touching and she could almost feel his shallow breaths on her skin.

"Cy," she said, her voice squeaking. A nervousness filled her, she tried to banish it and reclaim the peace she just had, but Cy was too close to comfort. How had she allowed this closeness to even happen, she wondered.

His stare was burning holes into her and she attempted once more to convey the Maker's blessing of peace, "The Maker will help us, He will show us how to figure this out."

Not able to bear his scrutiny, she shut her eyes and had almost turned her head when she felt soft, warm lips on hers. Stiffening, she tried to lean back, but he wouldn't permit her escape. He kissed her a moment more then slightly loosened his arms.

Questioning him with her eyes, she hoped she was communicating her shock with her glare. Cy was a stranger to her. She had been drawn to him, that was true, but she didn't think she had done anything to ask for a kiss. Trapped in his embrace, however, she had nowhere to go. Feeling uncomfortably hot, Ari tried to wiggle out of Cy's arms.

"Am I so revolting that you have to be free of me?" Cy asked not loosening his grip anymore than he had already. His voice carried a desperation she didn't understand. It was almost as if he expected her to acknowledge a connection between them she didn't know existed. But, her mother claimed something would develop in time. Ari didn't want to believe that.

She just realized, he might agree to her mothers ideas. The thought frightened her. It meant she had no say in this and staying on this route meant she would become Cy's wife in two days.

"But, I don't know you," she whispered desperately searching his eyes for some kind of agreement. "We can't get married when we don't even know each other."

"We can change that," he said, his eyes suddenly reflecting a fierce determination.

Her eyes widened and she covered her mouth. Anger viciously coursed through her, leaving her reeling.

His face suddenly revealed his vulnerability as he asked, "Why am I not an option, Ari? Let's see where this goes. Maybe we are meant to be together." Grabbing her hands, he reminded her, "You Caught my dream, remember? I had been trying to stay away from yours for months, and you," he emphasized, "came to mine."

She searched for something to say, but found nothing. He was right, she realized with a sinking heart. Could it be possible they were meant to be together?

"Will you please let me go?" she asked quietly her heart hammering in her chest.

His arms finally did and she scrambled out of his arms as quickly as she could.

"It's not you, Cy," she said, willing him to believe her, "It's me. I need time." She cringed when she realized that was what she told Del when he revealed his bond with her. Her voice shaking, she continued, "Time is our only option." A plan formed in her mind and she grew more hopeful as she spoke.

"We can leave the castle and not be forced to marry." At his expression she added quickly, "right now, but maybe, after getting to know each other, in time we will."

She forced herself to half believe it herself because he was never going to go along with her plan if she didn't believe in it first. Facing him, she pleaded, "Why rush this? This is a commitment we need to be sure of before jumping into."

Her eyes begging him to believe her impassioned speech, she waited for his response.

"What do I need to do for you to trust me, Arella?"

Taken aback, she paused before she said firmly, "Escape with me. Let's leave from here and change the course my mother has set before us. I don't want to lead the Outcasts, do you?" At his doubtful expression, she grew braver, "She is arranging not only for us to marry but to lead a group of crazed nightmares, Cy! That's not in my plans and it never will be."

Looking up at her, he asked, "You promise to allow me to protect you, to keep you safe?No one else?"

At his question, she looked up. "You're talking about Del aren't you? You don't want me to see him?"

Giving her a curt nod he said, "Not now, not yet."

"And you will agree to leave?" she asked skeptically. "You will leave the castle and escape if I agree to that?"

"Yes."

Recklessly, she nodded her head and agreed. Wondering how on Earth and Oneiro she was going to explain this to Del, she said instead, "Let's make our plans."

"Fine," he said reluctantly. "How do you propose we get out of here?"

Making a Break

The outside air chilled Ari inside and out. It wasn't really cold, but the enormity of what she was doing was making her whole body tremble. She was starting to rethink her decision.

She and Cy were crouched down behind a turret that jutted out of the east side of the castle. Cy had just told her they weren't too far from the ground. She could think of several choice words to say to him about that. He was out of his mind to expect her to jump down from this height. She could just imagine a broken leg if she attempted this mad leap from the second story.

As Cy watched the company of soldiers patrolling this side of the castle, she looked longingly at the forest beyond the walls. Its safety seemed so far away. It was just before dawn and she could barely see the trees. They were like arms waiting to take her into their safety and lead her home.

They had finished orchestrating their escape in the long hours of the night. She had been shocked at how well Cy knew the castle. He had said flying over the castle on display had had its advantages. She had been impressed he had used that embarrassment for their benefit. He then said he had been trained well on how to do that. He wouldn't elaborate more, but she hoped to ask him later what he meant.

Dismissing that train of thought, she concentrated on Cy's plan of escape. First they informed Gran of her mother's scheme to see them married and leading the Outcasts. Gran watched Cy closely as Ari explained everything to her.

Gran had finally agreed to divert Mother's attention as they made their escape. Ari was disappointed at Gran's lack of comment. She always had an opinion, Ari had complained. Gran had just shook her head and walked away, but not before she turned and reminded Ari she couldn't make Ari's decisions for her. It was the hardest part of being a parent, she had said sadly.

Anything was better than marriage to someone she barely knew Ari had thought then and even now. She still couldn't believe she had convinced Cy to leave. There was a recklessness to him she wasn't sure she trusted. But taking a quiet breath, she realized she had no choice now.

Cy had Caught Gran's dream and asked for her to meet them in his room and to bring rope. After Gran agreed to help in their escape, she said she was where the Maker wanted her. She could not go where Ari was going. Gran really had been instrumental in this breakout she thought, trying not to cry at leaving Gran behind.

Once Gran led the guards on a fool's errand, they had crawled out the window Ari thought was impenetrable. When she had told Cy that, he had just given her a small smile and made quick work of dismantling it. Starting with one loose brick, he then made a hole in the brick wall next to the barred window. He tied the rope tightly to her waist and connected the other end to himself.

Like a crazy person, she had followed him out the window and talked to the Maker like never before. Cy had led her up and down walls she thought would be her death and a couple of times, nearly were. Yet here they were. He had proven he could do his part, she thought, but she had proven she could follow, like she had promised him after their disastrous Catch. That Catch

257

seemed to be one of her biggest mistakes, she thought grimly. She resolved not think about that now, she had an impossible jump to make.

Cy took her hand without taking his eyes off the soldiers.   Squeezing it gently, he stood and turned, gesturing for Ari to jump. She tried remembering what he had told her to do.

"Go with the fall, if your body wants to roll forward, allow it. Tuck and roll into somersaults, several if needed, until you stop."

Before she could remember more, Cy jumped, pulling her with him. She hit the ground and rolled just like Cy had said. After somersaulting several times, she finally came to a stop. Before she could rest, Cy grabbed her and pulled her up, pushing her to run.

'He's trying to kill me', she thought as she ran. Not believing her body capable of bearing such brutality, she ran as fast as she could.

She turned just as she saw Wuz yelling at the guards that were patrolling the area they were escaping. 'He's distracting them!' she thought with triumph.

Still holding her hand Cy pulled her into the woods just as she heard a shout coming from the top of the East tower.

"Keep running, Ari!!" Cy shouted and together they pushed through foliage jumping over roots and fallen branches.

Ari ran until she couldn't run anymore. Time inched by. She concentrated on moving her legs that burned like twin fires as she fantasized about resting. the could imagine jumping ina cool, clear lake where she could quench her thirst and rest her aching body.

Instead she kept running. Dodging tree limbs and hanging vines she kept her focus on Cy's back until her vision blurred. Not able to breathe, she finally had to stop. Holding onto a tree trunk, she grabbed her side and heaved in lungfuls of air.

Sweat pouring off his brow, she saw Cy stop and come back to where she stood. "Ari," he said with concern in his voice, "if we stop, we need to hide. I see a patch of bushes just ahead. Can you make it? We can hide in there," he said in a hushed voice.

Nodding her head she followed. Her one coherent thought was she needed to rest. Finally making it to their leafy sanctuary, Ari crouched through the opening Cy made for her and collapsed on the pine needles that covered the ground.

Making room for Cy as he crawled next to her, she concentrated on finding her breath again.

"Now we wait," he whispered. "Calm your breathing. We have to be very, very quiet."

'That,' she thought tiredly, 'won't be a problem.' And she lay her head on her arm and closed her eyes.

Forest Hideaway

They had been in the forest hiding in the thick patch of bushes without hearing any more Outcasts searching for about a half an hour. Ari wasn't sure where they went, but a group of Outcasts had passed by, but thankfully had not found their safe haven.

Leaning her back against a tree, she was about to doze off when after a few minutes of silence, Cy whispered, "Haven't you ever felt safe, you know, like when you were a kid?" And he turned his dark eyes to hers.

A look came over him, of a pain she could only guess about. "Safe?" she repeated quietly.

He turned and her heart clinched when she saw his expression. He looked haunted.

"I don't know why, but every time I see you, it feels right, like you are a refuge from my thoughts."

Not having anything to say in response, Ari looked away. After a pregnant pause, she finally said quietly, "Yes, I do actually."

With a question in his eyes, he nodded, which urged her to continue.

"Every time I am scared," she explained,"The Maker gives me a peace and strength I couldn't possibly have without Him."

"But, just look at your situation," he argued gesturing around them. "How can you feel safe right now?" Looking at her incredulously, he continued, "Your mother is the queen of the Outcasts, who are responsible for doing acts that are disgusting, barbaric even. And, I'm not talking about in her castle even. There are things going on out in Oneiro that are awful, terrible," he said angrily, his head hung low. " All disguised in the name of good," he added quietly.

His shoulders slumped making him look like he was drained. She knew he'd probably never shown this raw side of his feelings to anyone else before. Ari also felt this was a time when she could share how the Maker could heal him of whatever pain had been haunting him. She knew that pain, too, for she remembered carrying it for a year. Quickly, she breathed a prayer to the Maker and started speaking.

"Cy," she said quietly, "The Maker is the reason I feel safe."

"The Maker?" he spat out. "Who is this Maker anyway and where was he when a little kid was beaten so severely, so many times, that he hid better than he could read and write?"

Horrified, she breathed Cy's name, all her breath nearly gone. Tears began leaking through her closed eyes as she remembered the few times Cy had been in school and even then, with faint bruises. She realized he was too busy hiding or recovering from beatings to go to class. Her heart bled for a boy who never had a chance to trust.

He continued talking in a detached voice, "I can't believe in something or Someone who would allow that kind of life for a kid. The whole time, my dad quoted things this Maker said to justify the beatings he gave me. I learned to hide from his rages and then track him so I could see if he was safe to be around. I didn't know what safe was. I was just a kid," he said his voice cracking. "Safe was just another word to me."

Through her continued tears, she looked over at him and saw he had his back to her. His shoulders shook slightly. Shaking her head, she couldn't hold hold herself away.

She reached over and touched his shoulder lightly. She didn't expect him to turn and pull her to him in a quick, tight embrace.

Burying his tears into her neck, he began talking in a low and furious tone, "I don't want to talk to you like this, I don't ever want to talk about that misery of a life I had." Leaning back, his teary eyes burned into hers touching her deeply.

Just as quickly her heart dropped when he said meaningfully, "I just want a normal life,

with a normal girl and I'd like that wish to happen."

Not sure why it hurt her to hear that, she wondered what made him say such a thing. By then when she looked up to study his face, he had gotten control of his emotions concealing them once again. She would rather see one trace of emotion than none at all.

As she stood there, her eyes searching his, she considered his wish for a normal girl and realized she would never be an option. Despite trying not to, she looked down to hide a tear that leaked down her face.

She didn't like to be the girl who had enough baggage to fill a house. She wanted to be the girl who cared for her partner and led a life that involved tending a house with a family in it. But, that was a life she had never known, only would watch from a distance, she realized.

Knowing that, she knew she had nothing to lose when she voiced her thoughts, "You mean, you want someone the opposite of me."

Turning away, he said heatedly, "You heard me wrong, I will never quit wanting. Wanting..."

"Wanting what?" she whispered hoarsely, her mind spinning.

With a groan, he turned quickly and his hands slid around her neck into her hair as he took hold of her face. As he looked deeply in her eyes, she had her answer. He softened his grip and began kissing her softly in a way that was surprisingly sweet.

'He cares for me,' she realized. The shock of that tore her lips apart from his, but she was even more shocked when she could suddenly feel his despair of her pulling away, but that couldn't be possible unless he was starting to form a bond with her.

Overwhelmed, she looked up into his eyes and asked the only question she could think of, "Why?"

A small smile turned up his mouth into a crooked grin, saying simply, "I dreamed a dream. And you were in it."

"But, you never knew me," she whispered furiously, "How did you dream about

someone you never knew?"

Tracing her cheek with his thumbs, he said, measuring his words carefully, "I may not have known you well, but I am not blind, I can see, even from a distance. And then the dreams came and I had to know you, more about you. And then I ended up at the castle."

His expression said there was more to this story. But, what frightened her was the fact that a Weaver couldn't love two people at the same time. There was only one chance to bond.

But, she hadn't completed her bond with Del. And at that thought she froze.

Del has completed his bond with her. She couldn't encourage Cy's bond, knowing she may not ever return his love. She was attracted, that much was sure, but in all good conscious she couldn't let herself go too far. A kiss was a kiss, but this was more. She was unsure and for that reason, she had to get away from him and decide who she was meant to bond with.

Once she leaned back, however, he grabbed her arms and reached in for one more kiss. Softly, warmly, he kissed her, and just when she wanted to reach out and push him back, he released her.

"You have a choice Ari," he said quietly, "one that you don't want to regret. Just do me this one favor," he pleaded taking her hand in his, "keep me in mind, especially as you sleep, ok?"

With that question, Ari's life just got a lot more complicated, because she was considering it. Considering loving someone other than Del.

Insomnia

Cy's last words made Ari want to melt and scream at the same time. She was never going to sleep now. And this had just put her in a terrible position.

She was still in their hideaway, but Cy had left saying he was going to hunt for some food. He had been gone for a while.

She refused to sleep. She could imagine Del's hurt expression when she explained her predicament and feelings lately. But, what did Cy mean when he said to think of him? Did that mean, in her dreams also?

Was he going to Catch her dreams, too?

If Del Caught her dream and Cy was in it, there was going to be trouble. Just the

thought broke her heart. What was she doing with Cy? And why had she Caught Cy's dream and not Del's? She wasn't even sure two Catchers can find and be in the same dream. Cy was another Dream Catcher, so it was possible he would catch her dream too, she guessed.

Her head was spinning with all of these questions. But, she couldn't help them and she had more. She didn't know whether Cy would know if Del was in her dream, and would he wait or barge in not caring if he ruined her life? She couldn't predict what Cy would do and for some reason she found that interesting. But, should she?

Because of recent talks with the Maker, she questioned how she felt about Cy. He seemed to love her and wanted to be with her as much as Del, but with Cy, she felt torn and conflicted. There were feelings of excitement too, but if she really looked at this situation it was interesting to her because it was new and different.

The question she should be asking herself was where did Cy stand with the Maker? For Cy to ever be a candidate for her life and future, she had to know. Did he walk alongside Him as he lived his life out? When he Dream Weaved and had a difficult time purging a nightmare, was Cy going to the Maker for help and advice? It was impossible to Dream Weave on your own.

She remembered Alicia, the little girl she had helped, knowing it would have been impossible to help her if hadn't been for the Maker. And He was always available. Time spent with Him was necessary to being a Weaver or a Catcher. She left many matters in His capable and loving hands.

Reflecting, she realized these were questions that needed to be answered before she had any more thoughts about Cy.

Cy was different from Del, for sure, but should that make him a candidate for her heart?

Thinking about Del, she still warmed to the thought of loving Del forever. He knew her better than she knew herself, and she knew he would make her happy, he always had.

But, with Cy, he had a future she couldn't see. He said he wanted a family and a life of his own, but there was a barrage of painful memories she knew he needed to unleash before he started a new life. He was different from anyone she had ever known, and all she'd ever known was Del.

There couldn't be more of a difference

Del

One Hour Prior

It was like lightening struck Del's gut as he was helping to pack up the General's camp. Doubling over, he could only hold his head as every feeling of Ari's, her fear, exhaustion, and need overwhelmed his senses.

Terror for Ari took over and he jumped up. He could feel her emotions, he thought wildly. She must be out of her mother's castle. She must have escaped. Form him to reach Ari's emotions it could only mean she was out of her mother's reach.

"Reckless girl," he shouted, "what is she doing?"

He ran toward the General's tent. One thought screamed through his mind, Ari was in danger.

Bursting through the tent flap, his eyes sought out General Tom. Finding him in a dark corner, he said quickly, "Ari is no longer in the Outcast castle, but I am going to need help finding her. Are you coming?" he asked in an impatient voice.

He stood halfway inside the tent even though everything in him was desperate to be gone in search of Ari.

With penetrating eyes, the General studied him, then asked in a caustic tone, "Did you get this information from a source or is the source you?"

Suspicious this man could be Ari's missing father, Del sensed his answer would not be taken lightly. He couldn't leave without this man's permission, so he had to give him the truth. Ari needed him. His bond with her was allowing her terror to course through him, making him crazy with worry.

"Look," he admitted heatedly, "I love that girl, and will until my last breath. There's no reason to keep that a secret when she is in danger." Breathing heavily, he said, "I am leaving. Now the question is, are you coming?"

The General stood up quickly. "It's obvious you have accurate information. I must get two other men. Wait here," he ordered.

Waiting impatiently for just a few minutes, Del was surprised when General Tom returned with one of his men and Jack.

"Saving the damsel in distress finally, huh?" Jack said with a grin, but with a serious look reflected in his eyes.

Nodding curtly, Del appreciated the General's inclusion of one of his own guys.

Turning abruptly, Del said to their small group, "Let's go."

Running into the forest, Del focused all of his thoughts on Ari's emotions. He knew he headed their team in the right direction the more intense the feelings became. He felt panic and he tried to see where he was going in response to her pain. What could be happening? Running as fast as he could, he tore through the woods. Ignoring the fierce lashes at his face, arms and body, his one goal was to find her. For once he didn't care the trail he was making. He just needed to find her as quickly as he could.

He ran for some time, the minutes became a blur as did the branches and roots he continued to jump over. He felt with relief when he felt her finally reach a place of safety. But he wouldn't slow down, not until he had her in his arms. She was still at a distance, so he pressed on as he heard the General, his Lieutenant, and Jack still following behind him.

Finally, he could feel Ari was close. Slowing down, he raised his hand signaling the others to do the same. She was just ahead, he thought with relief. Stopping he quietly caught his breath and focused on not making any noise. He didn't want to scare her. The men behind him crept close to him without making a sound.

The General looked over at him, questioning him with a look.

Nodding, Del ran his eyes over the forest searching for where she must be hidden. He could see a trail made obvious by broken branches and crushed leaves on the forest floor. He knew the others could see it, too.

But inside of himself, everything crashed. He could feel her fright and something else. Something he didn't want to acknowledge. Jealous anger filled him as he felt her wanting someone other than him. Turning away, he met the General's gaze.

"Now what?" asked the General, for the first time waiting for orders. With a sympathetic expression, said, "It's your call."

"We wait here," Del said, feeling like he was just flayed alive, a fate he would prefer to this, anything but her betrayal.

His heart breaking, he crouched in the bushes willing himself not to tear off the face of whomever Ari was with. Whoever Ari was kissing.

"Care to tell me what is going on?" The General asked him quietly crouching next to him.

Closing his eyes tightly, Del said firmly, "No." He shook his head trying to force out of his mind Ari's curiosity, then finally, her blessed rejection.

Releasing his breath quietly, he hung his head wondering what he was going to say to her and his blood boiled at what he was going to do to the one she was with. He wondered who it could be as he ground his teeth together. That Wuz character was who he was guessing and he pictured just what he was going to do to that bear's face.

He hardly noticed as the General dispensed orders for the other two men to comb the area for Outcasts who were most likely searching for Ari and her friend.

Waiting to calm down turned out to be great timing as the object of his fiercest hate came out of the bushes. His eyes couldn't believe it. Cy straightened himself to full height. Outrage fueled Del as he followed Cy's path into the woods. Taking his hate with him, he began to tracking his former friend who was now his worst enemy.

Amazing Grace

'I must be incredibly stupid,' Del admonished himself as he quietly stalked Cy. He fumed as he thought of all the times he trusted him giving him information about Ari he would only share with a good friend. That trust was wasted he reflected bitterly.

While he dreamed with Ari, Del thought growing more and more angry, Cy must have plotted and planned. Was it a ruse for him to be picked up by the vultures, or another of his plans he questioned now. And how easy it must have been for Ari to depend on someone he so obviously trusted. Feeling this betrayal deep within him, Del regretted ever counting Cy as a friend, when all the time Cy wanted her for himself.

Del stopped and hid behind a tree when Cy paused. Cy had his weapon out, which meant he must have spotted something to catch. Now, it was time. Time for Del to end this charade.

Slowly, he pulled his hunting knife free from its sheath. He didn't know when he had decided, but he was going to kill Cy. Red hot rage filled him. He allowed it to lift his arm that held his weapon. He was not going to allow Ari to be lied to, himself tricked, the world abused at the hands of a worthless Catcher who means nothing.

At that, Del paused. His head pounded with the urgency of this moment. But, a memory of something the Maker had once said teased his thoughts. The urge to remember interrupted the demanding need to kill, and he knew he had to wait.

Calming down, a memory spoke to him. The Maker had once said, "My *grace* is sufficient for you, for my power is made perfect in weakness." In that instant, Del couldn't hate Cy.

Who was he, he asked himself, to kill a man for purely selfish reasons? Wasn't that what grace was, undeserved forgiveness? The Maker found a man inside of himself that was pleasing to Him. The Maker can see through the darkness of a soul, who was he to prevent that time for Cy? The Maker could restore this man to right, here he was about to end his life. The Maker may have plans for Cy, yet.

Easing his arm down, he knew he couldn't hate Cy, not when he, Delius, was full of struggles himself. He wasn't perfect. And by taking the life away from this man, he was proclaiming his complete innocence, which he was in no way perfect.

Cy's actions were those of someone who acted out of weakness. Selfish living had shallow consequences that Del pitied. The Maker uses weakness for His glory, Del thought, deeply ashamed of himself. Cy may not think anyone cares for him, but the Maker loves this man, Del believed, and He could change Cy's heart and life.

Now that his anger was gone, Del's hand hit the tree, his weapon clattering to the the forest floor with a thud. In a second, Cy was in Del's face with his knife at Del's throat. Del did not resist. Cy had a crazy look in his eyes, one Del had not seen before. He knew if he moved, he would die.

"What are you doing here?" Cy spat, shaking Del with a strong grip that seemed desperate.

Looking at Cy with new eyes, Del thanked the Maker for this moment, that he hadn't killed this man who was so lost.

Shaking him again, Cy roared, "So help me, Del, I will kill you. You cannot get in the way now!" Shaking him again, Cy lowered his voice, "I am going to ask one more time. What are you doing here?"

Feeling the knife nick his throat, Del answered, "Cy, I am here to protect Ari, even from you."

Loosening his grip in surprise, Cy regained himself then cooly looked at him, saying, "How do you know she wants you still?"

Del burned with anger knowing it was Cy who was kissing Ari in the bushes. Swallowing thickly, he answered, "I don't know."

Cy's face hardened and he asked, "Does she know that you are here?"

"I'm sure she does by now," Del answered quietly. "So, if you are going to kill me, be quick about it. But, don't think for one minute she won't remember me and mourn every minute of her life."

A murderous look of rage came over Cy's face and Del knew he had to fight. He wasn't afraid, he just needed a strength only the Maker could provide. Petitioning the Maker quickly, he inhaled deeply and felt a power fill him he knew came from the Maker.

Thanking the Maker, he allowed it to fuel his upper body, he pushed as hard as he could against Cy. Feeling momentum come over him, he continued to shove Cy away in this fight for his life.

In his last push, he grunted and succeeded in getting his knee and leg in between them. Using that to his advantage, he kicked Cy hard, sending him flying.

Picking up the knife he had dropped to the ground earlier, Del asked the Maker to intervene and not only to save his life but that of Cy's, too. He had just stopped himself from killing this man, and now they circled each other in a death match.

Forcing himself to empty his thoughts he watched Cy's movements. His stance and his posture could tell him where he would attack, so Del watched and waited, keeping his knife ready.

Cy attacked first, sweeping the air in front of Del's stomach. Too close, Del thought fiercely. A gasp sounded to his left, one Cy didn't hear, but Del had. It was Ari, and Del tried to block her presence out, but everything in him wanted to shield her. He called out to her projecting his deep love making it obvious how he felt, always would.

Cy punched a lightening quick jab at his chin and in a sacrificial move, Del absorbed the hit jumping away from Ari. Dodging another swipe at his body, Del grabbed the arm as it completed its deathly arc. Spinning it around behind Cy's body, Del forced his arm up making Cy drop his knife. Del's other arm wrapped around Cy's throat and he placed his knife this time, at Cy's throat. It was a paralyzing move. If Cy tried to move, he could break his arm because of Del's grip or get his throat cut.

Del held onto him easily, and spun Cy around to where he could now see Ari's horrified expression. She was being held by the General and her mouth was completely covered by the General's hand.

At Del's nod, the General let Ari go, her eyes were streaming tears. Del's gut clenched at her pain. She was staring at Cy with new eyes. She had seen Cy's true nature, beastly and unrestrained in his attempt to kill Del. Ari gripped her middle and refused to be held up by the General's arm. Del was concerned as she looked ready to drop.

Ari took a deep breath composing herself and then slowly began approaching Cy. Del forced Cy's arm up further to discourage him from trying anything desperate.

Looking up at Cy, Ari tried to speak, but her words wouldn't come. Hanging her head, she cried softly, then looked up again.

"You were going to kill him, Cy?" she said so softly, Del could hardly hear her. "For what purpose would you do that?"

The General had followed Ari as she had come closer and said when Cy remained silent, "Arella, you don't need to question him. He is obviously not in his right mind. He won't speak the truth."

Shaking her head slightly, she never took her eyes off of Cy's and she asked him again in a tight voice, "For what purpose, Cy would you kill someone I love?"

Del admired her strength, but did not want her to experience any more pain. "Ari," he said gently. "Let it go."

Her eyes blazed and she turned to Del and said, "I deserve an explanation of why he would kill you. He had his chance to win me. It's over now."

In a voice tight with emotion, Cy finally answered, "I only wanted..."

275

"Wanted what," she said hoarsely, looking tortured.

"To find love," he finished simply as he sagged in Del's arms. Del looked over at the General and flicked his head meaning for him to come and help hold Cy's heavey weight. Before the General could come to help, however, Cy delivered a well placed stomp to Del's instep. It loosened his grip on Cy's arm and Cy spun around with his free arm hitting Del powerfully sending Del to the ground. The punch had turned his vision black, but his rage came back in full force.

Trying to get up, he heard shouts and a scuffle, and when his blurry vision cleared, he saw the General down on the ground, with Ari tending to him. Cy was gone. The other two men must have gone after him, because he could hear a chase giving way in the forest ahead.

Warring with whether or not to stay with Ari or chase Cy down himself, Ari's soft crying answered his indecision.

Kneeling down next to the General by Ari's side, he checked the General's pulse. Relieved to find a normal heartbeat, he turned when Ari said softly, "Cy knocked him out. I think he is ok."

Grinning, he said chuckling, "I think it's good for him to be knocked on his butt. Maybe getting off his high horse for a while will be good for him."

Looking quizzically at him, she then studied the General and said, "He seemed nice."

Not wanting to reveal his suspicions with the General asleep, who couldn't speak for himself, he averted the conversation.

Turning himself to fully face her, he cupped her face in his hands. Grief was slowly filling her as her eyes took on a faraway look. Her feelings were something he was very familiar with and he was saddened for her.

Looking into her eyes, he decided to ask the question that had been tormenting him for days, "Ari, I am going to get to the point here. I know you have been through a lot. But, I need to know where to take you, with me or somewhere else. Please try to answer, if you can." Taking a deep breath he looked into her crystalline eyes that he loved so much and took a plunge by asking, "Do you want me still? Or do you need time, time to think about all of this? I can take you home and leave for a while."

A fearful expression came over her face, and she quickly reached for him pulling him to her. She buried her face in his neck and when she spoke, she spoke to his heart, "Del, if you leave me, I swear to you I won't survive. I won't survive," she repeated softly.

Holding her tightly, Del's heart swelled, love filling him completely.

"Ok," he whispered in her hair as she softly sobbed, "It's ok, my love, I won't leave you, I won't ever leave if you want me here. I've got you."

Del knelt on the ground holding Ari, rocking her gently. Embracing her, he vowed to keep her safe, safe from the Outcasts, safe from her Mother, safe now from Cy.

This was where he was meant to be, in her arms. He was overcome with gratitude.

Talking to the Maker, he said in a heartfelt whisper, "Thank you Maker. Thank you for Your love, for Your mercy, for Your grace. Thank you for being with us," he said. "I give you my life, again and again. I give you my love, and please, continue to take care of us."

And as he knelt on the ground, he knew the Maker answered. His peace covered him and Ari's sobs quieted as they both reveled in the Maker's love and grace. Del knew in the Maker's care, they would know fear, and they would know loss, but they would also know peace, joy and love. For it was always as the Maker said, "For the greatest of these is love."

As Del held Ari, he couldn't agree more.

A Peek in Book Two of

The Dream Weaver Series,

Dream
Taker

Castle Visitor

Emotions stormed in Del's chest when he first saw Ari being led into the throne room.

His eyes burned as he watched but he couldn't help her, yet.

The only comfort he had was that he could still feel her emotions. They swirled in a fearful pattern, but there was a sense of determination and will power that made him proud.

She focused her gaze straight ahead and his heart jumped right as she passed him.

Their bond soared and he could feel her excitement climbing. With a startled look, she looked at him, curiously at first, then her eyes filled with hope. She stopped and her guards bumped into her grunting in frustration.

"Keep going, girlie," one growled, a rhinoceros creature that towered over her.

Her eyes stayed glued on Del's. Raising her hand toward him, she whispered, "Are you...?"

Del strained to keep quiet. He did not want any attention brought to himself. But, here she was directing the spotlight right to him.

Keeping his eyes straight ahead, he kept quiet. He was thankful to be given the directive to remain silent for anyone except the queen; he knew her guards would also know this command.

"He has to keep quiet, missy, or he's as good as dead," said the rhino guard. " There's no one here that needs to remember their names, anyhow. They work and fight for the queen. That's it. No talking during their post," Rhino gruffly explained. "Now, keep walking," as he pushed her forward.

Del's anger burned at their treatment of her, but he committed the two guards to memory promising himself he would take care of them later along with Cy, who was responsible for all of this.

Del watched Ari in the corner of his eye until she left his line of vision. The memory of her stumbling away as she looked back at him burned in his mind.

Deciding right then, he promised himself if he were blessed enough to have a family with Ari, he would teach their children what the Maker had taught him. He needed to trust the Maker's words and no other voice.

Acknowledgments

to the Following cheerleaders ~

Randi Purcell, for my first edit so many years ago.

Lynne Mcnutt, for my last edit, thank you for giving so freely of your time.

Linda Barlow, Captain of the cheerleading squad, this novel would never have been finished without your sweet and unending encouragement.

Mollie Simpson, you were once told that you are a prayer warrior. I couldn't agree more. Thank you for your calm wisdom and valued advice on every corner this adventure took.

Jenny Hayes, how could this have happened without your unending advice? Thank you.

Dina Pilcher, my sister, my friend. Thank you for your support and belief that I could finish. But, believe me, I'm not the only "creative one."

"Mewissa" Sorensen, the newest sister in my family. How could I have done this without you? All of our talks and dissecting of characters, you were there for them all. There were times, I am sure, you worried that I thought Del, Ari and Cy were actual people! Thanks for keeping my head on straight and in the writing game! Love you, fwend.

To all my little teens who read my story, you made this story very, very real.

.

SOFIA SIMPSON

grew up moving constantly. Never in one place more than three years, there was plenty of time to daydream during car rides. College finally gave her a chance to study what she had always dreamed of doing, writing.

She obtained a BA in Journalism, married and had two beautiful children.

A big believer in dreaming big, Sofia loves speaking to youth encouraging them to find hope no matter what their life looks like. "Life always looks different when you dream," she says. Sofia is a daughter of the Lord first and foremost and prays this novel gives hope and peace to those who need it most.

Made in the USA
Lexington, KY
13 August 2016